Bee's Business

Ann Cobb

ANN COBB

Cover Art by Marielle Williams Singletary

Book Design & Production by WatersDesigns.com

Library of Congress Control Number: 2012949060

ISBN: 978-0-9883279-0-0

First Edition: September 2012

Please visit the author's web site at: www.AnnCobb.net

Printed in the USA by

I dedicate this book to my husband Jerry and to my children: Andy and Donna, Michael and Cara, Becky and Jim.

To my grandchildren: Megan, Jesse, Alli, Sydney, Mary, and Charlie. May they remember it's never too late to dream.

I also dedicate this book to the memory of my mother and grandmother. Writing has brought back many memories of their lives.

Acknowledgments

Gratitude and thanks go to those who helped to make this book a reality…

To Jessica Clark, who first read my story and told me not to give up.

To Lisa Johnson, who always took the time to help with computer problems along the way.

To Margaret Newberry, who read and reread, always giving me a thumbs up.

To Marielle Williams Singletary, who patiently listened and developed the book cover.

To Shari Waters, whose technical guidance and general encouragement has been invaluable.

To Sandra Ray, my editor, who came to my rescue in the nick of time. Her help and assistance were invaluable.

To Edna, my business partner for thirty years, and my sister for many more. Hopefully after she reads the book, our relationship is still intact.

To my husband, who has endured my absorption into writing.

To Mary, my ten-year-old granddaughter, who has cheered me on, always saying, "Granny, it's good." (I didn't allow her to read the juicy parts.)

CHAPTER ONE

When there's no one at home to complain to, you have to go somewhere else to let it go. I was at the beauty parlor, and boy, was I telling Thelma, my beautician, all about it. If one thing wasn't hurting then something else was. From the pain in my hip to the indigestion I felt every day, I was definitely feeling my age.

"Getting old just isn't what it's cracked up to be," I said to Thelma, who wasn't a day over thirty. "If you knew how good you were feeling when you were young, I believe you'd enjoy it more."

Thelma agreed, but commented that all the standing she did was already taking a toll on her. "I probably won't be able to walk when I'm your age, not that I think that you're so old, Ms. Bee."

At sixty years old, I certainly had days when I felt as if I were already over the hill. Being recently widowed, my life as I had known it was over. With these recent changes, I was struggling to maintain a good attitude. There was nothing much to look forward to anymore.

ANN COBB

Why, the obituary column in the local newspaper was filled with people much younger than myself.

"You better start taking care of yourself," I said, "before it's too late."

"And how am I supposed to do that?" she asked. "With Johnny Boy, my ex–and last–gone to who knows where, and not ever a check in the mail, this is where you'll find me every day 'cept Sunday." I knew Thelma had a hard time of it, and with two children to feed, she seemed chained to that revolving chair.

"You know, Thelma, I feel like I look a hundred years old. What can you do to give me a new look?" I knew there was only so much she could do with what I had, but I was willing to try just about anything. I knew that I would look a whole lot better if I would just lose about thirty pounds. No, make that forty, but I had given up on that ever happening. Maybe a new hairdo would help.

"Well, for starters, let's give you a trim and color some of that mousey gray away. Why don't you just go for broke?" Thelma asked, as she grabbed the scissors and started cutting before I could back out.

"Go for it, Thelma," I said as I was considering how much this was going to set me back. Times were hard everywhere these days, and I was certainly feeling the pinch. Just keeping my head above water was getting harder every day. I sure didn't want to burden Thelma with my problems with all that heartache she was toting around.

Wow! What a difference the color from that little bottle made. I walked out of The Cut and Curl a good hour later, just hoping to run into anybody that would notice my new look.

"Your hair color could run," Thelma warned me, "so don't get overheated today. Be extra careful to stay as cool as possible."

Now that was going to be a problem whether I was at home or in town. Although I didn't want to stay in the sweltering heat all day, I was dying to hear somebody say, "What an adorable new hairdo! I do believe it makes you look ten years younger." There was absolutely nobody at home to notice, so maybe I would make a round in town before leaving.

I was off to the public library and of all the people I knew, my old friend Shirley, the county librarian, would surely notice the difference. Shirley had never married and lived all her life in her parents' home. Her mother and father had both passed away, leaving Shirley in a big old Victorian house packed with antiques and art. Her father had been a very successful lawyer. Unfortunately for Shirley, he had spent half his life spending money acquiring fine things he loved and admired, while never giving a thought about his family's financial future. She was stuck now, taking care of that big old house surrounded by her parents' possessions. Maybe it suited her, but it seemed as if she never made a life of her own. Perhaps that was part of the reason she was so meddlesome. Never in a million years would she let my new hairstyle go unnoticed. It would give her something new to talk about. Why, everybody that came out of the library had some new information—and I don't mean the kind that came out of a borrowed book.

Shirley was sitting on a small stool surrounded by a set of encyclopedias scattered about the floor. Thin as a rail and wrinkled as a prune, never really looking too healthy on her best day, Shirley looked awfully peaked today. "Thelma was saying you've been feeling poorly lately. I hope you aren't coming down with some kind of bug you can't get rid of. Why don't you take some time off and recuperate at home where you can get some rest?" I wanted to say something about all those cigarettes she smoked, but I didn't want to hurt her feelings. Everybody knew she smoked all day long right there in the library. After all, every book smelled like a smokestack.

"You know there isn't another person in this town that knows how to run this place. If I went home, this place would just fold up. I guess I'll just have to suffer right here. I'd feel as bad if I were at home anyway. Oh, Bee, we just got a new novel in about a sizzling love affair that takes place in Paris. You want to give it a shot?"

"I might, if you think it's not too risqué. I really don't like anything too racy. I guess I could try it, though, if you recommend it."

I had to be careful not to check out anything too steamy because Shirley couldn't keep her mouth shut. It would be out on the street the next day that I was reading a trashy novel.

I could tell Shirley noticed the difference in my hair by the way she looked at me, but for the life of her she wouldn't say anything flattering. It just went against her grain to say nice things about anybody.

"Oh, Bee, did you hear about Old Man Peterson's break-in the other night? He had gone to bed early. You know he goes to bed as soon as the sun goes down. Well, he was lying in bed when he heard somebody moving around in the next room. He reported that he grabbed his shotgun and as he was running into the front room, he ran right into the intruder. The prowler pushed him down and ran out the door with all the cash he found stashed away in the secret drawer of the rolltop desk in the living room. Old Man Peterson said he staggered out the back door behind the thief, but a ninety-year-old man ain't no match for some young scallywag out there trying to get something for nothing. Can't you just picture that old man struggling to run on those spindly little toothpick legs of his? Old Man Peterson said he called the law right then, but it wasn't until the next morning Sheriff Ledbetter came out and investigated. After several hours, you know yourself the trail wasn't hot any longer. Don't that beat all, that sorry piece of a sheriff waiting until the next morning to even respond? We need to look into finding us some better law enforcers around here."

"Oh my, I just can't believe that. It's a wonder that robber didn't kill Old Man Peterson. How's he doing now?"

"As far as I know, he's fine. Just a little bruised up. Dorothy, you know, the waitress from the diner, said she overheard Sheriff Ledbetter saying that we all need to be a little more careful about leaving our doors open. Can you imagine how hot it would be all night long with the doors closed?"

I nodded in agreement and asked Shirley if the sheriff had come across any clues on his trip out to Old Man Peterson's the next morning.

"The only clue I heard about was that he found a greasy rag lying in the bushes next to the door. Old Man Peterson recently had electric power installed in the house, and Sheriff Ledbetter said it could have been accidently dropped earlier by somebody with the power company. His old dog could have found it, dragged it around and left it there. I guess we won't ever know."

I shook my head and said, "My, my, you know the sheriff ought to take this thing a little more seriously. Why he should have gone on out, checked to see if Old Man Peterson needed medical attention, and investigated the crime when he got the call. I'm glad Mr. Peterson wasn't hurt though. You know, he could have shot himself with that gun. He can't see two feet in front of him. I saw him in the grocery store the other day buying some canned soups, and he couldn't see well enough to even make change. The poor man didn't know a nickel from a dime. He doesn't really need to be driving either. Sometime I stop by his place on my way into town to see if he needs anything, but lately I've been pretty remiss about it." I didn't say anything to Shirley, but since Will had passed away, I got an uneasy feeling he might be feeling his oats and had intentions of courting me. "I wonder if there were any footprints left around in the yard," I quizzed Shirley.

"You know, Dorothy didn't say anything about footprints. She was probably so busy with other customers she missed part of the sheriff's conversation. She picks up on a lot of interesting stuff at the diner. She was telling me just this morning about an affair going on right down the road with Eunice Donaldson and some old buzzard."

"That's old news, Shirley. Anyway, it's Eunice's own business who she goes out with. Now I've got to get out of here and get home to cool off before the missionary meeting tonight. I hope I'll see you there."

"I doubt it. I probably need to go home and crash. You know I have to work, unlike some people I know who never had to make their own living or hit a lick at a snake."

She always gets the last word in. I wondered why I always allowed that woman to get under my skin.

As I walked to my car, I noticed how peaceful and tranquil our little town seemed, even with a thief running wild.

Jeffersontown, Georgia, is a continuous line of brick structures along both sides of two paved lanes that run parallel to each other. Most of the businesses along the streets have awnings or covered entrances across the front. Boxes of produce or racks of this and that are right out on the sidewalk for inspection by passersby. Right down the middle of town, between the two wide streets, is a grassy area with large oak trees gracefully extending their limbs to provide a nice shade on a hot day like today. At the southern end of Main Street sits our large brick courthouse with its manicured lawn, stretching all the way to the sidewalk that runs along the shady street. I understand plans are in the works to pave more of the streets in town, but right now only Main Street and a couple of the streets that lead to the downtown area are paved. Scattered around the hub of the main street district are homes, new and old, stately and modest. A gas station on the outskirts of town, several churches, a school, and a few more businesses make up the small community.

It only took a minute to get to the dusty road that leads toward my place. Reminiscing as I drove, I thought about the good life Will and I had spent together. We had endured both good and bad times. After forty years of marriage, Will suddenly had a heart attack and had not survived. The doctors just didn't know how to repair that old worn out heart. Those were some sad days that left me without a whole lot of determination to go on. I guess the mourning had just taken over my life. It had been a year since he passed, and the sorrow was still there. I guess I was just learning to deal with it.

Will had taken over the farm after Daddy had gotten up in years, and we eventually were able to buy the place. We had taken care of Mama and Daddy until they passed away. I had never lived anywhere except that one house. Will was a good farmer, and I had spent the better part of my life caring for our home and raising our daughter, Margaret. Margaret was an only child, so I suppose we spoiled her some. Now she lived over in the next county and was teaching school. With no husband, or even a prospect of one, I felt she might end up an old maid.

Bess, my older sister by only one year, had always been a thorn in my flesh. She had the power to make me feel inadequate in everything I did. Thank heavens she wasn't with me today or she would have already made some remark about my hair being too short or too red. Thelma had only cut a little off and slightly changed the color, but I'm sure Bess would have found fault with the results. I didn't always appreciate her comments, especially concerning my hair or my weight.

Bess lived in town in a neat little house her late husband, Fred, and she had built after they sold their place next to Will and me. Tom Wilson, a neighboring farmer and close friend, had bought their farm and now rented my farm land to plant corn and cotton. He was a thoughtful man, and I appreciated him helping me get the cotton picked and to market the year before. It had been more than I could have dealt with at the time.

Bess's brick house sat on one of the wide paved streets lined with oak trees. The house had a low-pitched roof and a wide porch that extended across the front. Bess and Fred had screened the porch and with the painted oak rockers and little tables placed around for flowers and ferns, it was a picture fit for any magazine.

Bess had such nice things in her house. Her drapes in the living room were store-bought from Sears and Roebuck. Her settee and chairs all matched and were covered with nice brocade fabric. If it wasn't for those sheets she used all over the place to keep the dust off her furniture, she would be ready to entertain at a minute's notice. She kept all her little 'sit arounds' dusted, and if anything got cracked or broken, she would have a fit. Bedspreads were always in place without a wrinkle or a crease. Clean sheets were on all her company beds. Her towels always matched, and her shoes stayed in a neat row in the bottom of her closet.

Bess kept herself up as well as her house. She never let her weight creep up more than a pound or two before she was counting calories to get it back down. Her hair was always just so, and she never went to bed without moisturizing her face. She made all her own clothes on the Singer Fred bought her for her birthday a good many years back. It was nothing for her to seam up something in a day's time. She kept up with all the styles in the *Ladies' Home Journal* she had delivered. Her Sunday shoes always matched her purse, and her hat always matched her outfit. All that sewing and fussing wasn't for me, though. A store-bought dress had always suited me just fine, and I didn't particularly care if all my chairs matched my settee or not. If Bess wanted to worry herself to death about appearances all the time, more power to her.

With all that daydreaming it didn't seem to take me long to reach my farm lane. My 140-acre farm was only three miles out of town on Rural Route 3. I had been driving slowly to keep the wind from coming in on the side of the car and messing up my new hairdo. Leaving the window up had not been an option since the day was sweltering hot. This July, 1946, seemed to be much hotter and more humid than ever before. The weatherman on WPEX radio was talking just this morning about how this was the warmest and driest July we had experienced for at least twenty years. I really can't understand how he knows anything that far back, as young as he sounded.

It never seemed as if I was hurrying to get anywhere these days. Time just didn't seem to matter that much. After driving down the dusty lane that was anchored between rows of cotton on one side and pasture land where my small herd of cows stood munching dry Bermuda grass on the other, I parked my dark green, seven-year-old Chevrolet Coupe in the shade of the big old oak tree Daddy had planted long before I was even a twinkle in my mother's eye and reached for my library book on the seat.

I sat there looking at the house. The tall pitched tin roof with brick chimneys jutting toward the sky and the wide wraparound screened porch was as familiar to me as the back of my hand. The house had a graceful look about it. Once a bright white, the wide board exterior now was a mossy shade of gray, weathered from many years of harsh winters and hot summers. Over the years, people had commented what a stately old place this was, but I knew it was going down.

Over to the back of my yard was a five acre pecan orchard. I loved to sit out on the side porch and watch the crows fly down under the trees and the squirrels romp around carrying their uneaten nuts to their secret hiding places. An old weathered barn, a patched up chicken house and a well-rooted hog pen—with all its pungent odors—sat over to the side. The sounds of the hogs squealing and grunting welcomed me back to my world. The sad feeling I always felt when it was time to go back into my big, lonely house crept up on me as I sat there. Instead of thinking how nice it was to be home, glancing up at the house, all I felt was despair. "Bee," I said right out loud, "get yourself together." I often talked to myself, and it seemed as if I was doing it more often these days.

Mama and Daddy had loved this place and were so proud that Will and I had taken over. Even in the last years when we were all here together, Mama always reminded me that I should take pride in the way things were kept up. Well, it had been quite a while since I really noticed the paint was peeling on that old porch. The front screen door scraped the floor every time someone went in or out. I guess the hinges were slipping and needed to be tightened. I hadn't noticed how the weeds were beginning to invade my petunia bed at the front steps. Those purple petunias had appeared every spring for as long as I could remember. Mama always said, "God's wonders are everywhere, if we just take the time to notice." I guess I hadn't done a lot of that lately. I said a little prayer of thankfulness and reminded myself to quit being so self-absorbed.

Well, I would have to get out there and attack those weeds soon, but not today. I was going in, cooling off, and later this afternoon I was going up the road to my old friend Vera's house to our monthly Baptist women's missionary meeting. It was always a treat to hear what everybody was up to these days and enjoy refreshments, even though it was probably just pound cake, and...oh, yes, hear about some Baptist missionary I didn't even know, in some foreign country I never heard of.

CHAPTER TWO

The telephone in the center hall started to ring as I was getting in the door. Two rings, one long, one short. That's me. Rushing over to pick up the heavy black receiver, I almost tripped over the stool I kept by the telephone to prop my tired legs and feet while I was sitting on the bench. Will had persuaded me several years ago we needed a telephone to get in touch with somebody in case of an emergency. Little did he realize how much enjoyment that telephone would bring. Many a day, my only connection to the outside world had been my telephone. If I wasn't dishing out advice or adding my two-cents' worth to some gossip that was going around, I was listening along with anybody else on my party line that cared to accidently overhear a conversation. Why, just to be able to talk to Margaret was such wonderment to me. I certainly felt safer with it in the house now that I was alone with my memories.

I picked up. "Hello, Bee Martin speaking."

"Hello, Henry Maxwell here. I hope that you're having a good day."

What a letdown. I had been hoping to hear from Margaret. I was way overdue a call from my daughter. I kept telling myself how busy she was, but I still felt a bit rejected when she didn't call a little more frequently.

I would have to get used to this new preacher. We had Preacher Jenkins for many years, but unfortunately, he recently passed away. Our little church had been assigned Henry Maxwell to fill in as pastor until we could find a permanent replacement. In my opinion, he was too young to know much about pastoring. He couldn't have been a day over twenty-five.

"Well, thank you for calling. I do feel a little wilted in all this heat, but all in all, things are going well."

"Ms. Bee, I have a little something I'd like to talk over with you, if you have the time. I had you on my heart today and wondered if we could speak privately."

"Well, you know this line is not private, so I suppose we'll have to speak later." I knew I didn't sound too charitable, but I was not feeling too generous with my time today. I had my mind on the meeting with the girls, and I didn't want to be detained.

"If it wouldn't be too inconvenient, could I run out to your house in about thirty minutes?"

Hesitating, I replied, "Come on out. I do have a meeting later this afternoon, but I'll be watching for you shortly." What on God's green earth could this young, fast-talking preacher want to discuss with me that was so important it couldn't wait, at least until tomorrow? I really didn't have time for this today.

We had only spoken with each other once outside the church doors since he first arrived. We had run into each other at Floyd's the other day while Elmo, Floyd's nice young cousin, was pumping my high-priced gasoline. He had nonchalantly commented, "I really want to visit and get to know each and every one of the church members as I find the time and hope to get out your way shortly."

"I look forward to a visit," I replied. Not really wanting any unexpected visitor when I might not be looking my best or was busy with some chore, I added, "But please call in advance if you don't mind."

I also mentioned while paying for the gas, that since Will had passed away, I had to be particularly careful with the little money I had, but was a tither. It wasn't any of his business, yet for some reason I let that information slip out.

It is with a heavy heart that I tell you, I was lying awake at night worrying about money, or the lack of it. I felt as if my finances were way out of line and if I could just figure out how to get a little more coming in and not so much going out, maybe I could get a little peace of mind. I knew I didn't need to do any unnecessary spending for the time being. I should have kept myself home today and not bothered about my hair, but a girl does have to have a little something to lift her spirits now and then. I'd have to come up with some excuse not to go with Bess the next time she asked me out for an afternoon of shopping.

Thinking about it now, I wish I had never opened my big mouth to the preacher the other day about my personal finances. I had known other preachers who didn't always keep everything confidential.

Why, I recall one preacher who was preaching about what a sin it was just to look at the opposite sex with desire. Everybody knew the mailman we had at the time delivering mail to the rural boxes couldn't keep his eyes off a particular woman on his route. He had been seen coming out of the preacher's office the week before the sermon topic was "Lust in the Heart." It was fairly easy to figure out where the topic of that sermon came from.

Knowing I only had a few minutes before Preacher Henry would arrive, I flung myself into action. I grabbed an old towel and dusted off the tables in the front room. Checking to see if all the pictures were straight, I noticed a cobweb in the corner, so I went for the broom. I didn't intend for the preacher to enter the front of the house, but I needed to be prepared just in case I couldn't keep him out. After attacking the cobwebs and thinking everything looked fairly presentable, I headed to the porch and swiped the middle of the floor a few times with the broom. Although all I did was stir the dust up a little, it made me feel as if the house looked a little more presentable. My time was running out so I hurried down the hall into the bathroom to check my new hairdo and see if I had any color in my cheeks. I dashed on a little lipstick, straightened my dress, and looked as good as possible considering I had dressed early that morning and the temperature was way above ninety degrees. At least my hair color wasn't running and I had on a decent dress. Normally, I would have been in an old housedress that had seen better days.

I was ready when I heard a soft knock on the screen door. Wanting to get this over with as quickly as possible, I hurried out to the porch and greeted the preacher as calmly as I knew how. I did wonder if he was going to notice my new look. Actually, he probably didn't even remember my old hairdo, so what was I thinking.

"Ms. Bee, I hope I'm not inconveniencing you this afternoon." He seemed fidgety and somewhat nervous as I held the screen door open for him to step in.

"No, not at all," I replied. In the back of my mind, I was thinking he better get on with this so I can get to my meeting on time. I didn't want to miss any of the chitchat before the actual meeting started.

"It's a scorcher of a day. I believe I heard somewhere today the temperature was almost a hundred degrees," Preacher Henry said, as he attempted to start up our conversation. I really didn't have time for a weather report, I thought, as I tried to relax enough to at least seem sociable.

Preacher Henry's unexpected visit reminded me of how Margaret, as a child, would always run out the back door when we saw the preacher come by for a visit. We wouldn't hear or see her until our visitor would leave. Margaret never was able to endure a long boring conversation about the weather, or how the crops were growing, or when we would have our next afternoon sing at the church. If the preacher brought his wife, we would have more endless chatter. It was almost more than I could bear, at times. I have never known a preacher that seemed to be in a hurry to leave after sitting down in a comfortable chair with a cool drink in his hand. I really don't understand why a preacher thinks it's necessary to visit every member of the congregation every month or so anyway. I guess they think they have to do something to earn their salary. Now, if somebody's sick or there's a death in the family, that's a different story.

Knowing if Preacher Henry got all the way into the house that afternoon, I might never get him out, I motioned for him to sit in one of the uncomfortable straight chairs on the porch.

"How about a cool glass of water, Preacher Henry?" I asked. I was not about to let him know there was freshly made sweet tea in the icebox.

Seeming a bit anxious, he answered, "No thank you. I had an Orange Crush down at the filling station with Floyd and Elmo just before I called this afternoon. They're two friendly fellers. We ended up having a short visit. You know they're both members of the church. I almost lost track of time until Floyd mentioned he had to leave to get cleaned up to attend his weekly merchants' meeting this evening. It sure has turned out hot today," he said as he pulled a handkerchief out of his back pocket to wipe his face.

I thought we had already established that fact, but responded, "Yes, it surely has."

That's when I noticed his left arm was a bit shorter than his right arm. I thought it was a bit odd. Maybe it was a birth deformity or perhaps his arm was withered and had just quit growing. Most preachers weren't able to do much manual work anyway, and I imagined this one was no exception.

Preacher Henry was not the kind of fellow that would stand out in a crowd. He was not good-looking. He wasn't really that bad looking, either. He had a long face with a dimple in his chin. His ears stuck out a little, and he seemed to always have a shadow of a beard. I thought he could have managed to use a little Brill Cream on that mop of wiry black hair that stood out at the sides where it should have laid down. He was very tall and lanky without much meat on his bones. The dark gray suit and dingy white shirt he seemed to have on every time I saw him was a little shabby and in need of a good pressing. I guess that was understandable seeing that he didn't have a wife to take care of the washing and ironing.

"That big, old oak tree there sure does give some nice shade up here around the porch," he said, as if he had all the time in the world for this visit.

"It does help on these hot days. My daddy planted that tree in o' four. It's been a blessing a strong wind has never taken it down." This conversation had really begun to lag.

"Well, Ms. Bee, I do have something on my heart that I felt compelled to come out today and talk to you about."

This was it. I braced myself for what I was about to hear.

"You see, I have a younger sister I feel responsible for, and she wants to come and visit a spell with me. She needs a nice, comfortable place to stay while she's here. As you know, the church frowns on a guest staying in the church pastorium for any length of time. Besides, there's hardly any space in that little four room house for me, much less somebody else. Why the church ever bought that place is a mystery to me."

I didn't think it was his place to start criticizing the church, especially when he hardly had time to unpack his belongings.

"Anyway, what I'm getting around to, I was wondering if you might find it in your heart to allow my sister to stay here in your home for a while. She only plans to stay two or three months at the most. I don't suppose you've ever considered a boarder before, but after hearing you mention that things might be a little tight, why, the idea just popped into my head. She would, after all, be willing to pay whatever you consider to be fair."

This idea of his really did take me by surprise. Why, I didn't know what to say, and I'm hardly ever at a loss for words. After hesitating a minute, I politely answered, "Well, I certainly will think about it, Preacher Henry. The idea of such a thing never entered my mind. I've gotten so used to being right by myself and not having to worry about what time to eat or go to bed at night. I might not be able to handle anybody else being around the place with me. It would be quite an adjustment. It is something to think about. Just give me a day or two and I'll let you know."

"It certainly would relieve a burden from my mind. I never mentioned anything about my sister and her situation when I applied for the position, and I'm sure the church hadn't planned on anybody else coming with me. I guess I should have talked to the board about this before accepting their proposal." By this time he was beginning to squirm in his seat and shift his eyes downward as if he were uncomfortable. "Well, thanks for letting me come over on such short notice. I hope I haven't taken up too much of your time. Tell Vera and the others 'Hello' for me." He stood up as if my answer was his cue to leave. What a relief he wasn't planning on staying any longer.

"I will, and come again when we can visit a little longer." I don't know why I added that, knowing full well I didn't really mean it. Trying to be polite can be so tiring sometime.

He was out the screen door before I could say another thing. As he folded his long, thin frame into his little black car and drove off, I stood there on the porch. The prospect of allowing a complete stranger to come into my home to live with me left me stunned. The longer I stood there contemplating it, the more it seemed like manna from heaven.

CHAPTER THREE

I knew it wouldn't be too long before Bess would fly down the lane in a cloud of dust and start blowing for me to come out. She always complained about the dust that blanketed her car every time she came out to the house, but she never understood if she would just slow down a little, the dust wouldn't fly everywhere. She always started blowing her horn about the time she turned off the big road. She was to pick me up for the missionary meeting, and I was going to take a chance with my life and ride with her. Running late was not unusual for her, but more than likely, she'd be on time today.

I sat there on the porch thinking about the preacher's proposal. Was the prospect of having a boarder something that could really work out? Well, it surely would help me to acquire a little money for my bank account. The account was dwindling faster than running water from a well going dry. Will and I had not been able to put a lot back for the future and the future was here. It was pretty dismal.

There she was now, coming down the lane like she was going to put out a house fire. Sister Bess was always in a hurry. I quickly ran in, picked up my purse, and pulled the door to. I never locked anything up. Will always said it was better not to have everything locked up like Fort Knox for some burglar to tear up while getting into. Under the circumstances, I might need to rethink that now. Anyway, there was nothing of value here, and a burglar would probably be quite disappointed.

Opening the car door, I remarked, "What's your hurry? We have plenty of time. It won't take us a minute to get over to Vera's."

My old friend Vera and her husband Tillman lived about half a mile up the road toward town. I could walk it in ten minutes and drive it in one.

"Well, you know we don't want to be late." Glancing over toward me, Bess said, "Goodness, what did you do to your hair?"

"I went to the beauty parlor today, and Thelma, well, she got carried away. I don't know, it feels good," I said, as I patted the top of my head to smooth it down a bit. I couldn't wait to hear what kind of comment Bess would come up with. When she didn't say anything, I finally said, "Well, what do you think?"

"I don't know. Let me get used to it."

Feeling kind of crushed, I decided to change the subject. "Bess, I was going by Vera and Tillman's house today coming from town, and I noticed Vera had Tillman out pushing the lawn mower around the yard in the hot sun. She probably had him washing that big old picture window in the front room and scrubbing the porch too. I feel so sorry for that man. Why, I was over there two or three days ago to borrow some lard, and she had him washing dishes. I never put Will Martin in front of a dishpan his whole life."

Bess nodded her head in agreement and said, "Wonder what Vera will serve for refreshments? I hope she didn't bake a pound cake like she did last time we met over there. I think she said she used Mildred's mama's recipe. I'm sure the recipe was all right, but Vera must have left something out. It was so-o dry." Bess started slowing the car down.

"Now Bess, we need to be a little more charitable than that. I do know what you mean though. Her tea is always weak. You would think she would try to make it a little stronger when she's entertaining. Anyway, what have you been up to all day?"

"Why, I've been washing, starching, and ironing all my doilies, and they look so fresh now," Bess answered proudly.

I just rolled my eyes.

"Your hair is beginning to grow on me. I do like the length. It probably won't look quite so bright after we get out of the sunlight."

Well, that was about as close as I was going to get to a compliment. It could have been worse though. I thought about telling her about Old Man Peterson's robbery but decided to wait and tell all the girls at one time.

There were already three cars in the driveway at Vera's, so Bess pulled over to the side of the house to park. You hate to drive on somebody's grass, but sometime you just don't have any choice. Grabbing our purses off the car seat, Bess said, "There's something I need to tell you. Don't let me forget after the meeting."

I can't stand for somebody to tell me to wait on any kind of news. Now I would have to endure the entire meeting, wondering what Bess had on her mind. I had something on my mind to talk to her about too.

As we made our entrance, I was on pins and needles waiting for one of the girls to mention my hair. Everybody must have been too preoccupied with other things because not the first one said a word about it. Maybe I had just wasted my money today, or it could have been they were all just jealous and didn't want to bring it up.

If the day had not been so hot, Vera's front room would have been much more pleasant. I knew she was doing the best that she could with all the windows up. There wasn't the faintest breeze stirring. Just sitting on that vinyl settee had turned me into a puddle. With perspiration running down my back, I tried to be attentive to Mildred's well-prepared program about the needs of some missionaries in South America. It wasn't easy.

I wouldn't have been caught dead at night wearing those pants Mildred showed up in. She had never been one to dress up, but this was ridiculous. She said she had seen knee pants in the circular from Pearly's Dry Goods on Main Street and just had to have them. I had also seen them in the *Sears and Roebuck* catalog, but they were advertised as pedal pushers. Whatever they were called, I didn't think they would catch on. The circular came out in the mail on Thursday, and she said she had beaten the bushes to get in there by Friday before they were all sold out. I don't really think they would have sold out in a month of Fridays, but then again, I don't really know a whole lot about fashion. She said she considered they would be so much cooler than a dress and stockings and caved to the temptation and bought a pair. Not only had she worn them to the circle meeting today, but she had also put on a sleeveless blouse. Now everybody knows that any woman over the age of fifty, especially a large woman like Mildred, doesn't have any business showing off her arms.

Vera did have pretty things in her house, and today I couldn't keep my eyes off the sterling silver tea service her mother had handed down to her and Tillman years ago. She had taken it off of the table in front of the picture window and put it on the dining table to use along with her sterling flatware. She must have been cleaning it half the day because it was shining like new money. Vera had used a lovely cutwork tablecloth over her dark mahogany dining table, and for a centerpiece, she had long-stemmed zinnias from her flower bed. She had arranged little blooming marigolds in with them. I must say, Vera did have a knack with flowers. Sitting on a clear glass pedestal was a pound cake with strawberries placed around the sides. Vera, with the help of Mildred, served the cake and sweet tea, which was a little too weak but still very refreshing in the heat. I was afraid she was going to give out of ice until I heard Tillman back in the kitchen, chipping away. Vera, being a good hostess, poured iced tea refills and asked if anybody wanted the recipe for the pound cake. Bess asked for it, just to be polite, all the while knowing that she would never, in a million years, use it.

"Did anybody hear about Old Man Peterson's robbery the other night?" I asked as we were sitting there balancing our plates on our laps and sipping tea. "You know, somebody has to be really low-down to break in on a poor old man like that."

After I gave the group my account of Old Man Peterson's robbery, Mildred added, as if she was disgusted, "I heard our sorry sheriff didn't even go out to investigate until the next morning."

Vera chimed in. "That's what I heard too. It's so scary to think about somebody out there trying to get something for nothing. Tillman said we're going to start closing our doors at night and maybe even lock them from now on. Bee, you better do the same over there by yourself."

"Lordy, I've got enough on my mind without worrying about somebody trying to break in, for goodness sake," I answered, as I was thinking Old Man Peterson's house was only about a mile from mine and even closer to Vera and Tillman's place. "Does anybody know if Old Man Peterson could actually tell who the thief was?"

"My information came from Dorothy over at the diner," answered Molly Turner, one of the newest members of the group. She and her husband, Sam, the new principal at our school, had recently moved to Jeffersontown from Atlanta. "From what I could understand, listening to Dorothy while she was waiting on tables at the diner this morning, Old Man Peterson told the sheriff it was either a colored man or a man with a black hood over his head. Why would somebody want to break in on Mr. Peterson, is what I want to know," Molly questioned.

Bess retorted, "Old Man Peterson has never in his life used a bank. He says he doesn't believe in them. He thinks they steal your money, so he's always kept his money hidden somewhere around his house. You know that old man was probably loaded too. Why, he probably hasn't ever spent more than five dollars at one time in his whole life."

Vera added, "You know he never gave his poor old wife any money to do anything with at all. I remember a few years before she died, she had to borrow a dress from me to go to her own nephew's wedding in Augusta. He wouldn't even allow her to buy one for something as important as that. I don't know how she ever endured living with that tight old buzzard."

Bess was really getting wound up now. She responded, "Haven't you ever noticed how he looks at that measly dollar bill he throws into the collection plate at church? Why, I actually saw him making change right out of the plate as it went by one morning. If he ever accidently gave anything larger than a dollar, he would probably have a heart attack right there sitting at the end of the third row from the back on the left side of the sanctuary. I've heard him say many a time his family's been sitting in the same pew for seventy years. Wonder what would happen if some stranger came in and sat down on that bench?"

"Why, I imagine he'd run them off and sit right down," I laughingly replied.

After we had run out of news and gossip, Molly Turner and Madge Bennett got up to leave at the same time. They both had husbands at home waiting for their suppers to be put on the table. That would have been me a year ago. Madge, especially, needed to be punctual about getting back home. Her husband, Harold, expected her to live by his rules, and I'm sure they had a set time for meals. Harold was one of those people that just didn't bend. There's only one way to do something—and that's his way. Poor Madge.

Vera asked Mildred, Bess, and me to walk out and look at her flowers in the yard before it got too dark. We strolled out into the back where her petunias, zinnias, and snapdragons were all lined up in little rows like soldiers. We raved about them and I asked Vera, "How on earth do you do all this?" I waved my arm toward the flowers and said, "Your yard looks so nice and your house never looked better." Bess gave me a sideways frown as I waited to hear if Vera was going to give poor old Tillman any credit at all. I knew Vera well enough to know she'd probably take all the credit for everything that got done around here. We knew Vera couldn't keep this yard up one week without Tillman.

Vera proudly replied, "It does keep me busy, but I can still manage it. I can't stand to think about anything being left undone. I'm sure there'll be a day when it'll get the best of me, though." We knew that she had Tillman out weeding that flower bed yesterday, as well as breaking his back doing for her around the house today.

Bess and I made our excuses to leave, telling Vera how wonderful everything tasted, and what a nice meeting it had been, and let's get together soon. You know, all that stuff that has to be said when you're leaving someone's house. We didn't get our car doors closed good before I said, "Okay, what gives?" I couldn't wait another minute to find out what Bess had on her mind to talk to me about.

Bess didn't answer; instead, she switched the car on, shifted into reverse, and started backing out when I yelled, "Bess, watch out for that light pole!" Bess slammed on the brakes, and we both jutted forward in our seats.

"I saw it, Bee. You scared the living daylights out of me! I can't figure why the light company has to put the poles right next to the road, instead of in the backyard out of sight, for heaven's sake," Bess replied in an aggravated tone. She never could back out of anywhere by herself. The dents and dings all over the rear end of her car was evidence of that. I really don't know how she ever managed when I wasn't with her to watch out.

"Okay, we can talk now," I said, as we were both settling back down.

"Wait a minute," Bess said, as she concentrated on getting the car onto the road. As she shifted into second from first, we heard that familiar scraping sound. Bess could not change a gear without all that noise. Finally we were on the road in high gear, so I said, "I know you have something to talk about, so let's talk."

As if bidding her time, Bess drove on without saying a word, just looking at the road ahead. She finally said, "I can't talk while I concentrate on this dark road. Wait a minute, will you?" As we were pulling into the lane, she finally said, "I can remember just like it was yesterday, Mama and Daddy sitting out on your old porch early in the evening. All the work for the day was done, except Mama might still have some dishes from supper in the pan to be washed. They'd be rocking in those same old chairs you have up there on the porch right now. Those sure are some good old memories. By the way, when are you going to give those chairs another coat of paint? I was noticing the other day they were looking a little scruffy."

"When I get around to it," I said, thinking it was none of her business when I painted my chairs. Well, she had put off this conversation as long as she could. I knew she was just stalling, so I said, "I have something to tell you."

"Okay, but me first." So with a deep breath, Bess clinched the steering wheel and said, "I have a new friend that I haven't told you about."

"Well, what is so earth-shattering about that? What's her name?"

"J.R.," she muttered, slightly under her breath. "Short for James Robert, J. R. Kitchens."

"You mean like a man friend! My goodness! What kind of woman are you anyway? Why, you and Fred were married for over forty years, raised the boys together, and now you want to start all over again! Are you absolutely nuts? Why, Fred hasn't been dead three years. Aren't you rushing things a little?"

"That's just it, he's dead now, and he isn't going to get any deader later on."

"Where is this 'J.R.' from anyway? I've never heard of him, and I thought I knew everybody around these parts."

"That's because he doesn't live too close around. He lives over in Wall County, if you must know, about fifteen miles away. I knew I shouldn't have told you. I knew you would have a conniption fit. Well, I've been out a couple of times with him, and he's asked me to go out again this weekend. We're planning on going to that new place out on the highway. Everybody says the food is good, especially the pork chops."

"If you want to go, more power to you. You won't catch me out with just any old man who wants to put his shoes under my bed, if you know what I mean. People are going to be talking about you like they do about Eunice Donaldson."

"You mean Eunice, the girl that comes in occasionally to help out when Thelma gets herself in a pinch?" Bess replied.

"Yes, I do. You know all about her. Why it's nothing for her to go out with anybody that waves a dollar bill her way. The other day while she was pin curling Mildred, she mentioned she was going out with that old crow, Mr. Rooks. You know, the night watchman over at the oil mill. Now, I ask you, what does she see in him? He's old enough to be her grandpa, and he is a grandpa to half a dozen young'uns around town. His wife's dead, but I don't imagine that has much bearing on the situation. If he's got his old pickup truck in running order and a few dollars in his pocket, Eunice is usually available, unless somebody better than him comes along first, if you know what I mean."

"Bee, really! I can't believe you would even compare me to Eunice," Bess cut in.

"Well, you know it's all true, and she brings it all on herself. Since her husband died a few years ago in that hunting accident, her mother looks after her and those two children. Without her help, I guess she'd be out on the street. Maybe I shouldn't be so critical of her. After all, she does work for Thelma. Thelma says she's preached to her until she's absolutely blue in the face, but nothing seems to sink in." I had to add, "She does know how to use a comb and a brush, though."

"Well, I'm not like Eunice, and this is just a friendship, someone to go out with every now and again."

I thought, *that's what they all say.* I guess there wasn't any better time than this to tell Bess about my news. "Why don't you come on into the house?" I asked.

"No, not tonight, I'm expecting a call from Freddy. I think he and Jean are planning a trip to Florida with the grandchildren. They probably want to ask me about borrowing my suitcases again. I don't know why they don't just get a new set, instead of using mine when they go somewhere, not that they go so much, just once a year to the beach at Tybee Island or somewhere in the mountains. I ought to just give them those old suitcases. I don't ever use them. You know, we ought to head out one day and go see Cousin Myrtle up in South Carolina."

"I don't know about that. What with my stomach acting up so much lately, I'd better keep myself close to home right now. It's a good idea, though. When have you talked to Myrtle?"

"I called her about two weeks ago, and she said the weather was extremely hot. She and her circle were busy gathering up clothes for the needy in her community. You know, we could be doing more charitable things around here closer to home instead of worrying about people halfway around the world." Sometimes Bess and I were on the same wavelength.

"Bess," I said, "I need to talk to you about something too. It's not nearly as interesting as your news, but...I might take in a boarder. Now don't say a word until you hear what I have to say. I really could use some more income. I'm tired of pinching every penny that comes my way. I'm not destitute, mind you, but I sure could use a little extra. Preacher Henry's sister is coming to visit him for a couple of months, and you know how the deacons frown on anybody staying in the pastorium with the preachers. Well, I haven't answered him yet, but I am thinking it surely would be nice to have a little extra money in my pocket. What do you think about it?"

"Well, I think you don't know what you are getting into. You never saw this person before. She could be an axe murderer for all you know. Why, I won't be able to close my eyes at night knowing you have some kind of strange woman out here with you. Besides, you don't even like to cook, and you know people do like to eat three times a day. What are you going to do about all those dirty clothes? Somebody will have to wash and iron them, as well as all those sheets and pillowcases. I don't know about all this. You know you can always come and stay with me if you're that hard up."

I had never even thought about such a crazy thing as staying at Bess's house. She would drive me to drink with all that cleaning and organizing. Why, if she could just see the inside of my underwear drawer right now, she would just shudder. I don't think the last time I put away my unmentionables I even folded them.

"I can manage with what I have, but I just never have any extra. Will always handled the bills and repairs and such, and I never had to worry. The roof needs patching right now, and I'm scared every time I turn the water on that the old well is going to go dry. I would never bother Margaret by asking her for anything, so what am I to do?"

We both just sat there and stared at each other, thinking things sure were changing.

CHAPTER FOUR

A fter a restless night, I awoke with a renewed eagerness to meet the day. My energy would be waning by lunch time so whatever needed to be done, I needed to jump on it. My decision had been made. Even though my little inner sanctuary was to be invaded, I thought I could deal with another person in the house for a while. After breakfast and a little Bible reading, I began to think about what needed to be done to ready the house for this unknown person. I knew I needed to get out there and attack the grass and weeds in my petunia bed by the steps. I decided to stir up a little dust in the house instead. After tying a cloth over my hair to keep the dirt and dust out, I started cleaning with a vengeance I had forgotten I ever possessed.

I kept going over the situation in my head as I worked. What was the worst thing that could happen? I guess Bess could be right and Preacher Henry's sister could be an axe murderer, but if that was true, I wouldn't live to regret it. I'd be dead. If things worked out, I would have the money to get my roof fixed and maybe have a little painting done. Maybe Bess would find it in her heart to quit complaining about the condition of the place if she knew I was trying to do something about it. Chipped paint and sagging doors were just not as high up on my priority list as hers.

I didn't want to appear too anxious, so I thought I'd put off calling the preacher for a while. Carrying my mop water out the back door to pour on my tomato bushes for a little extra drink, I noticed Vonion trudging slowly around out by the barn with a bucket and a stick in his hand. Vonion had worked alongside Daddy and Will for years. He and his wife Ora Lee lived down the lane in the little tenant house they called home almost as long as my family had lived in the big house. In return for the house, water, and a little electric power I supplied, Vonion helped me around the place.

Vonion had always looked the same to me—old and worn out. His dark skin was weathered and creased with deep wrinkles. His large calloused hands seemed to dangle from long arms that were always covered with a long-sleeved shirt—even on the hottest day. A smile exposing his large white teeth was generally plastered across his face, and a cap or a straw hat was always perched on top of his wiry grey hair. I couldn't remember a time he wasn't in need of a shave, except on first and third Sunday morning church days.

Ora Lee had been feeling poorly lately, and I needed to check on her that afternoon. Ora Lee was what you might call plump, not fat. She had begun to slump over as she aged, and even though she had not given in to using a cane, she shuffled around slowly with her head tilted downward. She was a constant reminder of what old age was all about. I don't know what I would have done without her. She had helped raise Margaret and knew as much about cleaning and caring for my house as I did. Mama and Daddy were always taken care of with the grace and dignity they deserved because Ora Lee was there every day to help. She was always genuinely concerned about our family, as we were about hers. When Daddy got to where he couldn't care for his personal needs, Ora Lee faithfully did everything that was required. Her family was our family and ours was hers. I don't think I had realized what she meant to me until recently as I watched her health begin to go down.

"Morning, Vonion," I called. "How's Ora Lee this morning?"

"'Bout the same, I'd say. She is stirrin' a little this morning. If she could get her mind off of Lettie and the chil'ren being so far away up in Atlanty, she would be better off. Can't tell her notin' though. I know they is fine, but she ain't had no letter in about a month. That sorry, good-for-nothin' husband of Lettie's ain't much help to her, so she's helpin' out in some rich lady's house, last we heard. Ain't much, but reckon it's the best she can get rat now." Glancing toward the house with his red- veined eyes, Vonion asked, "What I need to do up here this day 'cept my regular chores?"

"Well, I don't know. I guess you could get the mower out and spruce up the yard a little." I didn't have much grass, but in the spots where it would grow, Vonion had always been able to keep it trimmed pretty well with the push mower Will bought a few years back. When she was able, Ora Lee swept our yard around the porch where we never could get grass to grow. I never saw much sense in it, but she loved to use that handmade straw broom.

She always said a fresh-cleaned yard didn't look right unless it had broom marks in the dirt. "You know, Vonion, this porch could sure use some paint. Do you think you could handle the job if I bought a gallon or two?"

Vonion stepped back like I had thrown hot water on him and quickly answered, "I ain't never in my life had no paintbrush in my hand. I reckon we have to find somebody else to do that kind of work!" After thinking about it a minute, I knew he was right. Vonion would get more paint on the floor and himself than he would get on the porch. Painting was not in his job description.

Vonion ambled out to the barn for the mower, and I stood there watching as he sat on an old wooden crate and started sharpening the blades. Christmas would come and go before he'd be through. "Have patience," I had to keep telling myself.

Back in the house, I tuned the radio to *The Good Morning Gospel Hour*. My favorite quartet, The West Family, which included Mom and Pop West and two of their grown children, Orville and Irma Jean, were singing "Amazing Grace." As I hummed along with the song, I began to ponder whether I would go see Preacher Henry today or wait until tomorrow and maybe just call. Tomorrow won out. While listening to the rest of my program, I gave my electric stove a good scouring and defrosted the icebox. Beginning to feel a few hunger pangs, I fixed a sandwich of leftover meat loaf and ate it while standing at the window watching the birds fly down to the ground, looking for an insect or a fat, juicy worm for their lunch. Vonion was still piddling around out in the yard when I finished my lunch, so I took a couple of sandwiches wrapped in a tea towel and some ice water in a quart jar out to him and asked if everything was okay out by the barn.

"Well, that greedy old fox still tryin' to get in the hen house, but I fixed them holes again. Can't keep that ole chicken snake out, though. He been suckin' eggs again. Found a few empty egg shells. Hogs seem fairly contented and Hortence give plenty of milk today. I guess everythang is usual. Want me to take some milk down the road to Ms. Waters fer them chil'ren?"

Vonion had taught me a great deal about sharing. When he knew about a need in the community, he always wanted to help out. Carl Waters had run off a few months ago and left his wife and three small children to fend for themselves. Eve Waters said he would be back after he made some money, but Vonion and I thought she might be living in a dream world. "Take all of it today, unless you and Ora Lee need some. And Vonion, I imagine they need some eggs and maybe a few tomatoes. Take whatever we have. The good Lord has seen about our needs, and it's our duty to help out those less fortunate."

"That mighty kind of you, Ms. Bee."

"Vonion, did you hear about Old Man Peterson's robbery the other night?"

"Yesum, I heared about it at Floyd's yesterd'y. I meant to mention it to you, but you was off gallivantin' most all day. Poor old Peterson. He probably gonna mourn hisself to death about that money. Dis world is getting meaner, and it creeping to us."

"I don't want to worry you, Vonion, but we need to be a little more observant of what's going on around here, don't you think?"

"Yessum, we shore does."

I was anxious to get over to check on Ora Lee. As I entered their house that afternoon, I was distressed to find her hunched down in the big old overstuffed chair in the front room. Going into Ora Lee's and Vonion's home was like entering a dark cave. They never used any unnecessary lighting, and the windows were always covered with some kind of heavy fabric. The furnishings were familiar since Ora Lee had always been the recipient of Mama's or my castoffs. She had always gratefully accepted whatever we wanted to get rid of. Ora Lee could find a use for anything and never threw a thing away. When an upholstered chair became raggedy, she would spread an old blanket on top. Old rugs padded older rugs and broken table legs mended. The old iron bedstead that sat in the front bedroom against the wall had at least four homemade cotton-ticked mattresses stacked one on top of the other. Every surface in the house was covered with some inexpensive knickknack.

"Ora Lee, you just got to quit worrying about Lettie and the children so much. It's just getting you down, what with your high blood and everything. You're just making yourself sick. Now, it's not healthy, you being cooped up in here and not even setting eyes on that daytime sky. You got redbirds all over the yard you haven't even laid eyes on yet. Come on out to the porch. There's a whole slew of them out there right now, bossing each other around."

Ora Lee moved over to the window and pushed the curtain back to look out. "Ms. Bee, it be so hard to get my mind on anything 'cept Lettie these days. I just wish she bring them chil'ren on back here and let me help her take care of 'um. I know them chil'ren all getting big now, and they needs to get off them city streets. Lettie won't listen. The Lord did give us a brain and he 'spect us to use it."

Well, I expect Ora Lee was right about that. She could reason things out better than anybody I ever knew. Ora Lee had always been my savior when I needed someone with a little sense to talk something out with; it wasn't like her to let things get her down so badly.

After finally getting her out to the porch to sit with me a spell, Ora Lee looked over my way and said, "What you done did to yo head? It seem a might bright this afternoon." Well, finally somebody had noticed my hair. I just didn't know if it was in a favorable way. I was beginning to think I was invisible. I watched Ora Lee's expression as I told her about my trip to the beauty parlor, but she just got that blank look on her face again, as if to say she didn't really care.

After a final attempt to cheer Ora Lee, I walked over to the porch stoop to leave, and reluctantly added, "Ora Lee, stay outside a while and enjoy the fresh air. I can't be worrying myself about you down here brooding all day long. Now please, perk up and quit tormenting yourself about Lettie. She's a smart woman and she can take care of her own children. You know you raised her to know right from wrong."

"I did do that, but she so wrong to marry that sorry scoundrel and try to raise them young'uns in that big old sin town."

Thinking she might be right again, I turned and started walking back up the field lane toward the house, thinking to myself. Why did Ora Lee have to get old before me? With all that was on my mind, the peacefulness of the cotton field put me at ease with every step. How I wished Will could be with me now. He would reason everything would be all right. With Ora Lee off my mind for a few minutes, I started thinking about Bess.

I needed to meet this new so-called friend of hers and pass judgment. I couldn't imagine why she needed a man friend, of all things, to distract her. She had not been out to the house to sit on the porch with me all this week. We badly needed to clean the cemetery lot where all our people were buried, but every time I mentioned it, she said she was busy doing something else. Now I knew how she was filling her time. It wasn't cleaning and organizing her closets. I guess I better keep in mind her social schedule might be full before I popped in at her house from now on.

The telephone rang later that afternoon as I was watering my wilted potted plants out on the porch. Two rings, one long, one short. That's me. I hurried in the house and reached for the telephone.

"Hello, Bee Martin speaking." Preacher Henry was on the line again.

"Ms. Bee, how's everything out at your house today?"

"Hot as usual, but I'm doing okay. I hope you're feeling well."

"Yes, all is well here at the pastorium, but I did have our conversation on my mind today. I don't really know how much time you need to think about what I asked you, but I'm on pins and needles wondering about your answer. I hope I'm not rushing you."

"No, not at all. In fact, I've decided to agree to your idea." Bess was going to kill me dead as a doorknob, but I was going ahead with this. I sat down on the telephone bench and listened as Preacher Henry went on to tell me he was sure we could come together on my compensation.

I gingerly replied, "I think fifty dollars a month would cover everything nicely." I had my fingers and my legs crossed as I mentioned the amount to him.

"I think that sounds about right. I don't really believe she'll be any trouble. She won't expect you to do any entertaining, just supply her basic needs. She's coming in Tuesday on the eleven o'clock train. Would it be all right if I brought her out about four o'clock in the afternoon? We'll probably eat at the diner and then go by the pastorium before coming out."

"That sounds fine," I replied. Bess would just have to get over it. If she wanted to busy herself with some old man she didn't know anything about, then she would just have to get used to the idea of me branching out into the business world.

CHAPTER FIVE

Sunday morning came and the frustration of my hair along with it. I was trying to take extra care to make my hair look presentable today for church services, and it wasn't cooperating. I never felt as if my hair looked exactly right anyway. "Why hadn't I made another appointment with Thelma to get it done yesterday?" I asked myself. "Because I couldn't afford it, that's why."

Now, if Vonion could sell eggs each week, I could make enough to go to Thelma on Saturdays. If we could take on five egg customers and sell each one at least two dozen eggs a week, that would just about cover my hair expense. To sell ten dozen eggs a week would mean we would have to have at least sixteen more layers, and that would mean we would have to buy more chicken feed from Old Jake at the hardware store. That money would have to be deducted from the profit. "That just ain't gonna happen," as Vonion would say. I might as well learn to do a better job with my hair and not worry about more chickens. That old fox would probably kill them anyway and besides that, Vonion would fuss and fume about all the extra work required by having more chickens to feed, more eggs to pick up and wash, and deliveries to make. It wasn't worth the effort.

A few of the girls had already seen my hair. Sitting on the fourth section of pews where my family had sat my entire life, I knew everybody in the Jeffersontown First Baptist Church would have a good view of it this morning. Even with it partially covered with my little pink pillbox. My pink and lavender dress was old, but I had taken care of it and never worn it anywhere except to church or a wedding, so it had kept its shape pretty well. I wish I could say that about myself. After I added white gloves and tucked a little lace handkerchief under my belt, I thought I looked fairly presentable. "If I could just lose that extra weight," my mind kept telling me.

Sitting alone on the pew with just my thoughts, I glanced around at the cracked plaster walls and scratched hardwood floors. The deacons were in constant battle to keep the church maintained. A few members of the church felt we needed cushions for the hard pews. Some members were in agreement we needed the interior walls patched and painted. We were all painfully aware the old furnace didn't work half the time, and the windows were so warped they couldn't be budged. Will had been a deacon, but unfortunately, he and I had always been on different sides when it came to the church spending money. Like most of the other deacons, he considered money spent for comfort or paint was an unnecessary expense. I guess we'd have to swelter to death in the heat of summertime or freeze to death in winter to get those few stubborn men to even consider a remodeling project.

Bess soon found her way over to our pew and sat down. After adjusting her wide-brimmed hat adorned with an abundance of fruit and flowers, and smoothing her pale yellow dress, she leaned over to me and said, "Bee, I hope the preacher keeps the service short today. It's stifling in here." My mind snapped back as Bess picked up a cardboard fan with a picture of a stream flowing through the woods on one side and Lawson's Funeral Home stamped across the other and started fanning furiously. One negative remark about my hair from her today and I knew I would want to crawl under the pew and never come out again. So far so good, Bess hadn't said a word about it.

Our little choir sang "I'll Fly Away" to a fast tempo that morning. I noticed that just about everybody was tapping their toes and some were even clapping their hands. Millie and Tillie, the elderly twins who always sat in the front row of the choir were really letting it go. It's amazing how good music can help revive a service. Preacher Henry preached on "Disobedience to God, Joshua 7" but never really got into that fire and brimstone mode. He appeared nervous, but I guess that was understandable since he was still new. His sermon was terribly dry, and it seemed he was reading part of it from a paper he had tucked into his Bible. Even his short prayers sounded rehearsed and memorized. He was just a temporary replacement for Preacher Jenkins so I suppose we couldn't complain. We would just have to bear up under him until our pulpit committee could find a suitable preacher for the church.

We had a fairly good crowd this morning for worship even though Sunday school attendance was off. Some of our youth were on an organized trip over at

Antioch Baptist Church. They were to participate in their service and then enjoy a social in the afternoon. I remembered fondly all the good times Bess and I had as youngsters, meeting other groups of children from nearby churches on those so-called organized trips. Bess had actually met Fred when our youth invited some teens from Rosemary Church to a peanut-boil down at Simpson's Lake. After they set eyes on each other the first time, they never noticed anybody else. Now Bess was ready to change all that because some old fool was paying her a little attention.

After the service was over, I stopped in the front door of the church to shake the preacher's hand and then quickly moved on out to the front of the church as other members were beginning to crowd up behind us. I looked around for Bess and finally spotted her over by the cars talking to Madge Bennett and her husband, Harold.

I waved and walked over to them and asked if they had seen Old Man Peterson since the robbery. Harold answered that he noticed Peterson hadn't been in church today, but he had driven out our way the day before and had stopped in to check on the old codger. "That man is going to grieve himself to death about that money. He needs to look to keeping his money in the bank from now on. Some people can't ever learn and he's probably one of them."

"Did he tell you how much money was taken?"

"No, he didn't say the exact amount but I'd say it was considerable..."

Madge glared at her husband and interrupted as if she was aggravated with Harold about something. "It's a shame he never saw fit to spend any money on his wife or children. They did without all those years, and now all that money is gone and they are too. What good did it do any of them? All it's done is line the pockets of some good-for-nothing thief," she snapped. "We can all learn a lesson about using our money for what we want and need and not pinching it as tight as a rubber band."

I decided to change the subject before Madge got any more carried away. "The song service was wonderful this morning. Tillie and Millie really belted it out."

"They sure did," Bess agreed. "The music was really inspiring. The sermon left a little to be desired, though, if you ask me."

"I know what you mean," replied Madge. "But I thought it was just me."

I turned to Bess and said a little forcefully, only for the benefit of Harold, one of our stubborn deacons, "Maybe he's just not used to the heat."

"Well, if he plans on staying here for any length of time, he better get used to it," Harold responded vehemently, as if to make a point.

I could feel the tension beginning to build, so I hurriedly asked Bess if she'd come on out to the house for a while this afternoon. I suggested we could take a walk and then relax on the porch with some iced tea.

"I feel a little fatigued today in all this heat. I think I'll just go on home and rest awhile. Thanks for the offer, though. Maybe we can get together later in the week." She didn't look tired at all to me. In fact, she looked pretty refreshed. I stood there with Madge and Harold and watched as she climbed into her car and disappeared in a cloud of dust and a grinding of gears.

Harold shook his head and said, "She's going to tear up that gear shift if she doesn't learn to change those gears properly. Does she do that all the time?"

I nodded and said, "All the time."

Harold shook his head and muttered, "Women drivers."

* * *

Top on my list of things to get done before Tuesday was to call Margaret and listen to her give me twenty reasons why I shouldn't go into my new vocation. I was dreading the thought of telling her, so I put off the call. It might soften the blow if I told her about Bess's new friend first. Bess having a boyfriend was as unbelievable to me as someone flying off into space, and we knew that wasn't ever going to happen.

Readying the house for the arrival of my boarder was really beginning to overwhelm me, but I jumped into action Monday morning. I still had sheets and pillowcases to wash and iron, and I wanted to put a shine on Mama's bedroom suit in the guest room. Every time I thought I was getting to the end of my to-do list, there seemed to be more to add to it. Why, I had completely forgotten to air out the mattress and pillows. It would have been so good to have Ora Lee up here telling me what needed to be done and doing it before I could even think about it. I'd have to see if I could get Vonion up here in a few days to help me take the mattress out in the yard to air properly. With everything else that had to be done today, it was just too late now.

I had not done any extensive cleaning since Will passed away, and you can't catch up on everything in one day. I kept telling myself that I was going to get this house back in good order—even if it killed me. I wanted to mop down the porches and clean the screens, but that would have to be another day. Maybe I could get Vonion to help with that. My windows needed a good scrubbing, and the curtains desperately needed to be washed and starched. The list just went on and on. Maybe if I just thought about one thing at a time, I could deal with it better. As exhausted as I was Monday night, I realized I couldn't put off calling Margaret with my news any longer. She answered after two rings. We talked about her new school year, which would start soon, and all her preparations for it. We were having a perfectly normal conversation when I started with news from home.

"Margaret, I know you're going to have a hard time believing this, but your Aunt Bess has a suitor now, of all things. I haven't had the pleasure of meeting him, but if Bess likes him, he's probably nice. I don't know much about him yet, but as time goes by, I'm sure I'll learn more. He seems to be taking up all her time, though. I hope she knows what she's really getting into."

Margaret didn't seem shocked at all and said, "Mama, it's perfectly natural that Aunt Bess would want to entertain a friend at this time of her life. Now you need to be a little more patient with her. She's got every right in the world to do what she wants. I'm happy for her."

If that little piece of news didn't shock her, I knew something that would. I hurriedly began telling her about the preacher's proposal, knowing that if I could tell her everything without her interrupting, I had a better chance of her understanding the whole picture.

Well lo and behold, she replied, "Mother, that sounds like a brilliant idea. I think you should jump on it. I know it'll be a lot of work, but you're still young and you do have Vonion and Ora Lee to help out. I wouldn't worry nearly as much about you if somebody was there at the house with you."

Well, I never expected that reaction, and, I must say, I was floored. I guess I had raised a modern woman after all.

CHAPTER SIX

Isabelle Newsome and the preacher arrived Tuesday afternoon. Preacher Henry drove down the lane and pulled the car over into the shade with my boarder in tow. I was standing at the window watching as the car drove up. I wanted to get a good look at Isabelle before she saw me. I noticed them look at each other, give a nod and a grin, as if to say, "We're here at last." She stepped out after Preacher Henry came all the way around to the side of the car and opened the door for her. I knew I should come away from the window and go out to greet them, but I watched as he walked to the back of the car to get her luggage from the trunk. She never once moved to help with all the paraphernalia that needed to be brought in. Laden with the suitcases, he followed his sister to the steps where he dropped everything and knocked. I slowly moved away from the window and walked out to the porch with a smile on my face and dread in my heart, saying to myself, "You can do this."

"Hello, Preacher Henry. I see you made it," I said, as I opened the screen door for the two to come in.

"Ms. Bee, I'd like to introduce you to my younger sister, Isabelle Newsome." Preacher Henry reached down and picked up the luggage and followed her in.

"I'm glad to meet you, Isabelle. I hope the trip on the train wasn't too taxing. Please, come on into the house." I could see that Isabelle was quite pretty with deep dimples set in an oval-shaped face. Her dark complexion was highlighted by shoulder length wavy brunette hair. She couldn't have been more than twenty-two years old.

"No, not at all. I'm glad to meet you as well. I do hope this arrangement isn't too much for you. Henry didn't tell me you were elderly."

"That's because I'm not elderly. Maybe I'm just looking tired today after all the time I've devoted to getting the house ready for you." This is not starting out well, I thought to myself. I quickly added, "I do hope everything will be satisfactory."

"Oh, I didn't mean you looked old or anything like that. I'm truly sorry if you misunderstood my meaning. I'm quite sure everything will be fine. I'm really not that hard to please." We all just stood there for a moment like knots on a log, when finally I gestured for them to come on into the front room. Following them in, I couldn't help but notice Isabelle had an angular and lean body. She had a lengthy stride and could probably walk a great distance without nearly as many steps as most would take. I was sure she never had to hem any readymade dress. Instead, she probably had a time finding one long enough. She didn't seem to favor Preacher Henry in the face, nor did their mannerisms seem similar. I imagined she looked like one parent and he looked like the other. They did have their height in common.

As we were sitting down, I asked if they'd like something to drink.

"We had a drink over at Floyd's a few minutes ago, but thanks just the same," answered the preacher.

We discussed the weather and with the conversation dragging, if you could call it one at all, the preacher asked if there was anywhere in particular I'd like Isabelle's luggage left. I offered to help him take them into the guest room, and as we walked back into the front room where we left Isabelle, I noticed she was still sitting on the settee with her hands folded in her lap. Preacher Henry looked at Isabelle and said, as if to only be speaking to her, "I need to be going now. I have some visiting to do before dark, dear."

Isabelle gave him a helpless little look and stood up as he walked toward the door. "I thought you'd stay awhile and not leave me alone my first night way out here in the country."

"You're not alone. I'm quite sure Ms. Bee will be more than happy to keep you company tonight. You'll be fine."

He opened the door to leave, looked back and in an encouraging voice said, "I'll be back tomorrow afternoon and maybe we can go for a walk if it's not too hot out. You two have a nice evening getting to know one another now." He walked over and gave Isabelle a little peck on the cheek, me a nod and was out the door.

We heard Preacher Henry's steps cross the porch floor and then the screen door scrape against the floor. Looking very uncomfortable, Isabelle finally said, "I'm awfully tired and need to freshen up now, if you don't mind. Where did you say the bathroom is?"

"I'll show you around the house later, but for now, your room is right down the hall, and the bathroom is next to it. If there is anything at all you need, just ask."

She nodded and excused herself saying, "I'm sure everything's fine. I hope I won't be a bother. Do you happen to have some aspirin? I seem to have developed a slight headache."

"Maybe it's the strain of getting here today and being so unsure about all these new surroundings and developments. There's a bottle in the bathroom medicine cabinet. I'll get a glass."

Isabelle took the glass and said, "By the way, I seem to have forgotten hand lotion. Do you think I could possibly borrow a little of yours until I can get to the store?"

"There's some in the bathroom closet on the top shelf. Use all you need. It might not be the kind you use, but it was on special at the store the other day."

Isabelle went into the bathroom and closed the door. She spent the rest of the afternoon in her room with the door closed. As evening approached, we ate a light supper of chicken salad sandwiches, chewy cake, and iced tea. Afterwards we each headed into our bedrooms to retire for the evening. Before lying down that night, I walked over to Isabelle's room and tapped lightly.

She opened the door right away and stood there with the hairbrush in her hand. "Come on in, Ms. Bee. I'm just trying to get the tangles out of my hair."

I glanced into the bedroom and couldn't help but notice all the clothes strewn over the chairs, shoes all over the floor, and opened suitcases left on the bed.

"No thank you, I just wanted to see if you had everything you needed before I lie down," I said from the hallway.

"I could use something to read. I seem to have gone off without anything to entertain me. Anything will do."

"I do have a book I picked up at the library you might like. I'll get it for you. It's a romance."

What have I gotten myself into? I thought to myself as I was finally lying down that night. Why that girl hadn't even made any attempt to have a decent conversation all during our meal. She could have at least commented on the chicken salad. Ora Lee had gone to a lot of trouble chopping chicken and pickles, cooking that cake on her old wood stove, trying to have something a little special for Isabelle's first night. Ora Lee had warned me that young people didn't have any manners anymore, and I was beginning to see what she meant. Isabelle had not even seen fit to bow her head for grace. I actually had to mention I always had a little prayer of thanksgiving before we ate our meal. Maybe she was just nervous; after all, tomorrow was another day.

Sleep didn't come easily. I began to make a mental list of all the things that could go wrong. I could have an invasion of mice, the plumbing could start leaking or get stopped up, and the milk could go sour at any time. The last thing I remembered thinking about as I dozed off was what on earth I would do if my old washing machine conked out.

Can you imagine anybody sleeping until eleven o'clock in the morning? Isabelle did. I had laid her breakfast out at seven, eaten mine, and gone on about my morning routine. After whispering on the telephone to

Bess a while, I headed out to see if Vonion was still out in the yard or around the lot. I could see him with a bucket out in the garden, in his long-sleeved shirt and a big straw hat, picking on the butter bean row.

Knowing we would have fresh butter beans tonight, I decided right then to ask the preacher to stay for supper. I walked out to the garden and asked, "Vonion, you finding anything? As dry as it's been, they're probably drying up."

"They's a few, enough for a couple a messes, I reckon."

"Good. How's Ora Lee this morning?"

"She a might better. She done got the washin' on the line, that somethin' for her."

"I'll be over to help shell the beans in a while," I said, and turned to walk back toward the house. I sat down on the back porch and glanced at a newspaper I had brought back from town a few days ago. I heard some movement in the house about the time I found a comfortable position and thought Isabelle was stirring around at last. I brought some frozen pork chops in from my porch freezer and placed them in the sink to thaw.

I had it on the tip of my tongue to say *Good afternoon*, but I didn't. "Morning," I said, as Isabelle walked into the kitchen. "I left coffee on the stove, and there's toast on the table under the dish towel."

"I normally don't eat breakfast. I was just looking for some coffee and maybe some more of that chewy cake," Isabelle replied in that squeaky voice that I was beginning to wonder if I could ever get used to. I could already tell my boarder didn't have good eating habits and probably didn't know the difference between a starch and a vegetable.

"There's plenty of food here in the kitchen. Eat anything you want. The chewy cake is in the bread box wrapped in wax paper. I'm on my way over to Ora Lee's house to shell beans for supper; so if you need me, I'll be down the lane. Ora Lee lives with her husband, Vonion, in the little house you can see here from the window. Supper is at six, and it would be my pleasure for the preacher to eat with us tonight."

She didn't actually reply, just nodded to me as if it didn't really matter one way or the other to her. I really thought she was still half asleep. I made my way out the back door and strolled down the lane.

"Ora Lee, how are you today?" I shouted, as I walked into the hard-packed dirt yard. Ora Lee was taking the wash off the sagging line Vonion had strung between the house and the chinaberry tree years ago.

"I's so much better and I got good news. You not the only one with people comin'. Got a letter from Lettie in this mornin's mail and she say she sending Roscoe here fer a stay. I be so glad to see that boy. He be a man now, though. Guess he going on twenty years. He should be here in a day or two, soon as he find a way. Lettie says she don't know 'sactly when. I guess we just have to wait and see."

Well, that was the best tonic Ora Lee could have had, just to know that Lettie's oldest child was on his way to stay. Maybe Ora Lee could get a little peace of mind knowing that boy was under her roof at night.

"Ora Lee, that's wonderful. It's going to be so good to see that young man again. Why, I guess I haven't laid eyes on him in at least a year. What do you reckon he'll find to do when he gets here? I do know Tom Wilson's always looking to find somebody to help him out, and you know cotton picking time's right around the corner."

Vonion came walking up about that time and handed the bucket of beans to me. I followed Ora Lee with her basket of clean laundry up on to the sloping porch. Feeling as if he had done his part, Vonion ambled on into the house, to rest his eyes a while, he said.

"I don't reckon I rightly know what that boy can do, but I just imagine he can shore learn somethin'. Come on now and let's get started on the beans or we's won't git done in time to cook them this evening." Then abruptly, Ora Lee changed the subject, "When the last time you he'rd from Margaret? It shore be good to see that girl."

"I talked to her a few days ago. I need to call her again and see when she can come. She's busy right now getting ready for the new school year. She needs to find a suitor, is what I think. She doesn't like to be reminded that she's not getting any younger and if she's gonna find somebody, she better get on with it."

Ora Lee and I jabbered and listened to Vonion snore from the front room while we shelled the beans. When our stomachs started growling, Ora Lee offered me a tomato sandwich. There's no way to describe how delicious that fresh salty tomato tasted between two slices of homemade bread. Maybe sitting out in the open air with good company had something to do with it. As we were finishing up the last of the beans, I glanced over and Ora Lee had dropped her head and was snoring in tune with Vonion. That's when I laid my head back and lost track of time too.

Later, as I walked back up the lane toward the house with my shelled beans in one of Ora Lee's bent up pans and a pound of butter Ora Lee had churned, I noticed

Preacher Henry and Isabelle out walking under the pecan trees, enjoying an afternoon breeze.

Preacher Henry did stay on to grace our table that evening. After he recited a pitiful little prayer, he ate as if he had a hollow leg that he was trying to fill. Now we all know there's nothing better than fried pork chops, mashed potatoes, fresh butter beans, corn bread, and sliced tomatoes; however, Isabelle just picked at the food on her plate. She explained that it was good, but a little rich for her delicate system. "It'll just sour in my stomach, as hot as it is in this house," she complained, as the preacher and I continued to eat as heartedly as two field hands. As I was serving peaches with heavy cream for dessert, I thought I heard a burp from the preacher's direction. He better watch that before sitting down at some of our more persnickety members' houses. A little unintentional mishap such as that could become a main topic of conversation around our church circles.

After the preacher had left for the evening and we had prepared for bed, I asked Isabelle if there was anything I could do for her before we retired for the evening.

"Not unless you can tell me how to sleep with this house creaking and croaking all night long. I've never been in a place that makes so much noise. My eyes didn't close at all last night. Between those creepy house noises all night long, those old crows cawing, the roosters crowing, the hogs grunting, and that cow mooing this morning, I couldn't even hear myself think."

"Well, you see, Isabelle, this is an old house and old houses creak and groan a lot. When we walk across the room, the floor squeaks. When we shut a door, the door groans. These are just sounds of age. The animals are waking up, and that's their way of letting you know that a new and fresh day is beginning. Maybe you'll get used to it as time goes by."

"I doubt it," responded Isabelle irritably. "I won't be here that long anyway."

"Well, try your best. Perhaps if you drank some warm milk before retiring for the night, you would rest better."

"I'd rather drink poison than warm milk. I can't stand that stuff."

"Suit yourself, but keep it to yourself. Hortence, our milk cow, might get her feelings hurt. She's real proud of her milk," I replied with a little playful smile behind my waning concern for Isabelle's comfort.

CHAPTER SEVEN

A few days later, Roscoe caught a ride on a produce truck from his home in Atlanta into Jeffersontown and then walked on out to Ora Lee's and Vonion's. Isabelle would sleep half the morning and read or just stare out into space except when the preacher would visit. He came every day and they would walk down around the pecan trees late in the afternoons or visit with church members. The pecan trees were putting on nuts and the cotton fields were blooming. Our garden was producing and Ora Lee and I were busy putting up butter beans and purple hull peas, using every jar we could lay our hands on for tomatoes and okra. This was a busy time for us and Ora Lee was coming around to her old self, especially now that Roscoe was staying with them. He seemed to be a bright boy, but without a job, he had too much time on his hands. Tom Wilson had not hired him, even though Roscoe had been over to talk to him several times. It would be September or October before the cotton would need to be picked and until then, he said he just didn't need him. With nothing much to do, he'd wander around the place or walk into town.

* * *

I was headed out the door one afternoon and asked Isabelle if she'd like to ride into town with me. I was floored when she answered in her squeaky voice, "You know, I think I would enjoy the ride. I've been cooped up here all day, and I really need to get out."

"I'm going by Bess's house for a few minutes," I said, as we were opening the car doors. "Would you like for me to put you off somewhere in town or would you like to visit with Bess and me?"

Isabelle immediately answered, "I think I'd enjoy seeing Bess's house and visiting a little with her. She seems to be a real nice person." We drove straight over and as we pulled up in front of the house, I noticed a strange truck in the driveway. I hesitated to stop, thinking it was probably J.R.'s. Why did he have to be here now? Well, I had to meet him sometime, I guess, and now was as good as later.

I stopped the car in front of the house and began thinking to myself how I wished I had taken the time to dress a little better. Isabelle looked fresh as a daisy in her pretty blue shirtwaist dress with the little round collar, and if Bess was entertaining, I knew she would be wearing something nice, not a housedress like I had on. Oh well, there just weren't enough hours in a day to coordinate your wardrobe all the time. At least my hair was holding its curl, and I had powdered my nose and put on a little lipstick.

As we walked up to Bess's side door, the one I always used, I thought I heard a giggle. Never in all my life had I knocked at her door and she had never knocked at mine; we generally walked in unannounced. After hesitating just a second, I did tap on the door a little timidly and stuck my head inside. "Yoo-hoo, Bess," I called.

That was when I knew I heard a giggle, then a whisper, more giggles and then a masculine voice, saying, "Cuddle Bumps, don't answer that. Whoever it is, they'll go away."

"Is that you, Bee? Wait a minute and I'll let you in," I heard Bess call from the other room.

I was already halfway in, standing in her doorway, and had heard more than I intended. Standing there with Isabelle behind me and waiting for Bess to come into the kitchen to greet us, I thought time would stand still. I was already mortified at what I had happened upon, and to top it all, Isabelle had to be with me today, of all days.

All in a fluster, Bess appeared in the doorway to the kitchen. She hurried toward us, straightening her dress and hair, looking guilty as sin. "Why Bee, come on in. And Isabelle, how nice to see both of you. We were just talking, and J.R. was telling me about a funny thing that happened to him yesterday." I hoped she didn't actually think we believed that. There was something funny going on here, and it wasn't J.R.'s story.

"Oh, Bess, I should have called. I never in a hundred years considered you would be entertaining in the middle of the afternoon. This is just an imposition. Isabelle and I can come back another time when you aren't so busy."

"Well, as a matter of fact, we aren't doing anything in particular. Come on in and let's have a little visit," she said a little half-heartedly.

"Well, if you're sure we aren't interrupting anything, we'll just stay a few minutes," I responded, knowing full well there was a lot more going on here than met the eye. Bess never could fool me about anything.

I walked into the front room behind Isabelle and Bess, not really knowing what to expect. Bess had never described J.R. to me other than to say he was a handsome middle-aged businessman from Wall County. All I can say is, I knew Bess was far-sighted, but I didn't know her sight was that bad. J.R. was a barrel-shaped, bald-headed old man, sitting in Fred's chair, the very chair that Bess had never allowed me sit in once since Fred had passed away. Why, I had always considered that chair to be downright holy. The very idea that she would let anybody lounge in it, with his shoes off and his shirt unbuttoned, was as farfetched to me as Bess growing collards, instead of flowers, in her front yard. It was far too late for him to try and tuck his shirt back into his pants or put his shoes back on. Looking like somebody who had been caught with his fingers in the sugar jar, he pulled himself out of the chair and extended his arm to shake our hands. Bess took charge and started introducing everybody. Why, I could even smell cigar smoke in the air.

"This is a real unexpected pleasure having the two of you drop in today," Bess nervously said, glancing over toward me. "Y'all sit down a spell and I'll bring in some homemade lemonade. It won't take me but a minute," she gushed, as if she were out of breath.

She headed back into the kitchen, and I popped out of my chair and said, "I'll help, Bess. J.R., excuse me. You and Isabelle just sit here and visit a few minutes together." I followed close behind Bess, and we made it through the kitchen door just in time for Bess to turn around and give me a look that made me want to dissolve into her recently cleaned woodwork.

Bess closed the door, turned around and locked eyes with me. Trying to defend herself, she whispered, "This is not nearly as casual as it seems. J.R. was hot and I told him he could cool off awhile before we went out to eat. He is usually well dressed and neat. We were just relaxing a few minutes and, well, you know how it is."

Yes, I knew how it was, all right. I knew Bess never let Fred sit around with his shirt unbuttoned in the daytime, or the nighttime, for that matter. I'm sure she had never allowed him to take his shoes off and throw them out into the middle of the floor. Fred had always lived by Bess's rules and standards.

Speaking as quietly as I could, I replied, "Well, I guess we really shouldn't have popped in on you without calling first, and we surely will knock the next time. But Bess, I hope you know what you're doing here, allowing a man into your home you hardly know anything about. I think maybe you're just lonely, but you aren't gonna find another Fred. Fred was a jewel. Don't let the likes of J.R. Kitchens knock the good sense right out of your head. I'm not telling you anything you wouldn't tell me under the same circumstances and you know it. You're treading in deep water here, and you might be getting in over that permed up head of yours."

"Let's discuss this later. Now grab those glasses and let's drink some lemonade so y'all can go. I don't like leaving Isabelle in there with J.R. too long. I don't imagine they have a thing to talk about. They surely don't have a thing in common. What did you bring her over here for anyway?"

"She said she wanted to come, and she needed to get out of the house. Is there anything wrong with that?"

"No, but I would have liked some advanced warning," Bess snapped right back at me.

"Well, next time I come, I'll send a card in the mail to give you plenty of notice," I said in a sarcastic voice that Bess had heard before.

"Whatever," Bess mockingly answered.

Isabelle and J.R. seemed to be having no trouble at all finding a topic of conversation and were having a little chuckle as we entered with the lemonade. After a little more chitchat, Isabelle asked to be excused, and Bess showed her down the hall to the bathroom. As Bess sat back down, J.R., sounding as if he knew something about farming, started asking me how the crops were growing this dry year and if the cotton out our way was putting on many blooms yet. He explained that he had been a fertilizer salesman for thirty years before he retired and was always interested in what was going on out on the farms around the county.

Bess broke into the conversation, as if she were proud of all of J.R's accomplishments, "J.R. always was a hard worker and had such a fine income. He's still able to live very comfortably in his well-deserved retirement." I was to learn later from Bess that J.R.'s wife of thirty-two years had died three months earlier, leaving J.R. comfortable with insurance money, and free as a bird. It sounded to me as if he was a fast worker, as well as a hard worker, him being a bachelor for such a short time and already out looking around for a replacement for his late wife, Minnie Lou.

With Isabelle still down the hall, Bess craned her head in that direction and finally got up to check on her whereabouts. Bess walked down the hall and stopped in the doorway to her bedroom. I heard her say, as she looked through the open door, "I wondered if you were okay. We missed your company."

Straining my ears to hear, I heard Isabelle answer from Bess's back bedroom, "I was just admiring your lovely bedroom. You have such a lovely bedspread, and I just love your curtains."

Bess glowingly replied, "Why, thank you. I've always loved to decorate, but with a limited budget, it's a little frustrating. My nicer things were all inherited from Fred's mother and father. The silver comb and brush set on the dresser is just one of many things they left us. They also left us quite a bit of silver and cut glass. They were fairly well off before the depression, and even though they didn't have much money left afterwards, they were able to hang on to some nice things."

"Well, you certainly do have beautiful things, and I can see why you'd be so proud of everything. I know I would be."

I knew that they were speaking Bess's language in there, talking about silver and cut glass and all that fancy stuff. We could hear them talking away about the rest of the décor without giving another thought about leaving us alone with not one earthly thing to talk about except the weather and crops.

Finally, as they returned to the front room, I immediately stood up, annoyed at both of them for leaving Bess's lover boy and me alone for so long. I firmly said, "Isabelle, I really need to get started on my errands before it gets any later. We don't need to take up any more of Sister's time anyway."

"Well, I have enjoyed the visit, Ms. Bess, and I just love your house," Isabelle gushed, as we headed toward the door to leave the lovebirds alone to resume whatever it was they were doing before we barged in.

Bess stood in the doorway as we were getting in the car and called out to Isabelle. "Come on back soon, and I'll show you the rest of the house."

"It would be my pleasure," Isabelle called back. "You just name the time, and I'll find a way to get over. You and I have such similar taste. It's so good to find someone around here that takes the time to make her home so charming." With a bat of the eyelids and a smile, Isabelle called, "Bye now." I didn't know how to take that last remark, so I just let it drop.

Isabelle tagged along with me to the public library to return my novel. I hadn't had a chance to even read the first page, but Isabelle had devoured it from cover to cover. Shirley, with a halo of cigarette smoke circling her head, greeted us as we walked in the front door. You could tell she was glad to see Isabelle, and she was obviously enchanted by the new preacher. "The preacher is so good to visit," she immediately started saying. "He's already been by my house twice this month, which was more than any other preacher ever has." I knew that had to be an exaggeration. Preacher Jenkins used to stop by and visit Shirley quite regularly. Shirley was just one of those people that loved to have anybody, even a preacher, give her the slightest bit of attention.

Isabelle seemed very proud of her brother, and gushed, "Ms. Shirley, that's so nice of you to say that. The next time he comes visiting, maybe I'll just tag along."

"Why, I would just love to have the both of you anytime. In fact, why don't y'all come on over for supper tomorrow? The library's closed all day and it's my day off. I'll have all day to ready the house and cook something special."

"Well, I believe I could go ahead and say yes. I know we can make it. Do you have a time set, so I can inform Henry?"

"Six o'clock will be good, if you think y'all can get over that early?"

"Oh, yes ma'am. That would be perfect for us. Henry generally tries to do some visiting late in the afternoons as many days as he can. We both have fairly busy schedules, but that sounds about right for us, that is, if it's not too much on you?"

If Isabelle had any kind of schedule, it had escaped my notice. Maybe sleeping fifteen hours a day did limit a person from some activities, but as far as I could see, Isabelle never exerted herself too much, anyway. She had not lifted one finger to help me do a thing around the house since she had arrived. I personally thought it had been impolite of Shirley to ask them over for a meal without extending the invitation to me as well. I wouldn't have accepted her invitation anyway. I happened to know that Shirley relied on one menu for guests—baked chicken and English peas, which I didn't even eat. But it is good to know that you are at least included.

As we were walking out with a couple of books to read, Shirley followed us to the door and smugly said, "By the way, Bee, I believe your hair has toned down a smidgeon since the other day. It doesn't seem quite so bright." As usual, Shirley had gotten in the last word.

After running by the grocery and drugstore, we finally pulled out on Route 3 towards home. About a mile outside of town, I noticed Roscoe hiking along the road. I slowed the car and pulled off the road beside him. Sticking my head out the window, I called, "Jump in, Roscoe. It's too hot to be out walking today. It must be ninety-eight degrees out here in the sun. You could have a heat stroke if you aren't careful."

Dripping with sweat and smelling to high heaven, Roscoe pulled his handkerchief out and wiped his brow as he got into the backseat. "Thank you, ma'am. It's hotter than a firecracker on the Fourth of July out here. I been 'bout everywhere I can think of huntin' a job, and it don't seem like there's notin' out there. I been round to five or six houses just today huntin' somethin'. You reckon Mr. Tom might reconsider 'bout hiring me if I go by there again?"

Isabelle never turned her head toward Roscoe or greeted him in any way, but placed her hand over her nose. Surely Isabelle wouldn't be so impolite as to say something about the strong odor coming from the backseat of the car, so I answered immediately, "Roscoe, I don't think it would hurt to check back with him again just to let him know how serious you are about working. What have you been doing with yourself these last few days besides looking for work?" I asked, as we rode along.

"I been helpin' Pa around the place some. He tried to teach me to do the milkin' the other day, but old Hortence, she wouldn't cooperate too good."

"That's something I never learned to do. Mama didn't want me to milk cows. She said it wasn't ladylike, and if I learned, Daddy might expect me to do it regularly.

"That so?"

"That's so."

"What about Ms. Bess? Did she ever learn to milk?" Roscoe asked.

"Ms. Bess? Why, she would never touch anything like that. I doubt she's ever touched a cow tit in her whole life. I'm not real sure she even knows where milk comes from," I kidded Roscoe. With a smile on my face, I added, "Daddy told us one time that the mama sow would rout her piglets up from the mud to birth them, and I think to this day she still believes that." Roscoe laughed while Isabelle rolled her eyes and gave a bored sigh.

As I pulled the car into the yard under the oak tree, I asked, "Roscoe, would you mind taking Ora Lee's medicine on down to her? Tell her she best better be taking it. She's always saying how that 'doctor medicine' just makes her sicker, but she just doesn't realize the full benefit of it. I don't want her to get down again like she did a week or so ago. I was so worried about her."

"I shore will, but first, I'll help with these grocery bags," Roscoe eagerly answered.

Isabelle didn't take time to offer to take one grocery bag into the house. Instead, she marched up the steps and onto the porch without one word of thanks for the ride to town or saying she enjoyed our time together. Being extremely annoyed with her for being rude to Roscoe, I wanted to call out, "Don't let the door hit you where the good Lord sits you." But I didn't. I presume her busy schedule didn't include offering to help with the groceries or being polite.

CHAPTER EIGHT

My days had settled into a routine of activities and chores. The preacher had promptly picked up Isabelle Sunday morning for Sunday school and church service. The two were out visiting—making their regular rounds—almost every afternoon and evening. Many of the church members even invited them to stay and eat. Isabelle was always chatting about how well somebody could set a table or what attractive homes a few of the members had. Roscoe was helping Vonion around the barn and yard. Ora Lee was feeling well again, and I was struggling with the idea I was completely being left out of Bess's social schedule now that J.R. was in the picture. Margaret had called the day before to let me know she would be coming in Friday afternoon for the weekend, so at last I had something to look forward to.

My desire to talk to Old Man Peterson about his intruder was stronger than my desire to avoid his unwanted advances, so I stopped by his small rundown place as I was driving by on my way to town one especially hot morning. One of his suspenders hung loose and the side flaps of his unbuttoned overalls gave me a whole area of his exposed anatomy to avoid looking directly at as he walked across his dirt yard, carrying a dented galvanized bucket. From the scowl on his unshaven face I could tell he was obviously still grieving about his stolen money.

I opened the car door and called out. "Morning, Mr. Peterson. Is it hot enough for you today?"

After his usual greeting, which was always only a nod, he answered, "I reckon so." He must have been on his way to slop the hogs. He put the bucket down on the ground, and the aroma of something that had been fermenting in the heat for a while filled the air. He took his faded blue handkerchief out of his back pocket to wipe the sweat that was dripping down his dark tanned face and boney neck. "We could use some rain about now. Maybe it would cool thangs off a little. Everybody's cotton's wilting in the field from this drought."

"Nobody can argue with that. Rain would surely be a blessing from God about now." Enough of this chitchat. I was ready to get down to the real reason I had come by.

After he offered me a seat on one of the old rusty chairs under the magnolia tree up next to the house, I said, "Mr. Peterson, you need to be thankful you didn't get killed or seriously injured the other night. I hope you've learned a lesson from all this. Your money would have been safer locked up in the bank, and your life is much more valuable than all the money on earth."

"Well, I ain't so sure about where my money would have been safer at. I probably should'a buried it, now that I think more on it. If'n I'd been ten years younger, that low-down thief wouldn't be walkin' around today, either. I'd have beaten him to a pulp!" he excitedly stated, as he looked over toward me out of the corner of his eye. "And if my arthritis hadn't been actin' up the other night, I could'a wrestled him to the floor and got all my money back, right then and there!" he added, as he beat his fist against the palm of his work-worn, gnarled hand.

"Mr. Peterson, you need to calm down right now! This thing isn't worth getting yourself so worked up that you have a heart attack just thinking about it."

"Easy fer you to say. It twern't your money that were stole," he replied, with an irritated tone in his voice. "I was a savin' that money fer something special. It were a motorcycle. I always wanted one, but my late wife wouldn't hear of it. She said it were a foolish dream of a foolish old man. Now that I think back on it, I imagine she were right about it. I won't ever be able to get one now, anyway. My money's all gone."

"Your wife didn't want to see you get hurt. She was just thinking of your safety. Do you even know how to ride one of those two-wheeled contraptions, Mr. Peterson?"

"Well, I ain't never rid one, but I'm sure I could'a learnt. I done plowed two old ornery mules all my life. What with Thisum wanting to go in one direction and Thatum wanting to go the other, I 'spect I could handle anything. I'm fairly sure I can manage a motorbike with just one engine. You just sit in the saddle, gun the motor, and hold on. It'll take you where you want to go, and you'll get there fast too. I 'spect I could have learnt the thing in a matter of a day or two. You know, two people can ride them thangs together, one drivin' and the other sittin' behind, holdin' on. I could'a come by your place and picked you up, and then you could'a enjoyed a ride along with me. We could'a raced all over the county."

Stricken with embarrassment at what he was implying, I gently added, "It is a nice dream all right, but Mrs. Peterson might have been right. You know, your eyesight isn't what it used to be." I wanted to add that his body and mind weren't what they used to be either, but I held my tongue. I came to the conclusion that perhaps that robbery had saved his scrawny hide from being splattered for a pack of buzzards to pick at. It also saved his feelings from being hurt after I had refused to straddle the thing.

I shuddered as I began to visualize this decrepit old man and me, huddled on from behind, with my dress tail flying in the wind, riding on one of those high-powered machines. That certainly would have given Nellie, our nosy telephone operator, a topic of conversation for days.

I was beginning to feel really sorry for my old neighbor by now. He had lost much more than just money as a result of the robbery. He had lost a dream.

Not wanting to sound too much like a busybody, but looking for some answers, I asked, "Is there anything at all you can remember about the intruder that you haven't told the sheriff? Was he big or small, short or tall? Did he say anything? Anything about him you can remember would surely help in the investigation."

"Bee, I told the sheriff everything I could remember. You know, with a black hood and black gloves on, I couldn't even tell if he was a colored man or a white man. He was strong though, and fast as a jackrabbit."

"Well, I tell you, it's not very comforting to think about some low-down scoundrel, who's too sorry to work for his own living, breaking in and robbing folks."

"Well, he's done got all my money now. That sorry, good-fer-nothing sheriff better come up with somethin' real quick or some other folks around here might wake up with that thief wandering around in their house in the pitch black dark of the night."

That sorry, good-fer-nothing sheriff was Earnest Ledbetter. Earnest was Etta Mae and Brinson Lee Ledbetter's only child. His daddy had always looked after him until Brinson Lee drowned while fishing by himself over at Simpson's Lake a year or so back. Earnest Ledbetter was on his own now, and for the life of me, I couldn't remember one crime the man had ever solved. Oh, he had picked up drunks off the street and arrested speeders, as well as a few brawlers that had gotten into street fights, but as far as using that space between his ears to solve a crime, he just didn't have a clue. He was always in need of a haircut, and his mustache looked like a piece of untrimmed shrubbery. He loved to hide behind a big old cigar he kept clinched between his stained teeth. Have you ever seen a man that wears his size forty-eight trousers pulled up to his armpits? I doubt any woman has ever given him a second look, except his mama of course. He still lives with her, and from what I hear, she still cooks and washes for her boy.

Not wanting to lollygag for fear Old Man Peterson might start giving me the eye again, I mentioned that I needed to get on to town. After asking Old Man Peterson if there was anything I could pick up for him at the store, I stood up and glanced around as I smoothed my dress back into place. That's when I noticed a small black button in the red clay right by the old worn-out steps to the house. I picked it up and rolled it over in my hand, trying to remove some of the caked-on dirt. I said, "Mr. Peterson, you must have lost a button."

"I reckon so, but I don't recollect losing one. I probably lost it a long while back."

"Probably so. Do you mind if I keep it? I'll put it in my button jar, and if you ever need a button sewed on, just let me know. I'll sew it on for you."

"Take it on. I ain't got no use fer it. Ain't nutin' I'm needin' from the store today either, but I thank you for the askin'. I might be a needin' somethin' next time you go, if'n you'll stop by again. Bee, I don't rightly know what it is, but there's somethin' about you that's not usual. I just can't put my finger on it."

"Mr. Peterson, I can't imagine what you mean," I answered, as I patted my hair. "I guess I'm the same as I've always been."

"Maybe it's yor hair? It don't seem the same. It looks like the sun is shinin' right through the top of it, real bright like. I like it!"

"Why thank you, Mr. Peterson. I'll take that as a compliment," I gushed.

I put the button in my change purse and wished Old Man Peterson a good day. As I was driving off, I began to wonder what I would do if I found a thief walking around in my house in the middle of the night. Maybe having Isabelle there with me at night was a comfort after all.

CHAPTER NINE

With so much to be done before Margaret comes for the weekend, I decided to make a to-do list before going to bed that night. I always sleep better if my thoughts are written down on paper—now if only I didn't lose the paper.

1. Bake caramel cake. (Margaret's favorite)
2. Spruce up house. (Boy, did I dread that)
3. Get Vonion to mow the yard and have a general yard clean up. (I probably had as much chance of getting him to move on that as seeing dogs fly through the air.)
4. Call Thelma for a redo.

First thing in the morning, I'd give Thelma a call, but right now I was ready to head for bed and lay my weary head down. It was getting a little late for visiting, and I noticed Isabelle hadn't returned to the house. Maybe they stopped off at the pastorium for a while. My little beauty regimen didn't take but a few minutes, and I was finally in bed, winding my bedside clock, when I noticed it was already ten thirty. It seemed I was tiring out much faster these days. I'd have to think about that tomorrow. Right now, I just wanted to say a prayer and drift off to sleep.

I could hear Vonion out by the barn talking to the squealing hogs and beating the bucket with a stick when I opened my eyes the next morning. The old roosters were crowing loud enough to wake the dead as the sun was making its way high in the sky. These were all wonderful signs of a good day coming. I was so grateful for all the things the good Lord had done for me, and not the least of these was my child was coming home for a few days. I prayed right out loud, "Thank you, dear Lord."

Breakfast was eaten and after calling Vonion's attention to the third item on my to-do list—and hoping he would take it seriously—I settled on the bench in the hall to put in a call to Thelma.

"Thelma, please," I said to Nellie.

"I'll try, but I imagine she hasn't started working yet. She's probably still getting those kids of hers off to school. You know, Bee, I'm not supposed to give out personal information over the telephone, but I feel obliged to let you know, for your own safety, mind you, there was a murder last night right here in Jeffersontown! I'm so jittery, I could just about jump out of my skin!"

"You must have dreamed about murder last night, Nellie. Sometimes things get mixed up early in the morning before a second cup of coffee. We don't have murder around here."

"Bee, I didn't dream any such thing! I'm quite sure of my information," Nellie snapped back.

Not wanting to get Nellie any more agitated before I got the lowdown, if there was in fact a murder, I apologized. "Nellie, I'm sorry I said that. You do such a wonderful job as telephone operator, and are always so careful not to ever repeat gossip." I had already said one prayer this morning, and now I'd have to say another little prayer to ask forgiveness for telling that little white lie. "You're absolutely the best operator in the world. I don't know what this community would do without your friendly voice coming through the lines. Why, you just brighten up my dreary days." *Lord, forgive me, again.*

"Why, Bee, how nice of you to be so flattering. Sometimes I feel as if people just don't appreciate my service to the community."

"Nellie, we do appreciate you, and we need to tell you more often too. Now what were you saying about a murder?"

"Well, if you're sure you want to know. Floyd was murdered sometime during the night."

"Oh, Nellie! No. That can't be!" I exclaimed, as I threw my hand to my mouth. "Are you quite sure?"

"Oh, yes! It's true all right! I overheard a telephone conversation early this morning between Sheriff Ledbetter and Roy, one of his deputies. That mechanic Floyd has down at the filling station, Elmo, was seen by a neighbor running like a wild man from Floyd's house about six o'clock this morning. Well, the neighbor reported seeing him, and Sheriff Ledbetter drove over and found Floyd's body inside his house. The sheriff picked up Elmo, in a panic, over on the next block. Elmo told the sheriff he had gone by to pick up the keys to open up the station and found Floyd dead on the floor, strangled with an electrical extension cord. The house was torn apart like somebody had been looking for something, probably money. Elmo claims he was running to find help. Can you believe that?

Poor old Floyd, who wouldn't hurt a flea, is dead as a doornail. From what I heard, Sheriff Ledbetter has Elmo locked up at the jail for questioning. He and one of his deputies, I think Vernon, are out looking for clues and other suspects. I don't know what kind of clues he has right now, but from what I've heard between the lines, he might be on to something. You know the murderer is probably the same crook that broke in on Old Man Peterson the other night. Lock your doors and don't open them to anybody you don't know real good. It looks like we're in the midst of a major crime wave!" Taking in a deep breath, Nellie added, "Oh, let me try to get Thelma for you. I totally forgot about your call. For heaven's sake, I don't know where my mind is this morning. This news about Floyd has just thrown me for a loop!"

I was still in a daze when Thelma picked up on the line and said, "Hello, Cut and Curl. This is Thelma speaking."

"Thelma, this is Bee Martin. I need to come in for some maintenance work, but after hearing about poor old Floyd, I'm just in shock and I'm terrified to come out of the house. Is Floyd really dead? Was he murdered like Nellie said?"

"Floyd was murdered last night or sometime early this morning, and Mr. Lawson already has him laid out at the funeral home! It's just unbelievable, isn't it? I was too scared to let the children walk to school this morning so I took them right up to the schoolhouse door in the car. Just keep everything locked up and get out your shotgun! Don't take any chances. I don't own a gun, but I've got my frying pan and a baseball bat right by my side, and I'm ready to use them if need be."

"My stars, what is this world coming to when a body can't be safe right inside their very own house? I'm glad I have Isabelle, the preacher's sister, staying with me now; not that I think she could be any real protection. It is a comfort to have somebody else in the house at night, though. You did know that I had a boarder now, didn't you?"

"Yes, somebody, I don't remember who, mentioned it the other day. That's real kind of you to be so helpful to Preacher Henry. I hope he appreciates you, is all I can say."

"I think he does. It's a challenge, but I'm up to it." Changing the subject, "Thelma, I do need to come in and get my hair redone. When would be a good time?"

"Come on anytime. No one else is getting out this morning if they've heard the news about Floyd. They're all locked up in their houses, scared to open the door. I guess you'll be just as safe here with me as anywhere else."

"If they've been on the telephone, they know all about Floyd's murder. News travels faster than a bullet with Nellie on the line." A cough came over the line, and it wasn't from Thelma. I guess I was in trouble again. "I'll tell Isabelle, and see if she wants to come with me or go over to the pastorium. I can't leave her here by herself. I'll be over as soon as I can."

As I hung up, I began to shake uncontrollably just thinking about poor old Floyd coming to the end of his life at the hands of a murderer who was still out there somewhere, roaming around free as a bird. Who knows when he might strike again?

I need to call Bess and make sure she's safe and knows what's going on before I do another thing, I thought to myself. I picked up the telephone and tried to get Nellie on the line again, but that was impossible. Every line in the county must have been busy. Nellie finally picked up. "Nellie, please connect me to Bess, and hurry. She might not know what's going on and could be in danger."

"Don't get your bladder in a splatter, Bee. I mentioned it before connecting her to some smooth-talking gentleman over in Wall County a little while ago. You know, it sounded for the world like he was her suitor. Whoever it was seemed to be mighty familiar with her by the way they were talking. Well, you know me, I'd be the last person to spread a rumor. Now let me see if I can connect the two of you. It'll just take a minute. I know she's home because she told the man she wasn't going out the door."

I had to grip the telephone and clinch my teeth to keep from saying something else I'd regret. At last Bess picked up.

"Bess, are you all right?"

"Bee, I was just about to call to find out if you knew about Floyd?"

"Bess, I heard. Can you believe a murder took place right here in our little town! The horror Floyd must have experienced before he died! I hope you're locked up tight. Thanks for calling and warning me before you called you-know-who. I swear, Bess, even with all this turmoil going on, you still have that Romeo on your mind."

"Bee, you ought to be ashamed. J.R. is very concerned about me. Now, you need to listen to me for once in your life, Bee Martin. Whatever you do, watch out for anything that looks unusual. I want you to get Vonion up there right now with the shotgun. He isn't worth much, but he can guard the place. Make sure Ora Lee comes with him, and y'all stay together until they catch whoever is running around murdering and thieving. You know whoever robbed Old Man Peterson probably killed Floyd. It sounds like he's on a robbing spree."

"Bess, you're probably right about that, but I'm not getting Vonion up here to stay with me, for heaven's sake. I'm coming into town to get my hair done."

"Bee, are you absolutely nuts? I swear I don't know what to think about you sometimes. I won't even try to talk you out of it because, as hardheaded as I know you are, there's no use."

"No, there's not. Margaret's coming home this weekend, and I can't let her see my hair 'til I can get it redone. I want it to look extra good."

"Well, everybody else has seen it. I don't know why Margaret is so different."

"Well, she is," I emphatically replied. "Do you think I need Thelma to tone down my color a bit, or just leave it like it is?"

"For pity's sake, Bee, I don't know. You should have thought about all that before you had her dye your hair the first time. I really don't think Thelma can take the color out after she's put it in, though. Your hair isn't like a radio that you turn the volume up and down on. Once you dye your hair, I think you're pretty much stuck with the results. Stop thinking about your hair for once and concentrate on staying alive. If you're dead, it won't matter what color your hair is. You always said you wanted a closed casket for your funeral, so nobody will know what color it is anyway. Now, whatever you do, be careful."

"Okay, I will. Bess, we probably need to get off the line now. We've tied it up long enough. Other people need to make calls too. Now you be careful too."

Feeling really anxious by now, I walked down the hall and tapped lightly on Isabelle's door. When she didn't answer, I cracked the door and said, "Isabelle, you need to get on up now. We need to go into town." When I didn't hear any movement at all, I peeked in and saw that she was sound asleep. I walked over and tapped her shoulder until she opened one eye. I looked straight at her and said, "Get your clothes on now. You can either go with me to the beauty parlor, or I'll take you over to the pastorium. You can't stay here by yourself. There's a murderer running around on the loose."

I told her what I knew about the situation, and she excitedly began quizzing me about the gruesome details, as she sat up in the bed with the sheet pulled up to her neck. "Ms. Bee, you mean to say poor old Floyd is dead? I just can't believe it. Maybe you heard wrong."

"No, it's absolutely true. Now get on up."

"I'm not scared. I'll be all right here. I really need a little more sleep."

"I'm not taking no for an answer. Now get ready right now and we'll talk on the way into town. I've got to go check on Ora Lee and Vonion before we leave."

The lock to the front door didn't want to cooperate as I attempted to turn the key as we were leaving. I don't know whether it was rusty from lack of use or my hands were just shaking so badly. After finally locking up, we dashed for the car. Not seeing Vonion anywhere around the yard or lot, I drove down the lane where I spotted him leaning over a fire, scalding some old roosters in an iron pot.

"Vonion, you and Ora Lee need to be extra careful today and watch out for anything unusual around here," I called from the car, after I hit the brakes. "Somebody broke into Floyd's house and strangled him to death during the night. Elmo found Floyd's body this morning. Can you imagine, right there in the middle of town!"

Vonion looked at me as if he couldn't believe the news. He shook his head sadly and said, "Almighty God. What this world coming to? You sure... Mr. Floyd, dead!"

"I'm sure, Vonion. It's just too horrible to think about," I said, shaking my head in disbelief. "Sheriff Ledbetter has a manhunt going on right now. I've got to go into town, and I'll be gone most of the morning. If you will, keep a watch out over at my house as well as around here."

Vonion stepped back from the fire and thoughtfully replied, "People dyin' now that ain't never died before. And for what reason, I just can't fathom why. I shore will be on the lookout though, but you need to be extra careful while's you in town. I don't like to think about you gallivantin' all over the place with a killer running round. Miss Isabelle gonna go with you?"

"She is and there shouldn't be anybody around the house this morning. Is there anything I can bring y'all back from town? Where's Roscoe this morning?"

"Ora Lee, she needs her snuff, that all. Roscoe, he got off early. I guess I missed him this mornin' when I got up. He was s'posed to go to Tom Wilson's to start workin' today. Tom Wilson come by yesterdee and give him the good news he could get started today. He was mighty proud he finally find a job."

"That's really good news, Vonion. Tell Ora Lee that Margaret is coming in Friday for the weekend."

"I got these two old roosters here, one fer you and one fer Ora Lee. You can make Margaret some dumplings. You know how she like them."

"Thank you, Vonion. I was wondering what to cook for Margaret. Now Vonion, do what I say and watch out for anything unusual. I've got a feeling that the crook that broke into Old Man Peterson's house is probably the same person that killed Floyd."

Feeling very nervous as things were completely out of control, I turned the car around in Vonion's yard, almost taking down the old chinaberry tree as we headed up the lane toward the road. Maybe I should have taken the shotgun from behind the bedroom door where Will had always kept it. I almost pulled over in the yard to get it but decided not to take the time. "I need to learn to shoot Will's shotgun as soon as I can get Vonion to show me how it works," I said to Isabelle as we passed by the house.

"Let's just get over to the pastorium as fast as we can so I can check on Henry," Isabelle impatiently replied, as if it was beginning to sink in that there was real danger out there. I was really beginning to feel her anxiety by then. That's when I decided to floor it. We made it in record time.

Leaving Isabelle in the capable hands of Preacher Henry, I drove on over to The Cut and Curl. After cautiously looking up and down the street in front of Thelma's little house, I vaulted from the car and sprinted around to the back of her house. "Thelma, it's me, Bee. Let me in," I yelled impatiently, as I knocked on the door to her little shop in the back room of her house.

"Ms. Bee, is it really you?" I heard Thelma whisper. She must have been standing right next to the door.

"It's me. Now let me in." I was so out of breath by then, I could hardly talk. I hadn't moved this fast since Vonion left the gate to the hog pen open accidently, and we had to drive the greedy hogs out of the garden a few months ago.

She cracked the door, peeped around, grabbed me by the collar and pulled me in. She looked as white as a tablecloth and was shaking like a tree in the wind. "Ms. Bee, get in here so I can get this door locked back up." She almost knocked me down trying to get the door shut.

"Thelma, get a hold of yourself. You're gonna make yourself sick. The person that killed Floyd is probably in another county by now. He's not stupid enough to hang around here for Sheriff Ledbetter to hunt down."

As I was saying that, my mind kept telling me that Sheriff Ledbetter probably didn't have a clue about how to go about finding any criminals. Everybody knew the only qualifications the man had was his daddy had enough money to buy the election for him three years ago.

"What in the world did Floyd have in that house worth killing him for? We haven't had much crime in our little community for years now, other than poor Old Mr. Peterson's robbery the other day," Thelma excitedly said, with her hands and arms shaking uncontrollably. "The only other thing I can remember was last year when some of Tom Wilson's hogs were stolen right out of the pen while Tom was gone over to Wall County to a revival meeting."

"Floyd probably kept cash from the filling station in his house all night, don't you think? I imagine somebody was after it and Floyd got in the way. I guess that's why they're holding Elmo at the station for questioning. He would have known about the money. But if you think about it, most people around here probably knew it too. Just like everybody knew Old Man Peterson kept his cash hidden in his house somewhere. He was always talking about how the bank didn't do anything but steal your money."

Thelma seemed to be getting more and more disturbed as we talked about the morning events. She was looking pale even with dark rouge smeared all over her cheeks. Her hands must have been shaking pretty badly earlier this morning from the looks of her eyebrows. Her left one appeared to have been penciled in at least half inch shorter than the right one, giving her a funny lopsided look. She began trembling as we talked and had to grip her cast-iron hair washing basin with clenched fingers for support.

"Listen, Thelma, do you think you can do something with my hair in the state you're in? I don't want to come out of here looking worse than when I came in. Do you think I need to come back when you're in better control of yourself?"

"Get your head over here and lean back. Have I ever messed you up?"

After thinking about that a minute, I answered, "I'm really not too sure about that."

CHAPTER TEN

B less her heart. Even with her mind a million miles away worrying about those children of hers and some murdering fool running wild out there, Thelma took extra care to make sure my hair looked nice. I believe the color had toned down some, and the length was a bit longer now. It really looks stylish, I thought, as I put my red earbobs on while looking in the mirror over the cluttered counter.

With no one scheduled to come in, I left Thelma at her beauty parlor all locked up, still armed with her frying pan and baseball bat. I drove over to Floyd's filling station not thinking for a minute it would be closed. Sure enough, it was locked up tighter than Dick's hat band. "This is going to really be an inconvenience," I said to myself as I drove on by. As far as I knew, there wasn't another gas station in town. I guess everyone would be walking soon. I better get over to the grocery store and then go straight home.

Entering the familiar store, I overheard that old busy-body, Mrs. Era Dukes, spreading gossip to somebody over by the canned goods aisle. "You know, they found out Elmo has a police record. About ten years ago, he was arrested and convicted over in Alabama for holding up a liquor store. Floyd knew about it, but he still hired him. I heard somebody say Floyd always boasted he was the best help he ever had. You know, he was Floyd's second cousin once removed, so I guess he was trying to give him another chance. It seemed as if he had straightened up until this."

Byron, the young store clerk, on the same aisle, was in on the conversation too. "I think Sheriff Ledbetter has him in custody, but no money has been recovered. I imagine quite a sum was in the house. Floyd did good business over at that station. That money might never be recovered."

"Well, thank goodness, Elmo is locked up. We can all breathe easier now with that killer behind jailhouse bars," Mrs. Dukes was blabbing to anybody who would listen.

I had known Elmo for five or six years now. He had always pumped my gas and wiped my windshield with a smile and a "thank you." It was hard to believe he was capable of such a horrible act. *He couldn't have been that desperate,* I thought to myself, as I hurriedly picked up a few items so I could get on back out to the house.

Will always said if you drive slowly your vehicle doesn't use as much gas, so I just poked along as I drove home. I kept my car under ten miles an hour until I heard a horn honking. That's when I noticed two cars, a big farm truck filled with chickens in wooden crates, and Cleo's rolling store lined up behind me. I sped on up to fifteen

miles an hour. If that didn't suit them, they could just pass
and waste all their gas, for all I cared.

* * *

Have you ever been scared, but you knew you had
to do something anyway? That's how I felt about going
back inside my house that day. I had stopped by the
pastorium to check on Isabelle before leaving town and
was in hopes she might want to come on back home with
me now. Since I had old Vonion as a watchdog, she said
she was going to stay in town all afternoon and go with
Preacher Henry over to Ms. Mildred's to visit with her a
spell. I thought that was a good idea since Mildred was
probably scared out of her wits by now. She always had
been scared of her own shadow. You know, she lives right
by herself, and Preacher Henry probably felt obligated to
check on some of the single ladies in the church.

Cautiously, I crept back into the house, looked in
the closets, and I even got down on my knees to look
under the beds. I have got to clean out from under these
beds and air these mattresses if I don't do another thing.
"I have absolutely put it off long enough," I sternly told
myself. I had left in such a panic that morning I didn't get
anything done, so I began making beds and straightening
up. I thought I would boil my chicken today and make my
dumplings tomorrow. After mixing up my batter for the
cake and putting it in the oven, I hurried down the lane to
give Ora Lee her snuff and get my chicken. I wasn't too
keen about walking down there by myself today. I didn't
have a lot of time until my cake would come out of the
oven, so I drove, knowing full well my gas supply was
limited. What on earth would I do if I couldn't jump in my
car and just go?

Wearing her old tattered straw hat that shaded her dark wrinkled face, Ora Lee was out sweeping the dry parched yard with her straw broom as I coasted the car toward the house. Vonion, with his cap perched back over hair that resembled a handful of dirty cotton, looked listless and contented sitting on the ledge of the porch with a pocket knife and a piece of poplar wood in his large rough hands. He said Roscoe was still at work, and they had not seen nary a soul all day. Vonion had finished scalding the roosters, and my chicken was sitting with its legs standing straight up in a dented dish pan on the porch steps. Despite his bad eyesight, Vonion had picked that chicken clean as a whistle.

I told them all what I had overheard in the store and Vonion wisely replied, "Now Ms. Bee, we got to stay watchful out here. If'n a man will kill one time, he'll shore kill again. We don't know notin' about his whereabouts either. I better go with you and check things out up to the house. You didn't have no business going back in there rat by yourself when you come from town. You knows, you shoulda' come for me to go in there with you, now don't you. I need to work on that yard anyways." Then as he glanced over toward Ora Lee, he firmly ordered, "Now Ora Lee, you stay put right here till I git back. I can't be worryin' 'bout two women at the same time. This thang is just frustratin' me." I handed Ora Lee her snuff and after she thanked me, I thought about my cake in the oven and hurried to my waiting car.

Picking up his shotgun and the dishpan with the rooster, Vonion opened the car door and climbed into the backseat. I had my mind set on asking Vonion to show me how to use my gun as soon as we got back up the lane.

Perfect timing! My cake was ready to come out of the oven as I walked into the house. I left the cake layers on the table to cool and placed the chicken in the refrigerator, then walked outside with Will's shotgun slung over my shoulder—ready for some target practice.

Vonion, surprised to see me carrying the gun, said, "You ain't got no business with that there firearm."

"Vonion, I feel unprotected. Maybe if I knew how to shoot this thing, I would feel a little better. Now is as good a time as ever for you to teach me."

"Mr. Will never wanted you to use that thang, but if you've got it in yor hardheaded mind to try it out, I might as well try to learn you." Vonion reached for the gun, and we walked over to the barn and picked up a few old rusty tobacco tins from the dusty shelf inside the door. Just to be on the safe side, we walked to the back side of the pecan orchard toward the woods for my lesson.

"You gonna shoot your foot off if'n you ain't careful. You know, a gun is a dangerous thing. It's best if'n you just know how to shoot it and don't ever have to," Vonion said as dead serious as he could sound. Vonion walked over to the fence by the woods and balanced the tobacco cans on the fence posts for me to use for target practice and walked back toward me. He showed me how to aim and squeeze the trigger on the heavy gun. I missed all the cans. Vonion said that was normal for my first lesson. "I s'pose you'll improve over time. We'll keep working on it, that is, if'n you don't shoot yorself in the foot first."

Vonion cleaned out my little petunia bed by the steps, and without being asked, he even watered my potted plants. I think he just wanted to stay up near the house for a while. I finished icing my cake, boiled down my chicken, and worked around the house all afternoon while fighting a heavy cloud of doom that had draped itself over me.

Isabelle and Preacher Henry came in late that afternoon, not long after I sat down on the porch with a cool glass of lemonade to rest a spell.

As they walked up the porch steps together, the worry on their faces was quite evident. "I'm so glad Sheriff Ledbetter is holding that garage flunky for Mr. Floyd's murder. It makes me feel a whole lot safer, don't you, Ms. Bee?" Isabelle asked, as she plopped down in one of the porch rockers.

"No, I don't. I don't believe one minute Elmo is guilty. I don't care what they say he did all those years ago. I can tell a man's character, and I know he wouldn't hurt a flea. They better keep looking till they find the real killer, as far as I'm concerned. I'm not saying this to scare you, but that killer could be anywhere around in these parts this very minute, just waiting to strike again."

"But Ms. Bee, Elmo had every reason in the world to do it. He knew all about that money, and he was there every morning. It was just luck somebody saw him running from the house," Isabelle sternly replied, as she stopped rocking her squeaking chair and sat up straight.

"Well tell me, why was he running from the house? He could have just locked it up and left. No one would have been the wiser until Floyd didn't show up for work. Where is the money? Sheriff Ledbetter didn't find it with Elmo. I believe he went in, found Floyd's dead body and was running for help, just as he said."

"He probably stashed the money somewhere before he ran. He had to act innocent," Isabelle replied, as though she had it all figured out in her head. "They've got the right man all right. I just know it," Isabelle snapped, as she started rocking again.

Preacher Henry calmly added, "We don't know what happened, and nobody else does—except the one who did it. You ladies need to be vigilant and don't go off anywhere by yourselves. Do you want me to hang around a while, Ms. Bee? I'll spend the night if it'll make you feel more protected. I don't mind a bit."

"No thank you, Preacher Henry. I think we can manage by ourselves. I have my gun and I can use it if need be. Vonion gave me a quick lesson this afternoon. I might not be able to hit a tobacco can on a fence, but I believe I could stop an intruder. We'll be fine. You go on and do what you need to do."

"Okay, but you know you can call on me day or night." As he shifted in his seat, he added, "I really need to work on Sunday's sermon. Unless the two of you need anything else tonight, I'll see you ladies tomorrow. By the way, Ms. Bee, Ms. Mildred sends her regards." Preacher Henry eased out of the chair, leaned over to give Isabelle a quick peck on the cheek, and walked down the porch steps to his car.

I watched him fold his long legs inside his dusty car and crank it up. He better ask the good Lord to give him that sermon, and it better be an improvement over his previous little sermonettes. I don't know what they teach in seminary or wherever he had gone to school, but I was beginning to wonder if Preacher Henry had missed a few lessons.

CHAPTER ELEVEN

F riday was here at last. I had been hoping for a little break in the current heat wave, but the temperature remained well above ninety degrees. I had finished everything on my to-do list so I felt fairly well-prepared for a good weekend. We'd go out tonight to eat and maybe shop a little tomorrow, and if Margaret wanted to, we'd see that new movie that was showing in town. It was starring Clark Gable, and if that couldn't get your blood flowing, I don't know what could. It's a good thing the theater is so dark when the movie is playing because Clark can just put a spell on you. We would eat our chicken and dumplings, and I would cook some cabbage and corn bread to have along with it. That caramel cake would top it off. If Isabelle wanted to follow along, I would just have to tolerate it.

My anticipation for the weekend visit from Margaret was overwhelming me. I wanted Margaret to know that I missed her, but I didn't want her to sense the isolation and despair I felt much of the time without her or her father here to share my life. I knew there was still a meaningful life out there for me; I just had to find it. "Enjoy the weekend," I kept telling myself, "and let time take care of the loneliness." I had thought the presence of Isabelle in the house would have helped me feel a little better. It seemed just the opposite. I just had to try a little harder.

Out on the freshly swept porch, I was putting zinnias from the back flower bed into one of Mama's cranberry vases. When I looked up, I saw Margaret's maroon Ford Coup stirring dust up the lane. Forgetting to take my apron off, I ran down the steps to greet her. I'm always in awe of how pretty my daughter is. She's small boned with sandy blond hair that she wears in a soft pageboy just to her shoulders. She always has a twinkle in the brown eyes she inherited from her daddy. She's quite an eye-catcher. We hugged and hugged again, and after getting her luggage into the house, sat down on the porch to catch up.

"Mama, are you sure you're doing okay? I know you're lonely here all by yourself with Daddy's memories surrounding you all the time. You know, I'd feel so much better if you'd come on and live with me now. You'd have so much more free time to do just what *you* want."

"Margaret, you and I have been over this time and again. I plan to stay right where I am. I'm perfectly content with my life just as it is." *What's another little white lie on top of so many others?* "On top of that, you know I feel responsible for Ora Lee and Vonion. They're family too. Now, I know you'd never want me to turn my back on them. Margaret, I do miss your daddy and sometimes the pain is overwhelming, but those memories that surround me really are so comforting. Remember, it is what it is, and you and I can't change a thing. We can only go forward and rely on our faith to carry us through. I do miss you so much, but just knowing that you're making a difference in all those children's lives you're teaching, and seeing how well you're doing makes me feel things are as they should be. Don't be a worrywart. Let's have a good weekend without all this nonsense. Now, do you have a special young man yet?"

Darn it! Right off the bat, I had already broken my promise to myself that I wouldn't ask about Margaret's personal life. She really didn't want to talk about it, and she readily changed the subject. She wanted to know all about J.R., so I told her what little I knew—and really more than I cared to know.

"It's perfectly normal for Aunt Bess to have a suitor, but I don't think you're ready for all that. There'll never be anyone to take my daddy's place in my heart or yours," she added, with a little too much determination. I don't know how she knew what was in my heart, but I readily agreed with her anyway.

"Where's Isabelle, Mama?"

"She and the preacher went over to Vera and Tillman's this afternoon to check on them. You know, with the murder and everything, everybody's a little skittish. After that, I believe they said they were going over to meet with Floyd's son about the service. Floyd was a member of the church, and I'm pretty sure Preacher Henry was called to do the funeral. He better improve on his delivery, though. His sermons are dry as a piece of cardboard."

Margaret stood up abruptly and exclaimed, "Murder! What in the world are you are talking about? Mama, Floyd's dead? Somebody murdered him?"

Oh, dear, how could I have forgotten to tell Margaret about Floyd's murder? After explaining all the details that I knew, she was horrified.

"Mama, this is insane and so sad. He was one of the sweetest men I ever knew. Why, he gave me a peppermint stick every time I went into that station with you or Daddy all the years I was growing up."

"I know. He was a fixture in this community and was always so kind. He will be missed by everyone. I've heard him say many times at that station, 'I'm here to make friends, not money.'"

"Mama, whoever killed Floyd is probably walking around here right now. Under these circumstances, maybe I should stay on until school starts. If I leave, I don't know if I can sleep at night, knowing you might be in danger."

"You are going back to work and you will sleep. Things will get better; they always do. Sheriff Ledbetter will find this murdering thief—sooner or later—and everything will get back to normal. I might as well tell you while we're talking. Old Man Peterson's house was robbed the other night. He was knocked down by an intruder but not seriously hurt. I feel as though the person that's responsible for Floyd's death might have also robbed Old Man Peterson. It's just a mystery, but I'm sure the sheriff will get to the bottom of it soon."

"Mama, why didn't you call and tell me all this stuff? Aren't you a little bit frightened?"

"Well, I have to say that it does concern me somewhat. I'm going to be a lot more cautious from now on."

"Well, I certainly hope so," added Margaret emphatically. "I don't know if I could live with myself if I left you here by yourself and something dreadful happened to you."

All of a sudden, Margaret jumped up as if she had forgotten something and said, "Oh, Mama, I've got a present for you!" She was out the screen door in a flash, yelling as she went, "I got you one and me one too!" Now, what had that girl gone and spent her money on now.

"It's a Brownie camera," Margaret shouted from the car. "Mama, we're gonna take some pictures this weekend. I want to show my new class pictures of my mama and my home." She dashed back up the steps to the porch carrying two brown boxes.

As she opened one of the boxes she said, "Mama, here. This one is yours. Now, I'll open mine and let's see if we can load the film. I don't think you'll have a lot of difficulty if you just watch me the first time. One of my fellow teachers showed me how to use this thing."

"Margaret, you know I'm not very mechanical. This is probably going to be more of a challenge for me than for you. But show me what to do."

"Mama, watch while I load mine." I watched and it really didn't seem too complicated. "Now load yours. It's easy."

"Yes, easy for you, but hard for me. I'm not so sure I can do this. Now where did you say to put in the film?" Well, lo and behold, after a little more instruction, the film went right in without much effort. I was so proud of myself. Maybe this was something I could handle by myself after all.

"Now, Margaret, what do I do?"

"Mama, take the camera and hold it like this. Now, aim it at what you want to take a picture of. Remember, you have to have light and you have to hold your camera level. Now, let's go outside. I want to take a picture of you by the old oak tree."

We walked down the porch steps, and I stood by the oak tree that Daddy had planted so many years before and smiled as Margaret took my picture with her camera. I held my breath with my stomach sucked in, hoping to look a little thinner. I don't know if it worked or not. Margaret said, "Mama, don't look so stiff. You're supposed to look natural." Well, my natural self is not looking so good these days. I have got to get on a diet soon. At least, she hadn't said anything negative about my hair. She hadn't said anything positive, either.

I wanted to take her picture too, so we changed positions, and I aimed and mashed the button on the camera. "Margaret, how do we get the film out and how many can I take with this roll?"

"Mama, I think there're twelve pictures on these rolls of film. Now when we take all twelve, we'll open this little compartment on the back of the camera, take the film out, and put it in this little package that comes with the film. Then we'll mail the film to the company to have them developed. Let's try to each take a roll this weekend, then I'll get them all developed and bring the pictures next time I come home."

"Oh, Margaret, what will they think of next? This world we live in is changing so fast. You know, I would have loved to have had one of these while you were growing up. We had to take you clear to Augusta to have you photographed. Why, I'll bet Vonion and Ora Lee have never even had their pictures taken."

"Mama, I know! Let's go down there right now and snap some pictures of them." With cameras in our hands and joy in my heart, we started walking down the lane together. I had to walk at a quick pace to keep up with Margaret and was a bit winded by the time we arrived at the little frame house. Margaret had a grand reunion with Ora Lee and Vonion that afternoon. We both took pictures of them grinning, standing behind those big white teeth. They smiled so big we could see down their throats almost to their tonsils. Margaret wanted pictures of the house where they lived also, so she made them stand by the front porch, and she snapped the picture. I don't think I realized how shabby everything looked around there until that very minute as we were all standing around taking those snapshots. Margaret would probably show those pictures to all of her friends at school and never even think to be ashamed of her family and home.

Sometimes I thought Margaret loved Ora Lee better than she loved me. She had, after all, spent just as much time in her growing up years with Ora Lee and Lettie. We didn't get to see Roscoe, but Margaret did ask about him, and she wanted to know all about Lettie and her other children. We stayed on a good while, enjoying each other's company, sitting contentedly on that old unpainted porch in squeaking rocking chairs and talking about old times and past adventures. Vonion finally stood up and said, with a little authority in his raspy old voice, "Y'all best better be gettin' on now before dark catches up with you. I can walk back with y'all if'n you wants me to."

"Vonion, you don't have to do that. We'll be fine. Mama and I'll walk together. We aren't scared," Margaret replied, as we were gathering our cameras and stepping off the old, sagging front porch.

"You know Mr. Will wouldn't never forgive me if'n I let anythang happen to the both of you," Vonion replied protectively, as we were about to walk away.

"Come on with us. We can use some protection," I replied to Vonion, knowing he wanted to feel needed.

"Y'alls come on back tomorrie and let me see you again fo you get on away, now Margaret girl, you hear me," Ora Lee called, as we were beginning our stroll back to the house.

"Yes ma'am, I will," Margaret called, and rushed back to give Ora Lee a bigger hug than she had given me earlier.

We could hear the telephone ringing as we walked through the porch screen door. Two rings, one long, one short. That's me. I hurried into the house and picked up.

"Hello, Bee Martin speaking."

"Hey, Bee. It's me, Bess. Has Margaret made it in yet?"

"She sure has. We're about to get ready to go eat out at the diner. Bess, come on and eat with us. Margaret wants to see you."

"No, I've already made a prior engagement to go out this evening. I'll catch up with you two downtown tomorrow morning, though."

I'd rather wonder about that prior engagement than to ask. After a short conversation, we were about to hang up when Bess asked, "Has Margaret said anything about your hair yet?"

"She hasn't said a word. Maybe she hasn't noticed the color."

"Oh, she's noticed it all right. She just hasn't said anything yet." Then Bess firmly added, "You know, there's a killer roaming around out there somewhere. You two need to be especially cautious going out this evening. I'm making J.R. stay over with me tonight so I won't be here alone. He'll be in the guest room. I know that's going to be your next question, so I'll answer it before you even ask."

"Well, I wasn't going to ask, but you know all your neighbors will see that truck there all night long, and you know how they'll talk. Bess, maybe you better come and stay out here with us tonight."

"I would, but with Isabelle and Margaret, you're going to have a full house. I guess I'll just take my chances here with J.R. My neighbors haven't had anything to talk about since old Mr. Hodges, across the street, went streaking last winter. I heard he got frostbite on his...you know. If it had snapped off, Mrs. Hodges probably would have cheered. The poor old man is so far gone now he doesn't even know his own name anymore."

"With circumstances as they are, maybe everyone will think J.R. is just being protective," I replied with a chuckle, knowing full well nobody would really consider it that way. Bess's neighbors loved to talk, and Bess and J.R. are going to give them something new to gossip about. Nellie's telephone lines will be sizzling tomorrow.

CHAPTER TWELVE

My evening with Margaret was a huge success. We went to bed with high hopes of having a wonderful day Saturday. Isabelle was in bed by the time we came in from the diner, and we tried to tiptoe around—not wake her. I did have the chance to introduce Margaret to Isabelle as we sat around the breakfast table the next morning.

Isabelle, with her hair disarrayed and a frown plastered across her face, walked into the kitchen as we were finishing up our toast and eggs. She was wearing only a lightweight cotton gown and seemed very unconcerned with modesty. As soon as she sat down, I introduced the two young women. Isabelle nodded toward Margaret. Margaret politely nodded back and said she was glad to meet her and hoped she was enjoying her stay. Isabelle mumbled something about that it was all right but just so hot. She dabbed her damp forehead with a napkin and started picking at the plate of food I sat in front of her.

"I hardly slept a wink all night. Maybe it's just the heat. There's just no way to cool off around here," Isabelle complained, as she sighed and began to fan herself with her napkin. "And those pesky crows out in the orchard just drive me crazy in the morning with all that noise they make. I wish old Onion would get his gun to them and shut them up for good."

"Vonion. His name is Vonion, and I would never want him to shoot God's creatures just for being noisy," I replied to Isabelle, as kindly as I knew how. "Now, what are your plans for the day? We're going into town, and we'd love for you to tag along." I felt a sharp poke in my left leg from Margaret's direction as I got the last word out.

"Henry's supposed to pick me up a little later to take me over to the church to do a few things to get ready for that boring funeral," she fumed, as though it was the last thing on earth she wanted to do. "That old funeral is going to mess up our whole weekend. We thought about having a picnic out at Simpson's Lake Sunday afternoon, but I guess that's out now."

Well, I guess, it was out, I thought. How selfish can you be?

Pulling her gown down over her knees, Isabelle continued to move her food around in her plate. "I just can't get used to this heavy country food," she complained, as she finished off her glass of juice and dabbed her forehead with her napkin again. "It just sits in my stomach like a brickbat for hours in this heat."

"Isabelle, have you ever considered country life might not be quite right for you? Mama doesn't have any control over the weather, and as far as I'm concerned, the food around here is the best," Margaret responded, and continued to eat with her head down so Isabelle couldn't see her roll her eyes. Lifting her head, she looked straight at Isabelle and said, as if to make a point, "You know, Mama's kitchen doesn't have a menu printed giving you a choice of foods. If there's something you want to eat that she doesn't have, all you have to do is go buy it, pay for it, bring it back, cook it, and eat it. You might even offer to share it with Mama. And, by the way, it's hot everywhere, not just under Mama's roof."

As much as I dislike any kind of confrontation, it was nice to hear my daughter defend me for a change.

"Well, I'm sorry if I offended you, Ms. Bee. I guess I just didn't realize I sounded so ungrateful."

"I accept your apology, Isabelle. Now, no more of this. Let's enjoy our day."

Later that morning after Preacher Henry—who had still not offered a red cent—picked up my spoiled boarder, Margaret and I met Bess in front of the drugstore in town. Looking all put together in a floral dress, matching pink handbag and heels, Bess greeted Margaret with hugs and kisses. Despite feeling rather dowdy in my beige shirtwaist and comfortable walking shoes, we walked into the drugstore to check if a new shipment of Evening in Paris perfumes had arrived. The drugstore is always nice and cool with the large ceiling fans stirring up a pleasant breeze and the aroma of all the perfumes and colognes filling the air. The soda fountain was installed several years before Bess and I became regulars. I was always game to try a new flavor of ice cream, but Bess always stuck to chocolate or vanilla. It was a temptation to order sodas for everybody and relax at one of the small round metal tables, but nobody was really hungry yet, so we passed.

When Dottie, the pretty young sales girl, told Bess that the shipment of perfume still hadn't arrived, Bess replied, as if it was a personal catastrophe, "I just hope my bottle will hold out another day or two. What in the world is the holdup?"

Now this could really affect her social life, I thought. Bess wouldn't even consider walking out her door unless she smelled like some exotic flower.

"Ms. Bess, we never know if a shipment will be in on time or not. I promised I would call you as soon as it arrives, and I will," Dottie answered, with more than a little irritation in her tone. I could tell Dottie had dealt with Sister a few times before.

The dime store had always been my favorite store in town. I could spend a whole day looking at all the new kitchen gadgets, tablecloths, dishes, and anything else you might need. You could even get clothes and shoes too, if you weren't too particular about them. Margaret needed hose, and I had seen some oilcloth I wanted to make a table cover out of. After idly browsing awhile, we made our purchases and then strolled up and down Main Street a couple of times just window shopping and cherishing the time we had together.

We stayed in town until lunch, and Margaret insisted Bess come on out to the house with us for a tomato sandwich and a little more chitchat. We all ate too much, but the taste of those fresh-picked tomatoes on white bread with mayonnaise was too good not to overindulge. We were stuffed but managed room for a piece of caramel cake. After lunch, we sauntered out to the yard to sit under the shade of the oak tree to chat awhile. We had taken Margaret's camera out to snap a few shots of the front of the house where the petunias were blooming.

Margaret had particularly wanted a good shot of Bess and me by her car. Bess was nodding off, and Margaret was talking about Old Man Peterson's troubles and Floyd's untimely death when Isabelle and the preacher rode up ahead of puffs of dust. After introducing Margaret to the preacher, we stood around talking when Margaret walked over toward the mailbox with the camera, and before you knew it she had snapped a picture of all of us.

"I really don't like having my picture taken," the preacher snapped angrily. "You should have asked for my permission first." He gestured toward Isabelle to come with him and haughtily added, "Now, if you ladies will please excuse us, Isabelle and I'd like to take a stroll down the lane before she goes into the house."

Watching them as they slowly walked away, deep in conversation, Bess asked, "I wonder why Preacher Henry is so touchy about having his picture taken? He isn't the best looking man around but he's not the worst, either. Maybe he just doesn't like the way he looks in a photograph. I guess you really should have asked his permission before you snapped it, Margaret."

"I guess you're right, but it's too late now. I'll put the camera in the car so I won't forget it when I leave tomorrow," Margaret replied, and walked over to her car.

I had cooking to do so I excused myself to go back into the house to chop the cabbage and start frying the cornbread for supper. I heard Isabelle slam the screen door and without a word, retreat to her room. I walked over to the window and looked out. The preacher was talking to Bess and Margaret. He wore a long, sad face, as if he was agonizing over something. I knew he had a lot on his mind right now with a funeral to preach tomorrow and a willful sister to take care of. With the weight of the world on his shoulders, he probably was in need of some reassurance. I came away from the window and went back to my work, feeling kind of sorry for that young man.

Bess and Margaret walked into the kitchen a few minutes later. Bess said, "Bee, the preacher apologized for his rude outburst. He said he just had too much on him right now and he spoke impulsively. I told him I would relay the apology to you."

"Thank you, Bess. I find that understandable. Bess, why don't you stay and eat and then go to the picture show with us? I know you like Clark Gable as good as I do."

"Why, Bee, you know I'd love to any other time, but J.R. is coming over tonight to play rummy and keep me company." She then sheepishly added, "Did I tell you he's planning on staying tonight again?"

"Bess, no, you didn't tell me. You're a grown woman, and you don't need my permission to do a thing. Whatever you do, remember to be careful, and I mean in more ways than one."

"Oh, I will. Now for goodness sake, let's change the subject and talk about something else. I've got to go in a few minutes. I still have to work on my hair a little and check my makeup before J.R. gets to the house."

Margaret and I were at the door waving to Bess as she walked to her car when Vonion came running around the corner of the house as if he was going to put out a fire. I could tell immediately that something was terribly wrong from the expression on his face. Margaret and I hurried out to the yard. "What on earth is wrong, Vonion? Is somebody hurt?" I anxiously asked. He was so out of breath he couldn't get out what he really wanted to say.

"Vonion, sit down here on the bench and take a breath and then tell us what's wrong."

"That sheriff done come and picked up Roscoe over to Mr. Tom's place today. He come to git Roscoe and take him to the jailhouse. Mr. Tom just come over and tells me that sheriff say he might have somethin' to do with that killin'. Ms. Bee, what we gonna do? Oh, Lordy, we got to go git him. We knows that boy won't do notten like that. Ms. Bess, we need Mr. Will, rat now. He always know what to do!"

"Calm down now, Vonion," Bess said, as she walked over to put her hand on Vonion's old worn-out shoulder to reassure him we were there for him. "We'll figure this out. We don't want you having a heart attack. Now go tell Ora Lee we're going to see the sheriff and get to the bottom of this right now."

Vonion readily agreed, and with what seemed to be the weight of the world on his broad old shoulders, our faithful friend trudged slowly back toward his house, talking to himself and shaking his head as he went.

Well, I tell you, we couldn't get into Bess's car fast enough, and Bess didn't take any time at all getting it cranked and headed up the lane. She was shifting into second when I shouted, "Oh no, I left the stove on! I've got to go back!"

She slowed down almost to a stop—but not quite—changed gears and whirled around faster than you could spell your name, narrowly missing the fence. That familiar grinding noise echoed in our ears, and we were on our way back into the yard like a ball being shot out of a cannon. I was in the backseat and all I could do was slide. I got in on the left side of the car and got out on the right.

I headed up the steps, lost my shoe, ran into the kitchen and turned the stove off. I flung my apron off, ran back through the porch and out to the car. That's when I remembered my shoe and had to go back after it. I was so winded by the time I got back in the car, Margaret scolded, "Mama, are you all right? Just that little bit of exercise has about done you in. We need to get you into shape."

"I keep telling her that," Bess remarked, looking over at Margaret in her little knowing way. I couldn't see her, but I was sure Margaret rolled her eyes.

"Y'all both need to mind your own business," I firmly replied.

Bess had turned the car around while I was in the house so all we had to do was speed up the lane. Bess was concentrating on that steering wheel, and Margaret was busy telling her to slow down before we all got killed. We pulled out on the road narrowly missing fifteen number one hogs in the back of a large farm truck. The truck driver hollered some choice words at us that I didn't even know existed, but Bess didn't let that faze her. She drove on like a trooper. An accident right then would have been completely inconvenient, and we surely didn't want to get mixed up with a bunch of hogs.

Margaret shouted, "Aunt Bess, for goodness sake, please watch where you're going! We want to get there in one piece, and not smelling like a truck full of hogs. It would take more than Evening in Paris to drown that pig smell off."

Bess looked over at Margaret for a second and as she clinched the steering wheel said, "You want to drive? I know what I'm doing. Just hold on and I'll get us there before you know it. I can't wait to tell that good-for-nothing sheriff how stupid he is to arrest Vonion's grandchild for murder. Why, that child wouldn't hurt a flea. He's been up to my house several times to help me in the yard and, I tell you, he's as harmless as a baby kitten. I bet that poor boy is scared to death."

"Bess, just watch the road, and when we get there, we'll find out why Roscoe's being held. I'm sure the sheriff isn't arresting anybody right now. I think he still has Elmo in jail, and I doubt that he can hold two people for the same crime."

"Bee, we don't know what that man can do. What kind of evidence could he have anyway? Where was Roscoe the other night?"

"I did hear Vonion say something about not knowing when he got in that night or when he left the house the next morning. He was going down to Tom Wilson's to start work."

Bess had her mind on getting to the station and wasn't really watching the road as closely as she should. She had to slam on the brakes to keep from going right into the back of Cleo's rolling store. As she attempted to pass, she had to swerve to keep from hitting an old dog lying in the road. I braced myself as Bess muttered something about what this town really needed was a dogcatcher. I noticed Margaret gritting her teeth and holding firmly to the dashboard.

"Y'all just hold on. I'll get us there," Bess said, as she changed the gears again and sped back up.

"Let's just hope it's in one piece," I muttered under my breath, as I continued to brace myself for Bess's next maneuver.

"Aunt Bess, what is that grinding noise your car makes when you change gears? There might be something

ANN COBB

under the hood you need to see about," Margaret remarked, as we flew down the road.

"Oh, it's nothing, I don't even pay any attention to it anymore," Bess answered, as she glanced in the rearview mirror to check her lipstick.

Margaret, in a very commanding voice, announced, "Now, we're almost there, so everybody calm down. Breathe deep and exhale. All right now ladies, let's just all go in there peaceful like and don't jump to any wild conclusions. Let's act like the ladies we are."

When Bess whirled into the parking lot at the jailhouse and slammed on the brake, I knew this was not going to be pretty. Evidently we forgot Margaret's lecture because we all jumped out and started for the door of the building with too much fire in our eyes and spring in our steps. I guess Sheriff Ledbetter must have seen us headed his way because he opened the door for us to come in, as if he was the doorman or something.

"Ladies, come on in. What can I do for you? It's always a pleasure to see all of you out together. Would anybody care for something to drink?"

All that deep breathing and exhaling didn't seem to have worked very well. "You can quit your politicking, Sheriff. We didn't come to hear a campaign speech. For starters, you can tell us why you've got Vonion's and Ora Lee's grandson locked up in this jailhouse of yours? Why, the very idea, he's just a boy!" I exclaimed.

"Ladies, as long as I think there's a killer out there or in here, I have to do my job and turn over every rock I know about. We can't take any chances right now."

"Well, I can tell you, you've turned over the wrong rock," I replied, with so much anger building up in me I was sure I was turning red as a beet.

122

"One of my deputies saw Roscoe roaming the streets the night of the murder. Therefore, we felt we had to bring him in for questioning. I've already turned him loose and told him to go home, but not to leave the county. I sent a deputy out with him to check out the house."

"Well, thank heavens, you used a little common sense and let the poor boy go. You had us all worried to death. Why Vonion and Ora Lee have been frantic," I retorted, as I was beginning to calm down a bit. "Your actions could have caused them to have a heart attack, and it would be on your shoulders. They could die from all this stress."

"Please, Ms. Bee. I'm just doing my job."

Bess, trying her best to control herself, snapped, "I'll bet Old Man Jernigan was out walking that big old black dog of his that evening too, but I'm thinking you didn't bring him in. What kind of justice do you pretend to have here?"

"I'll ignore that comment," he answered, with a bit of a superior attitude. "Now, I advise you ladies to go back home where you belong and be very cautious because there're some strange things going on around us. I'm not telling you this to alarm you, but there's been another burglary, this time over at Shirley's house. Somebody broke in over there and stole all of that art work of her daddy's, her jewelry and silver while she was at work. We're just all thankful Shirley wasn't at home when they tore the door down trying to get in. Whoever's committing these crimes probably wouldn't have thought twice about killing her."

Bess looked at me and I stared back at her. My knees felt as if they had turned to rubber, so I found the nearest chair and plopped down. "You mean to say another home has been invaded." Just shaking my head in utter disbelief, I added, "Poor Shirley, she'll never want to stay at home alone again. What in Sam Hill is going on?"

With her finger pointed right into the sheriff's face, Bess added, "Sheriff, you better do something about this, and you better do it now!"

CHAPTER THIRTEEN

A s I was climbing into the backseat of Bess's car, my dress caught in the door. When I snatched it, it ripped. Why am I so spastic, please tell me? Lord, I've got to calm down before Margaret sees how nervous and anxious I can get. Years ago I could keep myself together in stressful times much better than I do now. In addition to that, I get hot all of a sudden and just break out in a sweat when nobody else will even notice the change in the temperature at all. It's getting harder and harder to stay calm and collected. I wonder if they make a pill for what's wrong with me.

Bess was making a beeline back out Route 3 when Margaret turned to Bess and politely said, "Aunt Bess, I think you need to stay with Mama until they catch this deranged criminal. You know, with everything like it is, you can't really consider staying by yourself, and I personally don't think you need to even think about J.R. staying at your house. I'm a modern day woman, yet I don't think you should be entertaining a man twenty-four hours a day."

Bess slowly and thoughtfully answered, "You know, Margaret, I think you're probably right about that. I do need to go on by the house though and see if J.R. has showed up. If he hasn't, I'll just leave him a note telling him where I am." Bess would listen to Margaret, but I could have told her the same thing, in the same way, and she wouldn't have listened to a word I said in a million years.

Bess whirled the car around right in the middle of the road just like a stunt driver. I had learned a long time ago to always have something handy to grasp hold of when I was riding with Fireball Bess, so I reached over to grab the door handle and broke two fingernails. If I hadn't known better, I would have thought she was trying to get us all thrown out of the car, so Mr. Lawson would have to scrape us off the road and haul us away in his long black hearse.

I had to caution her, but unfortunately it didn't come out sounding too nice. "Bess, what in the world are you trying to do? You know you can't turn a car around in the middle of the road like that. It's illegal, for Pete's sake. Why, if one of those deputies saw you doing that, you would end up in the jailhouse along with those other criminals. I don't have enough money to bail you out, so I guess you'd just have to rot in there. Besides, they take a person's license away for less. Now, you would be in a predicament if you couldn't drive your car legally. Just slow down, for pity's sake. We're almost to your house. My nerves are shot to pieces, and I can tell you're a lot worse off than me."

"I'd get you out, Aunt Bess."

"Thank you, Margaret. At least I still have one person around here who cares two hoots about me," Bess replied sweetly to Margaret, but was looking straight at me.

"Keep your eyes on the road, Bess. I might be old, but I want to get a little older."

Bess drove up to her house and gave a sigh of relief when she saw J.R.'s pickup truck parked in the driveway. "What makes you think I'm nervous? I'm just fine. Guess I didn't miss J.R. after all. Why don't you girls wait in the car, and I'll tell J. all the latest." Then, after a pause, she added, "Bee, on second thought, why don't you and Margaret go on home in my car, and I'll have J. bring me on out in a little while. I'll bring some things with me and plan on staying the night."

I could tell by the way Bess was acting flustered she wanted to see J.R. all by herself. When had she started addressing him by J.? Lordy, this must be more serious than I thought.

Bess opened the car door and walked over to the truck where J. was sitting. We sat in the car and stared at them as they walked toward the house together. Bess kind of propped her head on his shoulder, and he put his arm around her for support, as if to be helping an invalid. Margaret seemed to be mulling something over in her mind when she said, "Mama, I'm afraid Aunt Bess is getting herself into something she might not be able to wrangle herself out of. We might want to talk to her a little about this. Men in this world today are out for just one thing, and that J. looks pretty mannish to me. I don't like this. Aunt Bess needs to think long and hard about where this relationship is taking her."

Without much effort on her part, Margaret slid under the wheel to drive, and I moved up to the front seat. "Now, Margaret, we're going to have to stay out of it if we want to remain on Bess's good side. I really do think Bess has good sense about most things, and we must respect her privacy. This could be the real thing, and maybe it'll give Bess a whole new lease on life. We don't know. I wish I could talk to her about all of it, but there are some things a person has to find out for themselves. I expect this is one of them. You know how you feel when I pry into your love life. You know how you resent it. Now, let's drive on down to Ora Lee's before we stop at the house and check on things down there. I hope Roscoe has come in by now."

Roscoe was leaning on the chinaberry tree out in the yard deep into conversation with his grandparents when we drove up. "Maybe we need to leave them alone right now," Margaret said thoughtfully as we debated about getting out of the car. We decided to veto that thought and barged right on in to give them our two cents' worth.

"Roscoe, thank God you're home. We were all so worried about you. What in the world's going on?"

"Mrs. Bee, they ain't got notin' on me 'cept I was walkin' down that street the other night just like lots of other folks. They questioned me 'til I thought I would just go out of my mind. They some mean folks down to that sheriff's office, just yellin' and gettin' all in my face, trying to make me say somethin' that just ain't so. I made it though, but they say I can't leave the county. I tell them I ain't going nowheres, and they can find me here or over to Mr. Tom's place. Now I be fine and I don't want any of y'all worrying no more about me. Everybody go home and let's get back to what we was doin' 'fore all this happened. They let Elmo go too. They say they don't have no real evidence on him either. They ain't found no money anywhere. They told him the same thang they say to me, 'Don't leave the county.' I did hear them talkin' and it seem to me they's feeling he might be involved with somebody else, and maybe he'll lead them to the others if he's out of jail. But we better not say notin' bout that outside of right here and now. They go through the house here, but they weren't notin' here for them to find. They take Elmo home too, and I 'spect they checked his house over good too."

"You're saying those deputies searched the house when they brought you home. Did they mess things up, Ora Lee?" I questioned.

"No, they kinda walk through and look around in the closet and under the bedsteads and around. They didn't tear up notin' or I would have gotten on to them. They was kinda nice and respectful. We didn't have no problem. They better leave Roscoe out of all this, though.

"Ms. Bee, I did heared that sheriff say they 'spect Mr. Floyd been dead quite awhile 'fore they found him early that morning. He still had his work clothes on, not his sleeping clothes. They was dirty and greasy like he done a day's work in them."

"Did you see anything the other night on that street that seemed unusual?" Margaret quizzed Roscoe.

"I didn't see notin' that I call unusual, Ms. Margaret, but they was some people out drivin' round town just like usual. I saw the deputies ride by, and they were a family with a bunch of kids in an old black Model T, and there was that man that I's didn't really know, walking down the street. And oh, yea, I saw Ms. Mildred drive by. I don't think they were notin' different from any other night I can remember."

"That man you saw walking, who was he?"

"I's don't know him. Ain't never seen him 'fore the other night. He was fairly young, probably 'bout thirty years old. He looked kinda poor; you know his clothes were torn and raggedy. He kinda seemed lost."

"That sounds mysterious," Margaret answered.

"I told the sheriff about him and he say that sounded interesting."

"Now Vonion, y'all have heard the boy, and I, for one, believe him, so let's all quit worrying about all this. The main thing is we're all safe right now. But we've got to remain careful about what we do and where we go," I said in a matter of fact way.

"You right 'bout that, I 'spect," Vonion replied. "I's keep telling you that, but you don't halfway listen."

"I will listen now, Vonion."

Margaret and I went on back to the house and we cautiously crept in. "Check all the rooms and closets, and I'll check under the beds," I said, after we opened the front door. "On second thought, I'll check the rooms and closets, and you check under the beds. I don't think I can get down that low today. My knees are a little stiff. I'll go out back and check around the yard when we're through. We surely don't want to take any chances that somebody might be lurking around out back in the bushes."

From her old bedroom, I heard Margaret say, "Mama, when was the last time you cleaned out from under these beds? Did you know you're breathing in all this dust? You need to take these mattresses out to air and mop under every bed. I swear it didn't look like this when

Ora Lee helped you in the house. Do you think she could give you a hand every now and again?"

"Margaret, that is the exact reason I don't like anybody snooping around my house. They find out too much about my housekeeping and it's not the best, I admit. Now, quit worrying about my dust and let's eat."

"All right, I am starving. Did you ever finish cooking that cornbread and cabbage?"

"I'll be through in a few minutes. Now you just go do something else, and I'll have it on the table before you can shake a stick." I examined my torn dress and thought maybe I'd ask Bess about repairing it while she was here. I hadn't worn that dress but a few times, and I certainly didn't have my money's worth out of it yet.

"Mama," Margaret called, as she was walking out to the porch. "Aunt Bess's boyfriend's truck is coming down the lane. It sure didn't take long for her to spend some time with J. Maybe she's going to bring him in to visit."

Dear me, I hope he doesn't think everything is going to be 'just so' over here like it is at Bess's house. I was past trying to impress anybody with my decorating and housekeeping. I snatched my apron off and ran to the hall to glance in the mirror. I certainly could run a comb through my hair, but it was far too late for that. *Good grief,* I said to myself as I stood there. When did I get so old? At least my hair was still that nice coppery color Thelma had put in. I guess I'd pass inspection for right now.

I immediately heard the truck door slam and then the screen door scrape. Bess, resembling a raging bull, charged in the house with fire in her eyes.

"You're not going to believe what that scheming old man just did!" she hollered, as if we were all the way down in the back field and hard of hearing. "If he thinks for one minute he can just move in and live with me without the benefit of a marriage certificate, then he is touched in the head! He not only thought I would let him live with me while his house was being fumigated for bugs, but he brought a tub of his dirty drawers and things for me to wash along with mine. If I didn't mind, he said. He had the nerve to say his washing machine was cutting up, and he didn't think he needed to have it repaired as long as mine was in working order. He is absolutely out of his cotton-picking mind! I told him he needed to find another place to stay while they were killing his bugs, and I did not intend to have an open door policy. Why, I'll bet his house doesn't even have a bug!"

"Aunt Bess, you need to calm down and take a deep breath. Maybe he just wanted to stay with you to protect you from this killer who's running around terrorizing everybody. I'll bet that's what he was talking about. Why are you so upset over this? You did ask him to stay overnight, after all. All you had to say was 'no' and that would have been the end of it."

"Oh, no, you don't understand. After I told him I didn't think it was a good idea for him to stay overnight and he would have to think of another alternative, he said if I couldn't be a little bit more charitable—if you know what I mean—he could find what he needed some place else. If I hadn't been stranded without any transportation, I would have told him to hit the road right then and there. The nerve of that old man! I told him I needed a ride out here and if he wasn't willing to bring me, I could walk. He said it was right on his way back to Wall County so he might as well drop me off. As soon as I was out of the truck, he drove off like he was trying to catch a moving train. Well, if he thinks I will, in a million years, entertain the idea of going out with him ever again, he has another think coming. I'm so grateful I saw what he had on his mind before it was too late. What kind of woman does he think I am?"

She was crying by this time and wringing her hands in anger. Margaret and I just stood there. We let Bess get it all off her chest before we tried to say another word. Boy, did I want to say, "I told you so." But she was brokenhearted and needed sympathy, so we gave it to her.

Margaret finally said, "Aunt Bess, there's somebody out there that's gonna love you for just who you are. It's going to be fine. You don't need that 'snake in the grass.' He was just out to get what he could, and he thought you were a pushover. But you showed him, didn't you?"

"Bess, just how much of a pushover were you, if you don't mind my asking?" I questioned, thinking if she was ever going to tell us the real nitty-gritty, this was the time.

"Bee, it's not what it's built up to be. I was perfectly miserable but was willing to bear up just to have a little companionship. Thank heavens I don't have to worry about shaving my legs or having on good undies anymore. It was just too much of a struggle to keep everything maintained all at one time. Now Bee, please don't let me get caught up in that kind of thing ever again."

"Bess, I don't recall you asking me about it the first time."

CHAPTER FOURTEEN

W e heard Isabelle come in a while after we had eaten, but she went straight to her room. Where were young people's manners? The least she could have done is to acknowledge us and ask to be excused for the night. I crept over to her door and tapped, "Isabelle, would you like to have a bite to eat? We have plenty."

"No thank you. I've already eaten with Henry. With all the preparations at the church for the funeral, I'm just give out. We cleaned the sanctuary and swept those church yards until I thought my arms would fall off. I never heard of a church that gets so wrapped up in funeral arrangements like this one does. I think I'll just lie on down and try to go to sleep, if y'all will try to be quiet."

"We'll try to hold it down." The nerve of that girl! Well, at least she did get some exercise today. "I won't bother you anymore tonight. Get a good night's rest."

I wanted to talk to her or her brother about the money due me. I needed it badly and felt they were avoiding the issue. It seemed strange neither she nor the preacher had even brought up the subject. I'd have to speak to Preacher Henry no later than Monday about that matter, but I would wait until after the funeral. He needed to have his full attention on what was expected of him tomorrow. I had my doubts he had ever preached a funeral service for anyone, and please tell me how any preacher really knows what to say about a person he hardly knew, anyway.

Bess still had the bathroom tied up, so being the last person on the totem pole, I'd have to wait my turn. Margaret, sitting on the settee in the front room, with her pajamas on and her legs crossed, was waiting for me to come in just like the old days. Will, Margaret and I always sat around together for a while to catch up on the events of the day before going to bed at night.

"Mama, I'm going to be so worried about you and Aunt Bess after I leave tomorrow. I know there's not a thing I can do to protect you from my house. Why don't y'all just pack up—the both of you—and come for a few days and stay with me, at least until everything settles down around here. You two could call it a vacation. Please! You could leave Isabelle in her brother's care, and Vonion and Ora Lee have Roscoe. Why don't you, just for my peace of mind?"

"Margaret, now I have already been through this with you. I'm not going to go anywhere, so you might as well not say another word about it. Your Aunt Bess and I are going to be fine, so let's change the subject and talk about something else. You know, I heard that Miller boy is back in town and is teaching here now."

"'That Miller boy' is married with two children, so I hope you aren't going where I think you're going with this. Mama, let me find my own man. I know what to look for, for Pete's sake."

I leaned over to her and whispered, "I hope your Aunt Bess has learned her lesson about men. You know what they say—*There's no fool like an old fool.*"

"Mama, we need to just drop the subject of Aunt Bess's romance and not even mention it again. I think she's through with men—for now—anyway."

We heard Bess moving around in the back of the house, so I walked to the bedroom door, knocked softly and called for her to come and talk awhile.

"I'm coming, Bee. I need to make a telephone call first. I'll just be a few minutes." Later as she walked in, she said, "I called Freddy, and he seems so grateful I'm over here for the time being. He said he had been trying to get me on the telephone tonight and was about to call out here. He wants us to keep in touch, and he said he'll come and stay if we need him."

Margaret jumped up and almost shouted, "Call him back and tell him to come on. You two need him now if you ever needed him!"

"We are not calling anybody. We're going to be fine; now get that through your thick head," I responded, almost too abruptly. "And when you leave tomorrow, I don't want you fretting yourself to death. That settles it. Now let's talk about something else."

"I won't say another thing. If y'all want to be hardheaded, then so be it. I just hope the next time I come home, it's not to another funeral."

Later on after everybody had settled down and retired for the night, I was lying in bed, wide awake, with Bess right beside me—and a little too close for comfort. I whispered, "Bess, you have got to move over a little.

There are two of us in this bed, so you can't just lie right down the middle. And quit gritting your teeth. Could you possibly stop shaking your foot, too?"

"Well, if you would just be still and quit rolling over every two minutes, I could get to sleep. Every time I get comfortable, you move, and you're creeping over to my side," Bess replied, as if nothing I had just said registered at all.

I sat up and wearily said, "This is just not working, Bess. What on earth are we going to do? Isabelle's in one bed and Margaret's in the other. We don't have another choice but to get through this night, so you have got to be still and I'll try to do the same. On second thought, I'll sit over in the chair for a while until you go to sleep, and then I'll try to get back into bed without waking you. Now, please don't do anymore of that snoring. And if you have to go to the bathroom, go ahead right now."

Bess rolled over and closed her eyes.

It was one miserable night. Bess went to the bathroom four times, snored in between each visit and shook her leg so hard it vibrated the whole bed, and that made the springs squeak. I sat in the chair dozing as best as I could, watching the clock. It was with much pleasure I watched the sun come up the next morning. There had never been a good time to lie back down the entire night with Bess stretched right down the middle of the bed. Feeling as if I was permanently attached to the chair, I slowly pulled my aching body up and walked to the window.

"Thank You, Lord, for getting us through the night," I prayed. I could hear the roosters crowing and Vonion hitting the side of the bucket with his stick while he slopped the hogs. This morning, I can truly say, those were welcoming sounds.

With lots to do, I was glad to be up early and get started on all my waiting tasks. After I made coffee and prepared a little breakfast, I called to everybody. Isabelle never got up, but Margaret and Bess ambled into the kitchen, both yawning. Bess sat down at the table, poured her coffee, and had the audacity to say she didn't think she had slept a wink all night. Sometimes it's just so hard to keep your mouth shut, but I did. I didn't want Bess to get mad and feel as if she wasn't welcome. I needed her and she needed me now.

It was custom for the ladies of the church to provide the grieving family a meal at the time of a funeral. "What can we take to church to feed all those people? We've got to come up with something fairly quickly," I said to Bess, as I stood looking into the pantry door.

Bess thoughtfully replied, "Oh, Bee, don't you still have some of those chicken and dumplings? We could heat them up and put them in Mama's big Pyrex bowl. Everybody will think you did them just for today. I just heard Vonion put the eggs on the porch a few minutes ago, so let's devil some. I know you've got plenty. Let's slice tomatoes and get a jar of your pickled peaches. We can go by my house and pick up the chocolate cake I made Friday for you-know-who. It'll be over my dead body that he gets a piece of that cake now. For heaven's sake, I think that's enough."

We all pitched in and before you knew it, we had the food prepared and the kitchen cleaned. Margaret said goodbye a little later that morning. Seeing Margaret drive off was a sad sight since I knew it would be at least three weeks before I would see her again. Even though I had gotten used to it, it was still hard to face her leaving without Will standing there beside me. Bess was a little more relaxed about going back into her house in the daytime, so she left to go home, and we planned on meeting at church for the morning service. The funeral was scheduled to begin immediately after the noon meal. The mourners would eat on old plank tables and sit on splintery benches that were permanently placed under the big oak trees between the cemetery and the small church sanctuary.

Isabelle finally got out of bed after Margaret and Bess left. With a sigh and a long face, she dragged herself into the kitchen where I was lining my picnic basket with a clean white tablecloth. As she opened the refrigerator to stare inside and feel the cool air escape around her into the room, she muttered, "Ms. Bee, I'm suffering with a terrible headache this morning. Would you please tell Henry I'll see him soon? I'm really not able to go anywhere today."

Oh brother, I thought. "Of course, I'll tell him. Is there anything I can do for you before I leave?"

"No, I'm sure it's just stress and I'll feel better after a rest. A little peace and quiet is all I need right now." She finally closed the refrigerator and walked back to her bedroom as if she were in a trance.

I wanted to check on Ora Lee and Vonion, so I needed to leave a little early. I really felt as if I had thrown myself together that morning with all the activity going on at the house. My black dress was getting a little shiny in the seat, and it felt as if it had shrunk a little across the hips, but it was what I had, so I had to wear it. Thank heavens, my hair seemed to be behaving itself for once. I dusted off my black shoes, black hat with the little veil, and put my handkerchief under my belt. Grabbing my good church apron, I hastily placed my basket of food in the car trunk and called out to Isabelle that I was leaving.

Ora Lee and Vonion were sitting in the old truck about to leave to attend their little church service as I drove up. Vonion was a deacon and also led the singing at the First African Eden Grove Primitive Baptist Church—about a mile down the road. I don't think they had missed a Sunday service in years, except when Ora Lee had come down with pneumonia a few months back. Vonion even preached a few sermons in between pastors coming and going. They were as faithful to the church as an old dog is to its master.

Roscoe, sitting on the tailgate of the old truck with his feet hanging down, was going along with them. He hopped off and walked over to the car. "Y'all ready to leave for church?" I asked.

Roscoe answered, "We's 'bout to go. Everythang all right last night to the big house, I guess? We were gonna stop by and check on y'all, but you beat us to the draw. Shore is gonna be a hot day. Notin' we can do about it though."

I agreed with that and told them to have a good day. Praying I had enough gas to get to the church and back, I left with a wave to Vonion and Ora Lee. I felt better about the day just knowing they were okay.

Preacher Henry had a big task in front of him today, and I was in prayer he was up to the challenge. His words of encouragement today would mean a lot to the family, as well as to the rest of the community. As far as him preaching a big funeral, I'm almost certain he had no previous experience. Why, I doubt he's ever preached a funeral before. I also was a little nervous we wouldn't have enough food for everyone. It was just like some of the women to have small bowls of vegetables and casseroles that wouldn't stretch very far. I don't know how you get it through some women's heads, if you're going to fix a dish for a crowd, fix something that will stretch and have a big container of it. I guess Bess and I should have done a ham, but it was a little too late to worry about that now.

After the morning church service was over, Mr. Lawson brought Floyd's coffin into the sanctuary, placed it on a sturdy table in front of the pulpit, and opened the lid for viewing. I had left my purse on the pew after the morning service in my haste to get my basket out to the tables, and hurried back into the church to retrieve it. I decided to walk over and take one last look at poor Floyd. I always hate to think about people being stretched out in a coffin for every curious person to peer down upon and then comment about how they never looked better or how bad they looked, but that was the custom. Mr. Lawson never could style anybody's hair or apply the right amount of rouge on anybody's face without making a mess. I had warned Margaret that she had better not let a soul see me lying in a coffin. I had a hard enough time getting my hair to do right while I was alive, and I knew for sure Mr. Lawson wouldn't be able to do a thing with it. Thelma had always refused to go near a dead person, so I knew she wouldn't be a bit of help.

Floyd looked quite peaceful stretched out in his good grey flannel suit and black necktie, with his hair parted right down the middle of his head. I had never even seen it parted like that; it always fell straight down over his forehead. He had a pink carnation attached to his lapel that was already wilted in the heat. Being curious if there were any markings left from the extension cord—and since there was nobody else in the sanctuary—I worked up my courage and gently reached over and pulled his collar out a little from the side of his neck. The strangulation marks were quite visible and appeared to travel higher toward the back of his head. I didn't know if that meant anything at all, but it seemed to me that it would indicate that the killer could have been slightly taller than Floyd. Floyd was a short man, so maybe that didn't mean a thing. Hearing the front door open and then footsteps, I quickly adjusted Floyd's collar, dabbed my eyes with my handkerchief as if to wipe the tears away, and walked away.

When there's a funeral for an important member of the community, as well as a murder victim, then you better watch out for a big turnout. We didn't realize everyone in the county was going to show up. Many remained standing out in the churchyard during the service since the church was too small to hold the crowd. We had already served the noon meal to the bereaved family and grieving mourners by the time the service was scheduled to start. There's something about food that's flavored by a few gnats, served on a hot afternoon on the church grounds, that makes it especially good. Ham, fried chicken, barbecue, peas, butter beans, corn, salads of all kinds, sliced tomatoes, pickled peaches, watermelon, and every kind of pie or cake known to man, were washed down by gallons of sweet iced tea.

I was dead on my feet by the time we put away all the dishes in the church pantry. I noticed Bess was dragging too. Since space was limited, Bess and I decided to wait out in the churchyard until the service was over out of respect for the family. After the service, we watched Mr. Lawson direct the pallbearers as they brought the casket out the front doors of the church and took it over to the cemetery. It is with special care a group of men of different heights can get a casket up a church aisle, out the doors, to the graveyard and keep it fairly level all at the same time, but they did. Mr. Lawson motioned to the pallbearers to place the casket on heavy ropes that had been placed over the empty grave.

By then the hot sun was beaming down and the temperature had risen considerably. My legs felt like rubber, and I didn't know if I could take much more of this standing in the heat. It was at least ninety-five degrees. One woman swooned and then another. Recognizing how hot it was, Preacher Henry didn't waste any time and said a few quick words of encouragement and had a short prayer. He asked the family to gather in the shade of the trees where there was a big washtub of ice water waiting for them. It was over except for the lowering of the casket into the grave. People started drifting away except for a few that stood around talking and shaking hands. I walked over toward Bess and some of the girls who were clustered together in the shade of one of the big, ancient oak trees, drinking ice water, and told them I was heading home before I fell out.

"I'll be back out to the house directly," Bess said, as she wiped her perspiring face with her handkerchief, "just as soon as I go back by the house to pick up a few things and get out of these hot clothes."

"Don't be too long. I don't want to start worrying about you."

Just as I was walking off, Vera called from the other side of the cemetery. "Bee, wait up." She hurried over, looking exhausted and on her last leg too. "Bee, could I possibly catch a ride home with you? Tillman has to stay with the other pallbearers and make sure the church is put back in order. It'll be a while before he can leave."

"Why, of course you can. Come on and let's go. Are you ready?"

"I'm ready. Tillman knows I was going to try to catch up with you."

"Let's get out of this sun then. My dishes are already in the car. Where are yours?"

"They're in our car. Let's go before we pass out. This heat is awful today." Then Vera added, as perspiration was popping out all on her face and beginning to run down her neck, "I know I don't want to go to hell if it's hotter than today, and that is what the good book says."

"It's just a pity most folks don't believe hell is hot. I, for one, don't intend to be there," I commented, as we walked past a group of teenage girls. Maybe we gave them something to think about. When you're that young, you think you'll live forever, but that's just not the case. Ask somebody that knows. Just ask me, I'll tell you the truth.

CHAPTER FIFTEEN

Vera and Tillman's place sits next to the road about a half mile from mine, as the crow flies. Vera had grown up there, and she and Tillman remained in the same house her parents left her, just as I had done. Vera had always been my closest childhood friend and other than Bess, my only playmate. We could walk through the woods to each other's house in no time at all. Most days, after we had done our morning chores, we would spend the afternoons together. We knew every tree and could walk those woods as well at night as in the broad daylight. As children, adventures were waiting for us every day, since we both had great imaginations and time to explore. We built playhouses, forts, dugouts and ate many a picnic lunch from a pail our mothers had packed for us. Our little one room schoolhouse was just over the rise beyond Vera's, so Bess and I would try to catch up with Vera and her older brother on the way to school most every morning and then race them the rest of the way. Vera's brother, Lawrence, always beat us, and most of the time, he'd hide behind the schoolhouse to scare us as we ran into the school yard. The memory of those days and the wonderment of childhood always gave me a warm nostalgic feeling.

Tillman had never farmed the land but sold insurance until he retired a few years back. He and Vera had managed to keep the land together much the same way I did now. Their acreage was rented out, and hopefully, every year they could manage to have enough income from it to keep the place up and pay their taxes.

My car was hot so we had decided to roll the windows all the way down and forget about our hairdos. We were both tired, ready to get home and cool off a bit. The day had been emotionally draining. We were both just wiped out. "Vera, where are you getting gas for your car? I need some badly and don't know what to do about it with Floyd's place locked up. I'm afraid to crank my car and go anywhere after today for fear of running out."

"You know, I really don't know. I always let Tillman worry about those things. I haven't even given it a thought." Those few carefree words made me just want to cry. Will's absence had changed my whole life in every way imaginable. In all the years of our marriage, there had never been a time I worried about gas in the car. The gas was just always there.

With a worried tone in her voice and perspiration popping out on her face, Vera wearily said, "Bee, all these terrible events are just about to do me in. I can't sleep at night, wondering if there's somebody wandering around outside trying to break in the house. Tillman has started sleeping with the shotgun beside the bed. I'm scared that I might get up during the night to go to the bathroom and get my brains blown out on the way back to bed. Just think about poor Floyd, lying in that graveyard right now because somebody wanted his money. You know Old Man Peterson will never be the same again. He'll probably grieve himself to death worrying about his stolen money. Shirley's scared to go back into her own home and is staying over at her Aunt Dora's house just to be on the safe side. Ms. Dora's so old and partially blind now. Maybe they'll get a little comfort from each other for a while anyway, until they start getting on each other's nerves. Ms. Dora probably won't allow Shirley to smoke in her house, so it won't be long before Shirley will have to move back home. You know Shirley can't go half an hour without a cigarette in her mouth. I don't think there's any reason for anybody to break into Shirley's house again anyway. Everything that was valuable over there has already been carried off. You and Bess better go ahead and get out the shotgun, learn to use it, and keep it where you can get your hands on it in the middle of the night, and do it pronto."

"Vera, I think you're overreacting a bit, but that stupid sheriff better start looking in the right direction for the real culprit instead of thinking for one minute Roscoe had something to do with all this business. He needs to use some real detective work and look for some real clues instead of just jumping to conclusions." Vera nodded in total agreement.

"Bee, look!" Vera exclaimed with a puzzled look spreading across her face. As we neared her house, she cautiously said, "There's something different about the house. I just don't know what it is." She sat forward in the seat as I pulled into the driveway and slammed on the brake, avoiding the light pole by only a slight margin.

"Y'all have got to do something about that pole, for goodness sake, before somebody knocks it over on the house." I think I'd warned Vera about that pole every time I had driven over to her place since the rural electric people had placed it there.

Completely ignoring what I was saying, Vera pointed toward the house. "Bee, look over at the side door. Is it closed or is it just pulled to?"

"Vera, I just don't know," I answered slowly, as I began to examine the way the house looked. I realized right then something was different about the place. Putting my hand to my mouth to try to cover my surprise, I asked, "Vera, when did you move your mama's tea service from the window?"

"I didn't. Why?"

"Because it's gone! Maybe Tillman moved it and you don't know anything about it."

"Are you out of your mind? Tillman wouldn't touch that thing with a ten foot pole without telling me first. He knows not to go near it. Oh Bee, it is gone!" Vera grabbed my arm and clamped down on it until I hollered with pain.

"Vera, stop squeezing my arm. You know how easily I bruise." Sensing Vera might want to investigate, I raised my voice and warned her. "Don't get out! I'm going to turn this car around and go back to town and find the sheriff. A burglar might be in there right now!"

"We aren't going anywhere! I'm staying right here! If somebody has my silver, he better watch out because I'm going in after him now! My mama would roll over in her grave if she thought somebody outside our family would be using that set! There's a short two-by-four that Tillman was using to knock a wasp nest down the other day over against the fig tree. I'm going to get it, and I'll use it over somebody's head if they're still in my house."

"A two-by-four? Are you absolutely nuts? That man probably has a gun. A two-by-four isn't a match for a gun. You aren't going anywhere!"

Just as I got the word "nuts" out of my mouth, Vera put her hand on the car door handle and was opening it with a look of determination that would make your blood clot. I reached over to stop her, but she was too fast. She jumped out of the car and headed over to the fig tree to pick up that piece of wood. That's when I realized she was dead serious about going into the house. I opened my car door a little more cautiously than Vera and followed her up the doorsteps. I couldn't let her go in the house by herself. How would I ever explain it if she got herself killed and I was sitting in the car? Lordy, how do I get myself into these kinds of situations?

"If I get killed, please don't let Margaret sell the farm, and make sure she lets Vonion and Ora Lee stay there as long as they live." I was steady mumbling to Vera as she pushed open the side door to get into the house. Glancing down, I noticed I still had my apron on. "Vera, how did I forget to take my apron off after we served all those people? I've got to get this thing off. If I'm dead, I surely don't want to be found with an apron on, of all things," I nervously said, as I attempted to untie it with my trembling fingers.

"If you're dead, I'm sure I'll be deader since I'm going in first. Don't be thinking you can write your Last Will to me right now. But if I get killed, tell Tillman I loved him, even if I have been pretty temperamental and bossy all these years."

"Vera, hush, and keep that two-by-four high so you can come down hard on this fool! Now, I'm right behind you, so don't make any fast moves I can't follow. Give me a little notice if you're going to attack somebody so I can be ready to back you up. I saw a movie one time with some karate fighting in it, and I think I can do it."

"Bee, after I use this board on somebody's head, you can karate chop him all you want."

We slowly crept over the house, me right behind Vera, and her holding that piece of wood in the air. After we had been all the way through the entire house, looking in closets, behind every door and under each bed, we let our guards down a little and surveyed the damage.

"Well, Vera, your mama's silver tea service is gone, and it looks as if somebody went through all these sideboard drawers and left everything in a mess."

"Oh no, Mama's sterling flatware is gone too!" Vera exclaimed, as she started opening more drawers. "I hope all the serving pieces wrapped up in the bottom drawer are still there."

Vera opened the next drawer and gasped. "All the serving pieces are gone, as well as my sterling salt and pepper shakers. Lord have mercy, what am I going to do? Mama would die all over again if she knew I let something happen to all her stuff. Vera's eyes were beginning to glaze, and she appeared to be in a state of shock by now. Vera grabbed me and put me into a bear hug that almost suffocated me. I pulled her away slightly and she grabbed me again. After she gained a little control, we slowly crept back into the bedroom where all the dresser and nightstand drawers were hanging out. Vera was behind me now and clamped to my back with her groping arms.

"Vera, you've got to move back some. I can't breathe with you so close. Now get yourself together. I told you we should have gone for the sheriff, but no-o, you had to come on in." Then, as I was beginning to feel really sorry for her, I added, in a little gentler voice, "Vera, it's gonna be all right. Nobody was home, so nobody was hurt or killed like Floyd. Count your blessings."

"Bee, that's easy for you to say. It wasn't your house that was burglarized! Oh, my gosh! All my jewelry is gone too. The ruby brooch my aunt left me and the cameo necklace Tillman gave me for our anniversary—it's all gone!" She clamped onto me again, and I stood there with her squalling against my shoulder for as long as I could stand it.

I pulled her back and sternly said, "Vera, I'm calling the sheriff right now. Wait here and get control of yourself!" I could feel the terror building up inside, too, as I started up the hall and grabbed the telephone. "Nellie, get the sheriff, now! This is Bee Martin, over at Vera and Tillman's place!"

"Bee, I will. But first tell me about the funeral. I couldn't get there because of this operator job. It is just so confining. Was it well attended? Did the casket look expensive? Please tell me Mildred wore something decent. You know she was in town the other day wearing those pedal pushers again! Can you believe that? Oh, and how did poor Floyd look?"

"He looked dead! Ring that sheriff right now or I'm coming over there and doing it myself! Now, do it! I'm fixing to hang up, so tell that sheriff or deputy, whichever one answers the telephone, to get a move on it and get over here as fast as he can! Do you understand that or do I need to repeat myself?"

"Yes, ma'am, I understand. And you don't have to be so bossy. I know my job! What do you need the sheriff for?"

Irritated is not the exact word for how I felt right then. I pretended I didn't even hear that last question and hung up. I tried to console Vera for the next few minutes, knowing full well she was on the verge of having a nervous breakdown any minute. She was heaving and said she couldn't breathe, so I told her to put her head down between her legs and to try to breathe harder. She tried it, but from the way she sounded, I don't think it was working. She was almost hysterical when I looked out the window to see Tillman riding up like it was just another day. Poor man, he was in for a shock.

The sheriff pulled in right behind him, and I saw him motion for Tillman to come over by the patrol car. After they had a few words, I watched as Tillman took out running for the house, and before you could spell your name, he was coming through the door with holy terror written all over his sweating face.

Vera just collapsed on that poor helpless man and started squalling like a baby. For the life of me, I don't know how he held that woman up as long as he did. He finally managed to get her over to the settee to sit her down. The sheriff walked in and checked the door to see what kind of damage had been done as Tillman started looking around at the disarray left by the thief. I found a piece of newspaper and started fanning Vera when the sheriff told me to get her some water to see if that would help. She drank the water and finally, after Tillman grabbed her by the shoulders again and shook her gently, she recovered enough to talk sensibly to the sheriff, explaining how we had come in and found this mess.

Tillman and the sheriff did a quick walk-through of the entire house, and I heard Tillman out in the kitchen, saying to the sheriff, "Evidently the burglar didn't know about our secret hiding place. We have considerable cash hidden right here in this old pickle crock. It's still here. Thank goodness for that."

All of a sudden, it dawned on me. I had left Isabelle home, unprotected and right by herself. I made a beeline out the door, yelling to them as I left that I needed to get home and check on things there as fast as I could. My car was blocked in by the patrol car, so I pulled over on the grass and made a u-turn right through Vera's daylily bed. Lordy, Vera was going to kill me when she saw the damage. Maybe she wouldn't notice it since there was so much other damage in the house to focus on. Thank heavens I missed the light pole again. When he has the time, Tillman has got to speak to the electricity people about moving that thing out of the way. I just know they can put those things in the backyard instead of the front if they wanted.

CHAPTER SIXTEEN

Only a few times in my entire life have I been really scared: the time we lost all our crops to the tumultuous rain that flooded our fields in September, drowning everything that had been planted; when Will died and I had to face the future without him; and now. Our community was being attacked by someone who had no respect for life or home. I was beginning to panic as I drove home. "Please, dear God, don't let anything happen to Isabelle while she's staying with me."

I was sure I'd give out of gas before I arrived home, so I let my car coast down the hill and went as far down the lane as it would go without applying the gas pedal. Thank heavens I made it into the yard. Maybe Vonion has a little gas in a can somewhere around the place. I had taken my last chance that I wouldn't give out on the road or in town. How inconvenient and embarrassing that would be. I wondered what everybody else was doing about their gas problem. I hadn't noticed anybody's car

ANN COBB

beside the road. Maybe everybody else kept a full tank all the time and didn't need any yet.

Everything looked fairly normal from out in the yard, so I walked slowly to the porch and stopped to listen for anything unusual. Those old crows down under the pecan trees, the hogs and chickens, and the sound of a big truck going down the highway were the sounds that made up the harmony of everyday life. It seemed as if everything was as it should be. Gathering up all my nervous energy, I walked onto the porch and then into the house, and called, "Isabelle, are you here?"

I thought I could hear something coming from her bedroom, so I walked on down the hall to her room and stood outside the door and called again. "Isabelle, are you in there?"

Isabelle answered, "Ms. Bee, is that you?"

"Yes, dear, it's me. May I come in a moment and talk to you? It's very important."

"Just a minute, let me get a little more presentable."

I could hear the bedsprings creaking and then her moving around. I stood outside the door until it opened. There she stood, with her hair disarrayed and a sleepy look on her face, wrapped in an old housecoat. "Ms. Bee, you look white as a ghost. Do you feel okay?"

"I'm fine, but I was worried something might have happened over here while I was gone. You haven't noticed anything out of the ordinary, have you?"

"No, nothing that I know about. Why?"

"There's been another burglary, this time over at Vera and Tillman's house. Someone broke in while they were gone to the funeral today and stole all that fine silver and some jewelry too. The sheriff is over there right now with Vera and Tillman looking for evidence. I was afraid we might have had some trouble too, with us being so close to them and all."

"Well, I've been resting all afternoon in my bedroom, and I haven't heard a thing except those pesky crows and hogs out there. Other than all those irritating animal noises, it's been as quiet as a tomb around here."

"Well, I'm glad you're safe. I think I'll have a good look around and then go check on Vonion and Ora Lee."

"Does the sheriff have anything to go on? Did the burglar leave any clues?"

"I'm afraid I don't know. I left in such a hurry I really didn't find out anything. I'll check with Vera later and find out more details. The best thing for us to do is just stay calm and continue to be cautious."

I walked all over the house and after being satisfied nothing was missing or rearranged, I changed my clothes and shoes, and walked down the lane. All the way down to the little frame house, I prayed that everything would be all right. Vonion and Ora Lee were sitting on the porch, Ora Lee with a little sewing in her lap and Vonion asleep, looking about as normal as ever. I tiptoed over to Ora Lee and whispered, "Have y'all seen or heard anything unusual around here this afternoon?"

"Everthang is about normal, I say. We just out here relaxin' on the porch. You seem a bit upsot."

"I am, and also a little nervous. I dropped Vera off at her house after the funeral, and we discovered their house had been broken into while they were gone. I guess it just scared me so badly that my mind went crazy worrying about something happening over here too. I'm so glad everything's okay."

Ora Lee looked at me with pure terror in those tired old eyes. "Lawsy me, what's to happen next? We is gonna be scerred to puts our hed on da pillow at night time. I know the good Lord is gonna look after us though. We is just got to keep on praying."

"You're right about that, Ora Lee. Now where's Roscoe?"

"That boy done gone to the river swimmin' with two or three other boys. They ain't got back yet, and I don't 'spect he be back fer a while."

We were whispering and trying to be quiet, but we evidently woke Vonion. He slid one lazy eye open and said, "Now, Ms. Bee, you know I ain't gonna miss nothin' goin' on around here. I been out here on this porch all afternoon a'watchin' and guardin' the place and ain't noticed nothin'. Miss Isabelle been out walkin' and Mr. Tom, he come by after church to check on us. He said he hurried home a few minutes before the funeral started to check on one of his brood cows that was about ready to drop a calf. Lordy, Ms. Bee, this situation done got serious. It seem we ain't safe no more. Sheriff Ledbetter better git to the bottom of all this. You think I needs to go over there and help out Mr. Tillman get everthang back together? I's knows Mr. Will, if'n he still be with us, he'd go straight over and help Mr. Tillman. Mr. Tillman got a lot to handle right now. You know Ms. Vera, she do get upsot easy, and him dealin' with her and this here break-in too, he probably don't know which way to turn."

"I think he probably would appreciate that. Vonion, is there any gas in the can? I know my car is on empty, and even if the gas station is open tomorrow, I'd be scared to try to make it there with what's in my tank."

"I think we got a little. I'll put it in your car 'fore I leave. They's a little in the old truck, so I think I'll drive over to Mr. Tillman's."

"Thank you, Vonion. Now Ora Lee, please stay close to home. We don't want to start worrying about you."

I stepped off the porch out to the hard-packed dirt yard, and thinking I needed a little exercise and alone time, I took the long way home all the way around the field. I was tired and it was hot, but I felt that getting out in the open was what I needed right then. Walking along the edge of the woods beside the field, I found myself actually enjoying the exercise. Just plodding along, one step after another seemed to comfort me. The woods were still, except for the occasional squirrel or jackrabbit and a gentle breeze that felt good against my body. I began to feel the peace that we all have within us, praying to God to protect us and to help Sheriff Ledbetter solve these crimes. I walked on and on until I had made it all the way around the field and back to my yard where I sat down under the big oak tree and began to doze. I guess I had slept a while because when I opened my eyes, Bess's car was parked alongside mine in the yard. I suppose someone could have taken the farm away and I wouldn't have known a thing. How I wish I could drift off to sleep like that at night when I lie down in bed.

Bess soon opened the porch door, and as she walked out, I noticed she didn't have that old pep in her step and she seemed rather stiff. "Bess, are you feeling all right?"

"I guess so, only a little tired."

"I know that you are given out. I know I am. Let's just sit a spell and not do a thing." Just as the words had come out of my mouth, I realized Bess probably didn't know the latest. I hated to be the one to tell her, but I knew she had to be told. I began the lengthy account of the events since I had last seen her at the funeral. After finishing the story, I said, "I wonder what in the world Vera and I would have done if we had encountered somebody in that house. I know we would have used that two-by-four if we had the chance, but we might not have been that fortunate. We could have ended up like Floyd or Old Man Peterson. The good Lord does look after us fools. That's for sure."

"Bee, I can't believe y'all went in there like that. Do you have any idea what could have happened if that robber had been in there? You wouldn't be sitting out here worrying about the color of your hair, that's for sure. Mr. Lawson would be trying to figure out which way to part it. You know he's completely useless with a comb and a brush. I, for one, am not about to tell Margaret what a foolish thing you did. She would have a conniption fit, and I wouldn't blame her a bit. How's this going to end anyway? We're all just sitting ducks, waiting for something else to happen."

"Bess, I don't know. But right now, I'm going in to find something for us to eat. Now, when you get hungry, come on in."

* * *

I knew I had a busy day tomorrow, so after supper I started sorting the laundry for the washer. I straightened my bedroom, putting all my church clothes away and changing the contents of my Sunday purse back to my everyday one. Where was the little cloth bag where I kept Mama's wedding ring and a little gold locket she had given me as a child? I always kept it in my everyday purse. I threw everything out of the purse onto the bed. My little cloth bag was not there. I absolutely knew it had been in there the last time I'd checked. I looked down in the bottom of the wardrobe under the quilts and spreads thinking it could have slipped down under something. Not a thing did I find except dust. I must have lost it after all. I'd go over the house and the car with a fine-tooth comb tomorrow. Maybe I'd come across them somewhere. Later that evening, feeling very irritated and confused, but expecting a better day to come, I finally closed my eyes and drifted off to asleep.

I did feel much better the next morning. Bess had already left for her house, and I doubted I would see her again until that evening. Breakfast and my regular chores went by without a hitch, and I started filling the washer with water when I heard a grinding noise coming from the motor. I was just holding my breath that nothing was wrong since I couldn't afford any repair bill right now, and I surely couldn't buy another one anytime soon, especially since Preacher Henry had made no move to pay me a red cent.

I wanted to get that mattress of Isabelle's out to sun today and clean under the bed, but I couldn't do any of it until she got up for the day. I gave the bathroom a good scrubbing and mopped the kitchen, all the while checking here and there for my little bag. It wasn't even eleven o'clock, but I was exhausted and needed a break. I thought about checking on Vera, so I gave her a call.

"Nellie, how about ringing Vera for me, please."

"Will do," she answered with a little abrasiveness in her voice. Vera picked up after three rings.

"Vera here."

"Vera, this is Bee. I was worried and thought I'd check on you and Tillman. Did you sleep at all?"

"Not a wink. Tillman and I both tossed and turned all night. Tillman has gone to town now to buy a new lock for the side door. We couldn't even lock the door last night."

"We were so lucky we didn't come in on that thief at your house yesterday, Vera. It just gives me the willies to think about what we did. I know I can't tell Margaret about it. I would hate to hear her reaction. I just hope some busybody doesn't tell her anytime soon." Maybe Nellie was listening and would take the hint.

"I certainly won't say a word to Margaret, you can count on that. Sheriff Ledbetter said he'd be back in touch with us if he had any more information about the burglary, but we haven't heard a word from him yet. I wonder if he's doing a thing. My mother would have left that silver tea service to Lawrence and his wife if she had thought I'd let something like this happen. I guess I should have kept it packed away and out of sight. Shirley called and said she hasn't heard a word from the sheriff either. She's still scared to death to stay at home by herself. You know she's terrified of her own shadow anyway."

"Vera, did the burglar take anything other than silver and jewelry? I know Tillman was still checking when I left."

"Hopefully that's all. We haven't missed anything else."

"Vera, it occurred to me that everything that was taken from Shirley was out for anybody to see, just like your silver. Her silver and all that artwork were all on display."

"I guess so, but do you really think that means anything? It was certainly common knowledge Floyd kept cash overnight at his house. Old Man Peterson's money was hidden away, but everybody around here that had ever had a conversation with him knew he didn't trust banks and kept his money hidden around there somewhere. Are you thinking that whoever is doing this breaking and entering is someone that knows what we have in our homes before he comes in?"

"It would seem so. But Vera, I'm just thinking out loud. Now, is there anything I can do for you?"

"We're okay now. We cleaned up the mess and did a temporary fix on the door with Vonion's help." Then with a good bit more emphasis in her voice, Vera said, "Bee, that sheriff ran right over my little daylily bed with his car when he left yesterday. He has a lot of nerve!"

Thinking fast, I answered, "He probably didn't realize what he had done. I wouldn't be so hard on him, Vera." My fingers were crossed and another quick prayer of forgiveness was sent straight up. These fibs of mine were getting to be more and more frequent. *I have absolutely got to work harder on being more truthful,* I told myself. *I'll start tomorrow.* "I've got to hang up and get busy. You know, my new little business venture has its responsibilities, and that means more housework. Having a boarder is more work than I ever figured on. I'll be seeing you and if you need me, don't hesitate to call."

"I will."

After hanging up, I sat there another minute thinking about the break-ins. Was there a connection between the burglaries? There had to be something everybody was over-looking.

CHAPTER SEVENTEEN

E ven after a good cleaning, my house still looked tired and worn out—much like I did. I hung out three loads of laundry, including Isabelle's things, which I finally got my hands on about noontime. Isabelle appeared late in the morning and said she was starving. After I heated a jar of my homemade vegetable soup and fried some cornbread, she picked at it and finally said it just wasn't what she had her mouth set for. I guess my homemade soup wasn't for everybody, but Will and I had always enjoyed it. After lunch, I took the clothes from the line and starched the blouses and dresses. Hoping Ora Lee would do the ironing tomorrow, I rolled the starch items and placed them in the icebox until I could get them over to her. Supper would be just for Bess and me since Isabelle had left with Preacher Henry to go visiting about one o'clock that afternoon. I had taken a beef roast out of the freezer that morning and now it was on top of the stove, simmering with potatoes and carrots. My old body was about to give out, so I decided to sit down a spell on the porch and rest before getting back to my tasks. Spotting Vonion out in the yard, hoeing out around the tomato bushes, I called to him to pick up the ironing when he left for the day. He gave me his old familiar nod and kept on working at a steady pace. Later he ambled over to the porch with a few nice tomatoes for me and two or three in his bucket to take home for Ora Lee.

As I walked into the kitchen to wash the tomatoes at the kitchen sink, I thought to myself, *I still haven't cleaned under the beds, but I'll just have to think about that another day. I'm just too tired today.* My mind was still on my little bag with my ring and locket when I realized I hadn't seen my new camera either. I thought I had laid it on the dresser in my bedroom, but I was sure I hadn't seen it since the other day. What in the world did I do with the thing? Maybe it was in the bedroom Bess was using. I checked around in there but didn't find anything but more dust. Bess could have moved it, but it didn't seem likely. I'd hate to tell Margaret I had misplaced it, knowing full well she would tell me I was getting senile in my old age, and she was probably right. Maybe Bess would know where it was.

Bess drove up about five thirty as I was watering the potted plants on the porch. I was trying to sound enthusiastic even with all the sorrow going on in my head. "Bess, hope you've had a good day," I called out as she was climbing out of the car. "We're gonna have roast with potatoes and carrots for supper. I was hoping you'd make a few biscuits while I finish up the watering. I want to sweep the porches, too, before I quit for the day."

"Sure, that sounds good. I haven't had a good roast in a while. You know, it's not any fun to cook just for yourself. Maybe I was too hasty about sending J.R. off the other day. I did enjoy cooking for him."

"As I recall, you didn't send him off. He left. And when did you ever cook for him? Y'all went out to eat most of the time."

"Bee, you don't know what you are talking about. Maybe I'll call him later and apologize. I really don't want any hurt feelings anyway."

"Bess, what was so wrong with your life before you met J.R.? I thought you were pretty content and happy. You have the boys, two grands, friends, the church, and me. That's not enough?"

"That's just it, Bee. I really don't have my children. My boys are so busy with their own lives that I don't see them that much. I guess after Freddy married, and Sam always driving that truck all over the state, they've just drifted in other directions. It seems to me they don't really include me in a lot of things they do. For instance, the other day my grandsons had a cookout in the yard with a bunch of their friends. They roasted hotdogs over a fire and played outdoor games. I told Jean that I would love to make a dessert for them and take it over and serve it to the boys. Do you think she called and invited me over with it? No, she did not. When I called a day or two later, she informed me they had eaten store-bought cookies instead. Now you know those boys would have loved to have had a nice chocolate cake or something homemade. I'll bet she didn't even bother to ask them what they wanted."

"Bess, for Pete's sake, it was a cookout. Nobody wants anything that requires a plate at a little boys' cookout. Those kids didn't know what they were eating, anyway. All they were thinking about was having fun and playing in that fire. You're making a mountain out of a mole hill. I really do understand what you're talking about and a lot of it is true. I wish I could be with Margaret more, but with her living off, that just isn't going to happen. We're going to have to be content with things as they are and make the best of it."

"Well, if you say so. I'm going on in and make those biscuits now. Anything else you want me to do, Bee?"

"Well, there're some tomatoes on the sink board for slicing, and if you would set the table, that would be helpful. Oh, Bess, have you, by any chance, seen my camera anywhere around here? I seem to have misplaced it."

"No, I don't think I've seen it since the day when we were taking those pictures with Margaret. Have you checked everywhere around the house?"

"I probably haven't looked as good as I should. I'm sure it's around somewhere. I'll ask Isabelle when they return from visiting this evening. Another thing I have on my to-do list is talk to the preacher about his rent obligation. You know, Bess, they haven't paid me one red cent yet. I don't feel like it's my place to ask them for it, but what else can I do?"

"It's not your place, but you better say something to them before more time goes by. Maybe they've just forgotten about it. Bee, maybe you're right and I need to just forget about romance. I guess watching Clark Gable should be enough for me. I don't know what to do with myself now. All the cleaning and organizing just isn't fulfilling me anymore. You know Fred has been gone three years now, and I don't feel as if it's time for me to quit living. I'm really not that old and I've taken pretty good care of myself, so my appearance isn't that bad. You know most women my age are either withered up or overweight. I've tried to keep my complexion and hair nice. I exercise every day to keep myself toned up."

"I don't know. I'm not the one to tell you," I said, while mulling over in my mind if Bess was trying to tell me something about myself without just coming out and saying it in so many words.

We ate supper and Bess enjoyed it. She didn't get good old country food very often. If she had been at home, she probably would have eaten a slice of cold ham and a few carrot sticks. After we cleaned the kitchen, I suggested we walk off a few calories. We started off down the lane toward Ora Lee's and Vonion's house and stopped only a minute to speak to Ora Lee as we passed by.

As we walked toward the woods, Bess said, "You know Bee, I think I'm going to stay at my house tomorrow night. I can't let some old crime wave keep me from my own home. I think I'd sleep fairly soundly if I knew you wouldn't be scared to death out here. Are you going to be able to sleep if I'm not in the next room?"

I answered as naturally as I possibly could with my limited breath. I didn't want Bess to think this little stroll was already causing me to gasp. "If that's the way you feel, I'll be fine. I do have Isabelle, if you count her as protection. I'm more concerned about you. You know you could stay with Freddy. That's an option."

"That is not an option. They don't have enough room for themselves, much less me. My two grandsons are crowded into one bedroom and with only two, I'd have to sleep in the living room on that lumpy old settee. That dog of theirs lies around all over the house carrying fleas and heaven only knows what else. I'd probably have him slobbering in my face all night. Just the thought of that makes me want to gag. I don't really feel welcome there anyway. Let's just try not to think about what's going on around here and go on about our normal lives."

"If that's the way you're feeling. I'll be fine. But I want you to call tomorrow evening just before you go to bed and then again when you get up the next morning, and that's final. By the way, Bess, I've misplaced my little bag with Mama's wedding ring and my little locket in it. Have you, by any chance, seen it lying around anywhere?"

"Heavens to Betsy, Bee! I can't believe you've lost something else. Maybe it's in one of your dresser drawers, stuck under something. Have you looked in the hall table drawer? You know you're always stuffing things in there. Keep looking. Surely it'll show up sooner or later."

"I hope so. I'm getting so forgetful lately. Do you think that's a sign of old age? I'm not ready to be over the hill. I don't feel as if I've even reached the top of the hill yet. There's got to be something ahead for us."

"I'm not ready to be old either, but it seems it just slips up on you. Bee, we're really not that old yet. We've got to keep thinking young thoughts."

"Give me an example of young thoughts."

"You know I can't do everything for you. Anyway, my young thoughts are probably different from yours."

"I was thinking about maybe buying a pair of those pedal pushers. How's that for a young thought?"

"That's a beginning. But my young thoughts are a little more shocking. Now think for yourself."

"I'm sure I don't really want to know about your shocking thoughts."

"Probably not."

We tried waiting up that evening for Isabelle and the preacher, but after about ten o'clock, we were both having a hard time holding our heads up. Between yawns, we told each other good night and went on to bed. I tried to keep from dozing off while listening out for Isabelle to come in but finally drifted off about eleven thirty.

Early the next morning, I put my ear next to Isabelle's door. Hearing a soft little snore, I was reassured she was home in bed. Bess was in the bathroom, primping, when I heard a knock at the porch door.

With her hair still in pin curlers and a worried frown on her face, Vera was standing on the porch steps, nervously running her fingers between the folds of her faded yellow apron.

"Morning, Bee. I know it's early, but I had to come over and tell you the dreadful news in person. I didn't want to call over the telephone."

Opening the door for her, I warmly said, "Vera, come on in. What in the world is the matter? You look as white as a ghost." Bess heard us talking and walked out to the porch.

"I can't stay a minute. But I wanted you to know that Earl Williford's place was burglarized sometime during the night."

"Vera, NO!" I gasped, and threw my hand to my mouth. "Please tell me Earl wasn't hurt." I immediately thought about Mildred and how she would react to the news. You see, Earl was her older brother and had lived almost like a hermit back near Indian River for as long as I could remember.

"Well, I don't have many details yet, but from what Tillman found out, Earl had gone to visit his son in North

Carolina for a few days and wasn't even there when the place was hit. Thank heavens for that."

"Vera, if Earl was gone, who discovered it?"

"Tom Wilson went over early this morning to feed Earl's dog and chickens. He noticed a window panel in the door broken out and glass scattered all over the side porch, so he hurried home and called the law. They came straight out and found a total disaster where someone had gone through the entire house, turning everything upside down. They've called Earl, but he hasn't had time to drive the distance back from North Carolina yet. Nobody is sure what was taken, only that the house was vandalized. It appears somebody might have been looking for something specific. I'm so glad Earl wasn't at home. He could have ended up like Floyd, dead as a door knob."

"How did Tillman find out all these details so early this morning?" Bess asked.

"Tillman went into town early this morning to pick up a hoe handle from Jake's hardware and heard about it there. I called Mildred right after Tillman came in with the news, and she said she was trying to get out the door then to meet the sheriff out at Earl's place. Poor Mildred, she's just beside herself with worry. You know, Earl's getting on in age, and she stays concerned about his welfare all the time anyway."

"Bess," I said, thinking Mildred might need some moral support about now, "we need to run over to Earl's place and check on Mildred." Bess was wringing her hands.

"I guess you're right. Mildred probably needs some reassurance." Then she exclaimed, almost as if the news had just sunk in, "This is just unbelievable! Girls, we are not safe anymore!"

"Calm down, Bess. It's not going to do any good to get so upset." Then turning to Vera, I asked, "Don't you want to ride over with us? We won't stay too long."

"No, I've got to get back home. I've already started cooking dinner. I just turned the stove off and came over after Tillman brought the news. I need to finish peeling potatoes for my salad and start frying chicken. Tillman still wants to eat, no matter what kind of turmoil the world is in."

"I know how that is. No matter what's going on, a man wants to know what's for supper," I added, remembering how Will was about his food.

"Tillman says to call if either of you need a thing. He can be here in a few minutes." Vera gave both of us a reassuring hug and opened the screen door.

"Thanks for coming over," I called, as she wearily walked down the steps into the yard and left with a slight wave.

Bess looked at me, and with a little quiver in her voice, said, "Bee, this crime wave is getting closer and closer. Having a man around to protect us would feel mighty good about now. What I wouldn't give to have our men back with us."

I hugged Bess, and with tears in my eyes, I nodded my head in total agreement. "There's a great many reasons I'd love to have them back with us. Protection is only one of many."

CHAPTER EIGHTEEN

B ess and I hightailed it over to Earl's place as soon as we were presentable, leaving Sleeping Beauty in bed. We had to travel down River Road a piece to get onto his road, which is really just an old washboard logging trail that winds back into the deep woods near the river. Bess drove her car and as usual, I had to hold on to the dashboard for support as we raced over the rutted, washed-out lane. Riding along, I felt as if we were entering a deep, dark cavern of foliage and tree limbs, which allowed only occasional sunlight to filter through here and there.

Earl's small farm is actually only a clearing where he had grown corn and cotton years back. As we were driving into the yard, we could see Mildred's old station wagon pulled up by the sheriff's car. Earl's place had run down considerably since I had been back there with Will years ago. Earl had never married, so there was definitely no woman's touch about the place. It appeared he had quit trying to keep anything up or make a crop on that old sorry piece of land. Word was his main business venture had been corn whiskey, which he sold illegally for years. His health deteriorated so badly he was no longer able to gather the corn or cook the mash. He was just getting by now, and I knew Mildred went over and helped him out frequently. She was always taking homemade soup or whatever she had cooked to him. I'd heard her say plenty of times that she did his washing and ironing.

It was apparent nobody had done any real maintenance around his place for some time. We had to step over tall weeds and uncut grass to get up to the old porch that was just hanging on to the small wood-framed house. I expect the house hadn't seen a coat of paint for many years. Here and there, along with crooked rows of protruding rusty nails, were flecks of dark green color that had managed to hold on to the old weathered boards running along the sides of the house. The dented tin roof was covered with mold and mildew that had worked its way up the single crumbling brick chimney. Two or three bricks from the chimney had fallen and were sitting on top of the roof along with fallen tree limbs and dried leaves. The yard was littered with trash Earl had thrown out the door toward a wooden barrel where—more than not—he had missed. In the weeds, a set of worn-out tires with dark sour-smelling water standing inside the rubber inner circles were propped against an old iron bed frame. A bird had made a nest in an old brogan that had been left out in the weather next to the rotting well house door.

Mildred, dabbing away fresh tears from her eyes with her handkerchief, was sitting on a small barrel in the front room talking with the sheriff when we entered through the side entrance. We gasped at the complete disarray of the house. The couch and chair cushions were ripped to shreds. Even the mattress was cut up and the cotton stuffing was thrown everywhere. All the dresser drawers in the bedroom were hanging out and emptied. Clothes, torn apart at the seams, were pitched everywhere. Every dish, pot, and pan in the kitchen was on the floor. Bags of flour and meal were all cut into and strewn everywhere. It looked as if not a thing was untouched.

I walked over and tenderly put my arm around Mildred and gave her a little reassuring hug. The sheriff asked us not to touch a thing until he had made a more thorough investigation. "Actually, I think it would be better if the three of you could wait outside, and I'll let you know when we're through in here." With a little more remorse in his voice, he added, "I'm not sure if I told you or not, Mrs. Mildred, but we found Earl's old dog out by the woods, dead. It looks like he was hit in the head with a heavy object, and the poor old thing was left to bleed to death."

"Oh no! That's gonna just kill poor Earl. He loves that old dog." She brushed away more tears and now they were beginning to flow like Niagara Falls. I offered Mildred my handkerchief since hers was completely soaked, knowing I probably would never get it back. I had loaned Mildred an apron once at a church social, and she had never thought to return it. "When Earl would visit, that dog would walk right into my house behind Earl, just like he owned the place, and I'd have to get the broom to him. Earl never could understand why I didn't want that old fleabag in my house. Well, I won't have to worry about that anymore."

"Yes, ma'am," the sheriff answered softly, and directed his attention toward his deputy. "Roy, grab that old quilt over in the corner and wrap the dog in it before those buzzards make a picnic lunch out of him. After you finish with that, get out your kit and start checking for prints."

We walked out to the yard and sat down on an old bench made of heavy boards and concrete blocks next to a snarled dogwood tree. Bess and I talked a little about the weather and avoided the subject of Earl and his immediate problem. I could tell Mildred wasn't in any mood for small talk. Between sniffles she muttered something about not knowing how on earth Earl could ever come back here to live. Bess put her arm around Mildred's shoulder and said, "Mildred, you've got to be strong now for Earl's sake. I know it's hard. Thank heavens Earl wasn't here when the break-in occurred."

Mildred nodded in between a few more tears and said she was thankful of that. "I think I'll see if I can wait for Earl back at my house. I'd really like to freshen up a little. The sheriff called so early this morning, I didn't have time to dress properly before I left the house. I just threw these old clothes on, and I'm not really dressed for the day." Mildred patted our hands and gave us a weak smile. "It's such a comfort that you two came out to check on me this morning. I don't know what I would do without my good friends."

She wearily stood up, as if she had the weight of the world on her shoulders, and we followed her onto the shabby porch and into the house. Sheriff Ledbetter was kneeling down and running his fingers through some of the white flour that was scattered across the front room floor. "Somebody made a real effort to find something in here. I wonder what it could be. Maybe Earl can shed some light on this situation."

Mildred cast a doubtful glance at the sheriff and asked if it would be all right if she left.

"Sure, go on home. Roy will stay and watch the place while I round up Elmo and Roscoe and bring them to the jail for more questioning. I think I'll look up Jupiter Johnson, too, and see what he's been up to these days." Jupiter was a seedy fellow who was always hanging around the pool hall in town looking for a drink. "I'll radio the sheriff over in Wall County to see if any vandalism is going on over there." Sheriff Ledbetter then looked directly at Mildred and said, almost as if he needed to explain himself to her, "We've already checked around for tire tracks, but there doesn't appear to be any in that weedy yard or on the road. It's packed hard as a brickbat."

"Let's go too, Bee," Bess despairingly said. "Roy needs to do his work. We're just in the way here, and Mildred needs to go home and get some rest."

As we turned to leave, I asked, "Mildred, do you think you'll be all right?"

"I'll be fine. Y'all go on and I'll be in touch later. I've just got to figure out what's best for Earl now."

As we rode off, Bess shook her head and gripped the steering wheel as if she needed to hold on to something for dear life. "My heart goes out to Mildred. What's she going to do about Earl? You know, he doesn't have anybody else other than that sorry son of his. Mildred's not so strong herself these days. She still hasn't gotten over losing Horace. Why do you think the Lord takes the man before the woman most of the time, Bee?"

"I don't know, Bess. That's not a question any of us knows the answer to."

"What in the world are we going to do?" Bess asked, as if she were really just speaking to herself. I didn't bother to answer and we rode home in silence.

Vonion was coming out of the henhouse with a bucket in his hand as we rode into the yard. Bess parked the car under the oak tree, and we walked over toward him. I knew I had to let him know the sheriff planned on picking up Roscoe again, and as soon as I got the words out of my mouth, he handed me the bucket of eggs and left in the truck without a word.

"I'm going into town to check on things at my house, Bee, and don't argue with me about it. I'll call after I let myself in and let you know if everything's all right. I want to talk to the neighbors too, especially Mrs. Hodges, and make sure they're all safe. I'll go by the grocery store on my way back and pick up a few things for supper, so don't worry about cooking anything. We'll make out."

I gathered Bess planned on coming back to spend the night. Thank heavens I didn't have to argue with her about that.

"I don't think it's a good thing for you to go back into the house by yourself, but I know better than to try to talk you out of it." After thinking a second, I added, "I don't think that sheriff has one lead. He's in over his head and needs to call in J. Edgar Hoover with the F.B.I. or somebody with a little police knowledge."

"I couldn't agree with you more, Sister."

Bess left after we put the freshly gathered eggs in a basket for her to take over to Mrs. Hodges. Isabelle's door was still closed and I assumed she was still in bed. That girl could sleep all day long. I didn't know when I would ever get a chance to air that mattress. If she wasn't on it, it was too late in the day to start airing it.

Isabelle appeared about lunch time, long enough to eat a toasted leftover biscuit with strawberry jelly and drink some sweet milk before picking up one of her beauty magazines and disappearing in her room again. She never ate anything nutritious, and I had just about quit worrying about offering it to her. She would gag at the sight of an egg, and she said she would throw up if she had to eat grits. Peas and butter beans reminded her of chinaberries, and okra and squash were too slimy. I don't know what city folks eat.

Bess called and reported everything was fine over at her house, and she'd be back after a while. To relieve my mind, I telephoned Mildred but didn't get an answer. Nellie said she was probably resting, and she never answered the telephone if she was lying down. I often thought Nellie gave out way too much information. I waited until later in the afternoon and asked Nellie to try again.

Mildred answered after three rings. Sounding as if she was out of breath, she said, "We've just walked back into the house. Earl came by and picked me up when he got back into town, and I went back out to the house with him. Sheriff Ledbetter was waiting for us out there, and he questioned Earl until Earl was just worn out. He's here now with me, and hopefully he can get some rest. I'm going to insist he stay on here for a few days. We just aren't up to starting a cleanup out there just yet. Earl's so upset about that dog, and he's just absolutely exhausted from all that driving. I think he's relieved to be home with me for a while."

"I'm thankful for that, Mildred. Maybe both of you can get some rest. Just take it easy and don't even think about going back out to Earl's house for a while."

As if Mildred needed to vent her frustration, she forcefully added, "Bee, I don't think Sheriff Ledbetter is a bit closer to knowing who's responsible for these crimes than he was last week. He wouldn't know how to go about an investigation on one of his better days. I don't know what the taxpayers pay him for. Whatever it is, it's too much. He doesn't know his head from a hole in the ground."

It sounded as if Mildred was at her wit's end. I had to agree with her but didn't want to start a long conversation now about the sheriff. She needed to rest and to get herself back together now just as badly as Earl did. After agreeing, I told her I'd check on them later, and in the meantime, take care of Earl.

I was still sitting at the telephone bench, deep in thought, when the telephone rang. Two rings, one long, one short. That's me.

"Hello, Bee Martin speaking."

"Mama, what in the world is going on over there? During lunch break, one of the teachers told everybody they had heard there had been more robberies!"

"Oh, Margaret, there have been." I had to tell her the latest happenings. I didn't know how much she already really knew, and I wasn't about to tell her about my misadventures on Sunday afternoon. I knew she'd find out everything sooner or later, but for right now I hoped it was later. "Bess is still spending the nights with me, and we're dealing with all this." I despairingly thought to myself, *We're fine, except there's a killer and a robber roaming around, and Roscoe is being held over at the sheriff station right now.*

"I could come if you just say the word."

"Well, I'm not about to tell you to come home right now at the beginning of your school year. There's not a thing you could do here to protect us. We're coping just as well as anybody else could under these circumstances."

"If you say so, but all you have to do is ask, and I'll be there. I'm worried to death about you."

"Now Margaret, if I need you, I promised I'd call."

"Mama, I did send our film off, and I'm having the pictures sent to your house. They should be there anytime, so watch for them in the mail. I hope they're good. Have you taken any more pictures since I was home?"

"No. I haven't really had time, but I want to get over to Freddy's house and take some of the boys." I still hadn't found the camera, but Margaret didn't have to know. I didn't care if the pictures came back anytime soon or not. Maybe, if I could lose some weight before I'd have to look at them, I wouldn't feel so bad. I knew in my heart that wasn't going to happen, but I could still dream about it.

After several more warnings from Margaret, we hung up. I hadn't seen or heard from Vonion since that morning, so I walked outside toward the barn to check on things. I imagined the chickens had been fed, and the hogs looked pretty contented for the time being. If that old cow hadn't been milked, she'd just have to wait a while. That was not something I intended to do unless I absolutely had to.

I sat down on the tree stump out by the barn to think. As I looked up into the cloudless sky, I thought, *Why would any burglar go out to Earl Williford's house in the first place? No one, in a million years, would suspect that old codger had anything valuable hidden away out there, unless somebody knew something that wasn't generally known.* I kept going over it in my mind all that afternoon as I went about my chores and came up with the same conclusion. There had to have been something valuable in that old shanty house, and whatever it was, the thief knew about it in advance and had probably found it. Maybe Mildred had an idea and hadn't said anything.

I was under the oak tree in the front yard rinsing my dusty car with the garden hose when Vonion came up later that afternoon and gave me a report. "Roscoe, Elmo, and Jupiter, all at the jailhouse. I hates to think about that boy bein' down there, but fer rat now, he better off. Lots of folks is lookin' fer anybody to blame, and that could put them fellers in danger."

"We certainly want to keep Roscoe and the others safe. It's a pity he has to be down there, but I'm sure it's only temporary. Vonion, did you milk Hortence? I wasn't sure, but I didn't really check either."

"You know I ain't left that cow unattended to. Now don't ya know that? She give some good milk, and I give it to Mrs. Waters fer all them chil'ren. Does you need any today? She probably give a little more if I try."

"No thanks, I've got plenty. Thank you for seeing about Eva Waters. I worry so about her and those children. We need to do all we can for them. She's what the Bible calls 'the least of them.'"

"Dat's right. Ora Lee, she sent a mess of okra from our little garden over there the other day, and Mrs. Waters say them chil'ren eat it like candy."

"Vonion, have you seen Carl Waters around town or anywhere? I could have sworn I saw him the other day when I was in town."

"No, I don't git to town too regularly, but I ain't noticed him. You know Mrs. Waters said he was gone."

"I might have been mistaken. You know my eyesight isn't as good as it used to be. I'm just thinking out loud, Vonion, but Carl Waters is pretty familiar with all these places that are being broken into. He's lived and worked around here all his life. Why, I imagine he's done some kind of handy work for every one of the victims. I really think I spotted him the other day walking down by the oil mill. You know, Eve says he's gone, but she's still feeding those children, and I've noticed she still has electric power running into her little house. Where is she coming up with the money? Do you think Carl is capable of doing these horrible things, Vonion?"

"I's don't reckon I knows anything about that. That be too hard to thinks about, I 'spect. I guess it be possible. He be a scallyway, but a murderer? Hit ain't likely, to my thinkin'."

"You're probably right."

"Give me that hose and let me wash yor car all the way, with a rag and soap. It been needin' it the longest time. Just rinsin' ain't doin' no good."

I relinquished the hose and went to get some soap, rags, a bucket, and a couple of whisk brooms. I couldn't just stand there while Vonion did all the work, so I started on the front and Vonion started on the back. We scrubbed the windshields and headlights until every one of those pesky dead bugs were gone. Vonion shined the mirrors and gave the chrome a little extra elbow grease. I swept out the floorboards and wiped down the dashboard while Vonion swept out the trunk. In no time at all, we had my old car clean as a whistle. If only I had somewhere exciting to go, and a little gas to get me there.

"Vonion, I'll help you wash the truck while we have the rags and soap out here." Then, after hesitating, I added, "That is, if you want to."

"No, ma'am! We ain't washin' the truck! That dirt probably the only thing holdin' that old truck together. The rust do help some too, I suppose. Ora Lee ain't complained one bit about it being dirty, and she rides in it ever Sunday to church meetin'. She always says it's better than walkin' or hitchin' up to a mule. Thank you fer the offer, though."

That settled that.

Bess came back out to the house later that afternoon, and I could tell she had a lot on her mind. She hated she didn't feel comfortable in her own home, and it was really getting next to her.

"It's apparent everywhere you go around town that everybody's on edge," Bess commented that night after supper while we were sitting around talking with Isabelle. "Nobody feels safe anymore. Most people are locking all their doors and have stopped leaving their houses unattended at night. They're loading their guns too, ready to shoot and ask questions later."

I didn't say anything about my suspicions concerning Carl Waters that night. I needed to concentrate on keeping Vonion, Ora Lee, Bess, and myself safe. "I wish now for the first time since I lost Rip last summer, I had found another watchdog to replace him. I still believe that dog died with a broken heart after Will passed away. I've got the shotgun loaded now, and it's where I can get to it fairly quickly. Don't anybody go walking around in the middle of the night unless you let me know. You might get your head blown off."

"Bee, I know good and well you don't really mean that," Bess replied, acting as if she was shocked at what I had just said. "Isabelle, it sounds as if we better keep a chamber pot under our beds for emergencies during the night. Going to the bathroom could be dangerous to our health."

CHAPTER NINETEEN

My mind was made up. I was going straight down to the jailhouse in the morning to see if the sheriff would let me talk to Roscoe. The child needed some support right now, and I intended to let him know I was there if he needed me.

As I was preparing for bed that night, I began to think about something else—my shotgun, and whether I could really use it in an emergency. I went over to the corner where Will always kept it and picked up the gun. Holding it in my arms a few minutes, I decided to go out to the porch and shoot into the air, just to let any close predators that might be in hearing range know that I was armed and ready for action. I aimed toward the moon and shot into the sky. Bess came running out of the house with her robe flapping in the breeze, with a look of panic written all over her face. "Bee, what's out there?" Isabelle, looking equally horrified, followed close behind and grabbed Bess by her neck, almost chocking the life out of her, and clamped on for dear life.

"Nobody's out here except me, I hope. I'm just giving a warning shot to let folks around know I'm ready for whatever comes my way."

Bess, trying to untangle Isabelle's hands from around her neck, collapsed on a rocking chair and began to breathe deeply.

I hurried over to her and started hitting her on the back. She threw her arms in the air and walloped me right in the stomach. "Get away from me before you kill me!" I jumped back before she let me have it again. She soon regained her breath and hollered, "Are you out of your cotton-picking mind, Bee Martin? You just about gave me a heart attack! I'm going to take that gun and toss it in the river if you ever do that again!"

Isabelle didn't say a word. She turned and walked back to her bedroom, shaking her head as she went. Bess gave me another look that said everything and stomped back into the house, leaving me alone to fight off any intruder by myself. I could do it too… *maybe*?

I leaned the gun back in the corner where, hopefully, it would stay permanently. Vonion had already given me a second shooting lesson. He had set up a few old cans on a fence and instructed me to shoot at them. After raising the gun and aiming at the target, I shot and missed every last one of them.

"Maybe it be the gun," Vonion had said, looking a little perplexed, as he took the gun and shot at the same targets to see if the gun was shooting accurately. Every target went flying in the air as he shot. He loaded the gun, handed it back to me and said, with a little smirk, "Naw, it twarnt the gun. Try again." Why anybody liked to fool around with firearms was a mystery to me. I would just as soon not ever see the thing again as long as I lived, but for right now, I was glad it was leaning against the wall in the corner of my bedroom, ready for action if I needed it— even if I couldn't hit the broad side of a barn. My second attempt wasn't any better, and Vonion had smirked playfully. "Maybe you do better to hit somebody over the head with the thang 'stead of shooting at him." I really didn't think that comment was very humorous, and I had thought at the time about hitting him over the head with it.

I finally made it to bed and was beginning to drift off when I felt a strange sensation that something was moving around right over me. I slowly and cautiously opened one eye and almost jumped off the side of the bed. Right in front of my face, not a foot away, was Bess's face, staring me down.

I jumped, trying to sit up too fast, and my body took a nosedive as I rolled over, catching the bedcovers as I went to the floor. My head bumped the headboard, and my backside collided with the bed rail on my way down. I was so tangled up in the sheets I couldn't move, so I just laid there for a moment trying to get my bearings.

"Bee, for goodness sake, whatever is the matter with you? You are so jumpy. Are you hurt? I came in here to tell you I was going to the bathroom, and for goodness sake, don't shoot me. I didn't want to get my head blown clean off, so I figured you needed to know it was me moving around in the house. Are you so tensed up you jump out of your skin if you hear any little old thing?" Bess bent down and started pulling me by the arms. "Here, let me help you up."

"Bess, you just get out of my way, and I'll get up by myself. You know I wouldn't shoot you. For heaven's sake, I can tell you from a burglar. I'm not completely blind. Now don't you ever wake me up that way again because next time I might grab you by the neck and body slam you to the floor!"

"Bee, you know you don't know anything about wrestling, and you better not lay one finger on me," Bess exclaimed furiously. She marched out of the bedroom, and I heard her slam the door to the bathroom. She came out a few minutes later, walked over to the bedroom door and announced, "You can get your guard up again now. I'm going back to bed, and please don't wake me unless it is an absolute emergency. How anybody can get any sleep around this house is beyond me."

I lay there a minute, thinking she had a lot of nerve, waking me and then telling me not to bother her. I wouldn't tell Bess in a hundred years, but it was such a comfort to have her in the next room, even if she did snore loud enough to wake the dead. Praying that I wouldn't be bruised up and stiff in the morning from the tumbling act I had just performed, I closed my eyes again.

I must have slept through the rest of the night because the next thing I remember was hearing Vonion out in the yard talking to the hogs and beating that bucket with a stick. I think he does all that just to make sure I wake up early enough to go out and talk to him at first light. He always was an early riser. All the years Vonion helped farm the land, Will never had to roll him out of bed in the mornings. I put my feet in my slippers by the bed, grabbed my robe, and walked out to the porch, thanking the good Lord for all his many blessings and the peaceful night, peaceful except for Bess's and my little misadventure.

Vonion was out by the barn having a conversation with the milk cow, Hortence, just as if she could understand every word he was saying. I called out,

"Vonion, can you come on over here to the porch for a few minutes, please?"

He ambled over with the egg bucket in his hand and wearily plopped down on the porch step. "I didn't sleep not one ary minute all last night, with all the thinkin' goin' on in my head. Ora Lee, she just as bad. Roscoe probably thinkin' we done forgot him by now."

"Now Vonion, don't fret. I'm going over to the jailhouse as soon as I can get off this morning and talk to him, that is, if those scalawags down there let me get in to see him." I saw a hopeful look come over Vonion's old weathered face.

"That be good. I could go with you, but I probably need to stay 'round here and protect the place."

"That's right. But first take all the milk you can to Mrs. Waters and ask her if there's anything else she needs. I imagine we'll have enough eggs to share with her today too. If there's a need we can provide for, let's do it. And while you are over there, check around and see if you see any sign that her sorry husband has been around. It's a mystery to me about his whereabouts. Does Ora Lee need anything from the store that you know of? I'll be glad to pick up anything."

"Yes, ma'am, I will. I's thinking you barkin' up the wrong tree though. Just tell Roscoe to keep the faith and we be praying for him. I might take Ora Lee to town later this afternoon just to get her mind off'a thangs." I expect Vonion had as much grief in his heart as Ora Lee, but him being a man, he was trying to hide it and hold up for Ora Lee.

I hurried around and was on my way to town by nine that morning. Bess and I left the house at the same time. I left Isabelle a note telling her I was going into town for a while and to eat whatever she wanted. As likely as not, she probably would still be in bed when I returned. I had given up worrying about her diet. She had never in her life had a regular meal time, I would bet on that.

Driving down the road that morning with the window partly down and my head held over to the side so my hair wouldn't blow too badly, I kept thinking there had to be something the sheriff was overlooking. I wanted to go by to see Roscoe and was also thinking about going over to Mildred's to talk to Earl, if he was up to it. First things first though. I was headed to the gas station to see if anybody was there to fill my tank.

Floyd's gas station was just a little old hole in the road. There wasn't anything fancy about the place at all. On the front glass window was a Champion spark plug metal sign lined up with a Railroad snuff advertisement and a flyer about a lost dog. A Lucky Strike cigarette sign dangled from a loose board over the side entrance. A drink box, a candy counter with a cash register, and a line of Prince Albert tobacco tins on top were all crowded into the front room. A few hard chairs surrounded a potbellied stove over in the corner. If that stove could talk, it would have many a tale to tell, true and untrue, I imagined. I had never sat around inside, but I knew Will had spent many a happy time right there gossiping and talking about whatever was on his mind, usually the weather. A telephone inside for public use was hanging on the wall, giving travelers and anybody around a place to make a call. We had been fortunate to have been one of the first families in the county with access to the telephone wires that were beginning to be strung across the land, while many families still had to rely on a public telephone. You could tell the old door to the inside of the station had been opened and closed a few thousand times from all the grease and dirt imbedded in it. There was a grungy garage over to the side where they worked on engines or changed tires. It was a sorry sight, I admit, but it was the only place around to get gas or service for my car.

Thank heavens, it was open! Elmo, dressed in his usual baggy coveralls with grease smudges, ambled out of the station when I honked my car horn. "How in the world are you, Elmo?" I asked, as I stuck my head out the car window to greet him. I was so glad to see somebody running the place, and I was especially glad it was Elmo.

"Well, I've seen better days, but it's good to be here right now. Floyd would have wanted the place to stay open, so for the time being, I'm gonna do my best. That lawyer feller from Augusta told me to hang in here for a few days until they could get all the legalities taken care of. What'll it be, regular or high test?"

"Regular, two dollars' worth please, and if you would, check my oil. I've been a little concerned about it lately. I don't remember when it was last changed. You know, Will used to take care of all that kind of stuff, and I'm still not sure how to care for my motor like I should." Changing the subject, I asked, "Elmo, how did you get out of jail so quickly?"

"Oh, that sheriff let us all go today. He said to stay close. He don't have enough proof to hold any of us. He needs to be out hunting up some real evidence. I don't have an easy feeling thinking about some killer roaming around these parts."

"I know what you mean," I replied. And then, a little more thoughtfully, I asked, "Elmo, who knew Floyd kept all that money in his house at night? Was it common knowledge around here or what?"

"I guess just about anybody could have figured he had to keep it somewhere. I've been thinking about things, and it seems to me he must have been murdered pretty soon after he got in from work, seeing as he still had his work clothes on and all. He always took his greasy clothes off and bathed as soon after coming in from work as he could. He knew he would get grease all over the house if he didn't." Elmo thought a moment and sadly added, "I tell you, I've got a mournful feeling that just follows me around, and it won't turn me loose."

"I know you do, Elmo," I sympathized. "You say Roscoe was let out today too. I was on my way to see him, but I guess he's probably back at home by now."

"No ma'am, he ain't ta home. Mr. Tom Wilson picked him up from the jail, and as far as I know, they've done gone back to work. Least ways, that's what I overheard Mr. Tom telling Roscoe. When they was getting in the truck to leave, I overheard Mr. Tom say, 'Now let's get back to the field. All this ain't nothing but a bunch of hogwash, and we got work to do. All we're doing here is killing daylight.' Roscoe sure is lucky to have a man like Mr. Tom stand by him."

Amen.

After Elmo gassed my car up and checked the oil, he wiped the windshield and the mirror with a smile on his face just like nothing was on his heart or mind. Trying to cheer him up a little bit, I said, "Let me know if you need anything at all. Maybe I can help. I don't believe for one minute you or Roscoe had one thing to do with these burglaries or Floyd's murder. I know Sheriff Ledbetter is barking up the wrong tree. I just wish I knew where the right tree was." I tell you, my heart went out to that man, knowing how he was grieving and worrying about his future.

As I was driving out of the gas station, I made up my mind to get over to Mildred's house to see if I could have a few words with Earl.

As I drove over, I began to feel a little uneasy about questioning Earl. There had to be some reason a burglar would pick his old run-down house over other residences that might appear to be a better choice. What was it about his place that enticed a burglary? How could I word my questions to him without him realizing that I thought his home was a dump and all it really needed was to be bulldozed? Was there a connection to Old Man Peterson, Floyd, Shirley, Vera and Tillman, and Earl, or was it all just a coincidence that these places were all picked for robbery? Maybe there wasn't anything Earl could tell me, but I was going to talk to him if I could ever get past Mildred. Earl was her baby brother, and I sensed that she had always needed to shelter and protect him. That was probably what was wrong with him. Mildred had always done way too much for him, and he had lost all his incentive to do anything for himself. I could get past Mildred, though. All I had to do was flatter her a little, and I knew I could handle that. I specialized in bending the truth. *Lord, forgive me, again...in advance.*

CHAPTER TWENTY

Mildred lived over on Green Street. She and her husband, Horace, had built that little cracker box soon after they married. They had raised a son there, and he had gone into the army and seen action in the big war. We had prayed for Horace Jr. and his safety many a time at church and our circle meetings. He had returned home in one piece and now lived out of state with his wife and children. Horace Sr. lived quite a while with cancer but finally gave up the fight and passed away a few months ago. He had supported his family for many years as the best house painter in our community.

Mildred, with a tired and worried look on her face, came to the door wearing a pretty appliquéd apron over her pedal pushers. "Come on in, Bee," she said as she opened the screen door to her little porch. "Sit down here on the porch if you can find a clean chair. Wait a minute, let me get a rag. I'll wipe one off for you. You know how hard it is to get a porch halfway clean. The dust just settles on everything faster than you can get back to clean it again."

She hurriedly went back into the house and was back again before I could say, "Oh, Mildred, don't worry about it. I'm used to a little dust." She gave a couple of swipes on the seat of a small rocker and gestured for me to sit down.

"Thank you, Mildred," I said, as I sat on the chair. Mildred had all kinds of potted plants out on the porch. She has such a way with them. I always admired how she can grow anything she set her mind to. "Mildred, the way your porch always looks so green and colorful, it's a wonder you have any time left for anything else. I would ask you for some cuttings, but you know as well as I do, they would probably die. I don't have a green thumb like you and Bess."

"Bee, you know your plants always look nice and healthy," Mildred said halfheartedly. I knew she was lying, but I accepted the compliment. "What about some iced tea, Bee? I just made a pitcher."

"That would be nice. I could use something cold to drink."

"Just stay seated and I'll bring it out." She was back through the door again. I glanced around the porch while she was gone. Mildred had let other things go quite a bit in the last year or so while she nursed Horace. Her porch was in as bad need of paint as mine. Dust covered every surface and cobwebs were in the corners. I had no room to talk, so I just told myself to mind my own business.

Mildred brought the tea out, and I took a sip while she sat down. She must have left half the sugar out again, but I acted as if it was delicious.

"Mildred, I meant to tell you how much I like your stylish pants. If I had the figure for them like you do, I'd be looking to buy a pair too. You always were a fashion leader."

"Why, Bee, thank you. I do pride myself on being a little forward thinking." Taking another sip, I asked how Earl was doing.

"He's doing as well as expected, I guess, just a little worn out from these upsetting events. He's out there at his house now with one of the deputies. They came by and picked him up a while ago. You know, they won't let us do a thing out there until they get further with the investigation. Earl is staying here with me for the time being, and I hope to talk him into staying on indefinitely. You know, I'd be scared for him to stay out there by himself. To be frank, I'm scared to be here alone. When the sun goes down, I start hearing imaginary noises and thinking any minute somebody is going to break in and beat me to a pulp. I can tell you one thing. A thief could tear this house to pieces, and he wouldn't find one thing of any value." Taking a breath, she emphatically added, "Bee, the taxpayers need to get somebody in this county with enough sense to catch whoever is terrorizing this place."

"You are so-o right. I feel the same way. You wouldn't believe how threatened Bess and I feel out there with hardly any protection. Isabelle is a danger to herself. Why, she wouldn't know which end of the gun to shoot. With Vonion down the lane most of the time, I could be dead and he wouldn't know a thing was going on."

"We're going to have to take matters into our own hands if there isn't an arrest soon. Bee, I'm just at my wit's end. Who knows what's going to happen next. We might all be dead before the sun comes up tomorrow."

I readily agreed. "I know just what you mean. We're all just wondering who's going to be the next victim." Trying to change the subject, I asked, "Mildred, do you have any idea why Earl's house would be singled out? I don't want you to think I don't think much of Earl's place, but there are more desirable locations for a burglary. You know that old Evans place over on Dukes road has sat there full of all that antique furniture all these years. Why, I've never heard anything about it being burglarized. It just doesn't make sense. There must be some connection between the incidents. I don't know, maybe I'm just whistling Dixie, but I believe there has to be something Sheriff Ledbetter is overlooking. Vera and Tillman had that expensive silver sitting there for anybody to see, and so did Shirley. Old Man Peterson talked about how banks always stole your money and how he would never put a red cent in one. Just about anybody could figure out Floyd had to keep a good bit of money in his house overnight. Was there something in Earl's house that was valuable or something somebody would go to extremes to find? It was evident somebody was looking for something specific. But what did Earl have? There has to be an explanation."

"Bee, I've got an idea about that, but you have to promise not to talk about what I'm going to tell you. Earl wanted to keep this a secret. He's kind of embarrassed about it." Mildred looked me squarely in the face and asked, "Bee, do you think you can keep a secret? I mean this is top secret. Nobody knows about this."

"Mildred, how can you ask me something like that? I've never told anything anybody asked me in confidence not to tell. Of course I can keep a secret! Remember when Mable Rooks had that hot affair with that married man that came around every month selling to the hardware store? I knew about that a year before everybody else in town knew a thing. Will and I had seen them dancing one night out at the dive on the county line when we dropped in to have a little supper after going to the livestock market over in Wall County. Anyway, I never once breathed a word of it to anybody, that is, until it was all out in the open. You know, Mable and Ed moved sometime later, and I don't believe I ever heard what happened to them. I wouldn't be surprised if they ended up divorced."

"Actually, I believe they did. Nellie said something to that effect one day when I was making a telephone call to…"

"Now, Mildred, I don't mean to interrupt, but I really don't have a lot of time today. What I want you to know right here and now is that if you have something to tell me that is not common knowledge, I'll uphold your confidence and not mention it to anyone, except Bess. She and I don't have secrets we keep from each other. But I promise if Bess and I know something you want to keep quiet, we'll respect it and keep our mouths shut." I was so anxious to hear what Mildred was going to tell me, I would have promised her that I would cut out my tongue if I blabbed a word.

"Well, in that case, I'll tell you what was stolen from Earl's house, but for mercy sake, don't let it go any further than to Bess. Earl is going to kill me now, as it is, for telling." Mildred bent toward me and lowered her voice, as if there was somebody that might overhear. "He had some very valuable coins he had come about illegally in a poker game years and years ago. He never told anybody about them as far as I know, except me and Horace. He said it was ill-gotten gain, and he just didn't feel right about selling them for profit. He had kept them hidden out there all these years. He'd worried about what to do with them now that he was getting on up in years. He had thought about giving them to his son, but Earl knew that Marcus would sell them and squander all the money. He and his wife can't handle money, and for every dollar they make, they spend two. Earl had given it some thought, and as of late he had been mulling over in his mind about giving them to some charitable organization where the money they would fetch could make a difference and do some good. Well, I guess he won't have to worry about that any longer because the coins are gone now. Whoever broke in tore the place up and found them. Earl's rifle and shotgun were stolen too."

"Oh my, that's just a shame, Mildred. How do you think anybody knew about those coins, if Earl never mentioned them? Do you think the crooks just came across them, or do you think they were looking specifically for them?"

"As far as I know, Earl never talked about them, but I don't know all his business, of course. It does seem as if the crooks were looking for something very specific and found it."

"How valuable were those coins?"

"I'm not too sure, but I believe Earl thought they were worth several thousand dollars. It was quite a nest egg. It's a real pity too. Earl could have used that money to fix up the place."

"Mildred, Earl lived just like he wanted to, I imagine. Don't worry about what could have been now."

"I guess you're right."

"Maybe Sheriff Ledbetter will come up with something. Listen, I would love to stay and talk awhile, but I really need to get on back to the house before it gets any later. If there are any more developments, please call me. And if there's anything Bess and I can do for you or Earl, please don't hesitate to ask."

"Thanks for coming over. You're always welcome. And remember, not a word."

She closed the screen door behind me, and I walked out to my car. I shifted into reverse and backed my car out of the driveway, hitting the curb with my tire. Narrowly missing an old truck parked across the street under a big oak tree, I drove off. I had been driving for years, but it seemed I had never been able to direct a car going in reverse or judge distances very well like Will could. He always said women drivers were a detriment. As bad as I hate to say so, I had to agree. My mind wasn't really on my driving anyway. I couldn't help but wonder about those coins of Earl's and who in the world knew about them.

Isabelle was gone when I returned but had left a note saying she'd be out until late. She was going with Henry to a meeting of the worship committee and act as hostess. I couldn't for the life of me imagine her serving refreshments with any grace, but maybe she was learning a few social skills after all.

CHAPTER TWENTY-ONE

Looking at the thermometer Will had put on the side of the house, it read ninety-six degrees—and that was in the shade under the tree. I couldn't wait to get into the house and cool off a little. We had a fan installed in the ceiling for those kinds of days, so I opened the side windows, pulled the curtains back, and turned on the big clunker. The breeze it stirred up in the house was so refreshing I sat down right there in the hall and just collapsed with a cold glass of water in my hand. It was too hot to cook anything this afternoon, so I decided we would have to make do this evening with a cold sandwich and some iced tea. I needed to eat something to tide me over until later, so I went on into the kitchen and found some leftover ham and ate it with a sliced tomato. After my midday lunch, I stretched out on the bedspread to rest my eyes and soon fell asleep. I must have slept quite a while because when I opened my eyes again, the sunlight had angled to a new position against the ceiling in the bedroom.

I could hear Bess walking around in the house. I was so groggy, it didn't dawn on me to call out to her and let her know where I was. I heard her walk into her bedroom and close the door. Then I heard the crying. I pulled myself off the bed, walked into the hall, and stood there not knowing whether to knock on her door. My conscience wouldn't let me go away. I knocked. "Bess, are you all right?"

"I'm fine, just so discouraged about everything. Come on in."

Well, Bess had a meltdown right then and there, and we cried together for a while. Then drying our eyes, we told each other we'd get through this and would be stronger for it. We could handle this. We had already lived through many difficult situations and had grown through them. "Lean on the Lord. That's what you do when things get tough. That's our motto," Bess said with conviction. "It's times like this that really teach us to be humble."

We ended up having a nice evening playing rummy and laughing together like old times. I guess we had released a lot of tension that afternoon.

It wasn't until about nine o'clock that evening when we realized Isabelle hadn't returned from her meeting. I never expected her to keep me abreast of her social calendar, but just for safety's sake, I wished she would be a little more punctual in the evenings. Knowing she was always escorted by Henry, I didn't worry quite so much. I had just lain down about ten o'clock that evening when I heard her come in and go straight to her room. I would sleep a little more soundly now that I knew she was safe and sound.

The morning came too soon, and I wanted to start my day with a good breakfast and a few minutes of Bible reading. I intended to find my bag containing my wedding ring and locket if it was the last thing I did today. It had to be someplace in the house, and I had just overlooked it. I had eaten, but Isabelle and Bess were still in their bedrooms when the phone started ringing just as I opened my Bible. Two rings, one long, one short. That's me.

"Hello. Bee Martin speaking."

"Ms. Bee, this is Sheriff Ledbetter. Is your sister, Bess, around there?"

"Yes, she's here. Let me see if she's up. Hold on a minute."

I called Bess to the phone and stood beside her as she held the receiver to her ear, wondering why the sheriff needed Bess this early in the morning. She put her hand over her mouth and gasped, crumbling to the stool. Shaking her head and tearfully muttering something I couldn't understand, she dropped the telephone back on its cradle and without looking up said, "Somebody broke into my house last night and tore up the place. Oh, Bee, I don't know if I can take much more."

I reached down to put my hand on her shoulder when she stood, and with conviction in her voice, said, "I've got to get over there now. The sheriff's waiting for me. Call Freddy while I dress and see if he can come over too. I imagine he's already left for work, but we might catch him."

I told Nellie to ring Freddy's house, but after six rings, I hung up. I knew if I hung on the telephone much longer, Nellie would start questioning me, and I wasn't in the mood. I scrambled to the bedroom, grabbed my purse, and tried to catch up with Bess as she ran across the porch. I was determined to go with her. "Wait for me," I yelled, as she sprinted down the steps. I hurried right behind her and around to the other side of the car to get in. "Let's go," I said. "But don't drive like a maniac. Let's get there in one piece. I couldn't get Freddy, but maybe we can reach him at work a little later."

I held on for dear life as she dashed down the road and then through town toward her house. Thank goodness there wasn't any heavy traffic on the road that morning, or we could have been smashed to smithereens several times, since Bess paid no attention at all to any warning or stop signs all along the way. Bess never did relax in the car but sat forward like she was ready to jump out at any minute. We pulled up to her house, and Bess stopped the car so abruptly it jolted forward. I hit my head on the windshield. I sat there a moment with my head swimming, and when I finally was able to climb out, I had to steady myself with the car door. This reckless driving of late was just too much for me. I was feeling as if I needed to keep my feet planted firmly on the ground for a while.

Roy, the deputy, was stationed at the door, and Bess made it over to him in record time. I was bringing up the rear when I heard Bess bark, "What in the world's going on here? Somebody broke into my house?"

"Yes ma'am, I'm afraid so. We had a call about two hours ago from the man across the street. He claims he saw someone leaving the residence with some sort of sack in his arms. We really thought he was just hallucinating, so we didn't respond until first light this morning. When we arrived, the door here was standing wide open. The sheriff's inside now, checking out the place. I'll call and tell him you're here."

"There isn't any need for that. We're going in and check it out for ourselves," Bess retorted, as we walked on up the steps to the house. I thought Bess was going to faint as we walked in. Closets were opened and drawers were hanging out. Things were scattered everywhere. Bess was staggering as if she might faint any minute as we made our way through the kitchen and the front room and on to the bedroom where the sheriff was standing, holding Bess's jewelry box in his hands.

"I'm sorry about all this, ma'am," the sheriff said, as we entered the room. "It seems you've been hit pretty hard. Is this where you kept your jewelry?" he asked, as he looked over in our direction. "It was sitting in the middle of the bed with the top pried off."

"Yes, just some costume stuff. I carried my good jewelry with me when I went out to Bee's," Bess replied, with a look of blankness in her eyes.

"Look around and see what's missing, please," the sheriff said, in a discouraging tone. "I won't know anything until you've gone through things. I'll walk out and give you time to check around."

"We'll do that now," I answered, seeing as Bess didn't seem to realize he had said anything at all.

"Bess, let's check the attic first," I said, as Bess steadied herself against the bedpost. She told me several nights ago she had hidden her sterling silver and other valuables up there.

I pulled the ladder down from the attic door, climbed up, stuck my head into the dark space over the ceiling, and pulled the light string hanging from a rafter.

"It's all right there in that big box to your left. I put an old sheet on top and then spread a blanket over it," Bess said, as I surveyed the space at the opening.

I immediately spied the box, lying empty on its side. The blanket and sheet were thrown over to the side. "Oh Bess, was everything in the box? I'm sorry, but the box is totally empty."

"It can't be. I put everything in that box. How could anybody know it was there? Oh my Lord! All Mama's silver, the sterling flatware, the goblets we got for wedding gifts, and everything else. Is it all gone? Are you sure there's nothing in the box?"

"Bess, there's nothing in the box. It's all gone."

I came back down and realized Bess was frozen in one position right there in the bedroom doorway. I grabbed her and we stood there hugging each other and crying at the same time. We tried to compose ourselves long enough to talk sensibly to the sheriff when he walked back in the house a few minutes later. As I began telling him about the missing items in the attic, he started taking down notes.

"I need a list of everything that's missing, ma'am, if you don't mind. Give me a few more minutes in here and then I want to talk to the neighbors."

It seemed to me Bess had gone into shock, and she didn't even try to answer. After a few seconds, reality finally set in, and she said in an agitated tone, "Okay, but I've got a lot to do in here, so hurry up. I don't want the sun to go down before I put this house back to order."

"I'll stay on and help," I readily offered, as I surveyed what I knew was going to be a whole day affair.

"I can't imagine how anyone would have known to go up into the attic," Bess told the sheriff. We had gone back out to the side of the house where he was standing with the deputy waiting for the list. "I had just put all that stuff up there a few days ago, and nobody knew it was up there, except Bee."

"Bess," I asked, "are you sure there isn't anything else missing? You know, I didn't notice your nice crystal lamps in your bedroom when we were back there."

"Oh, my goodness, I think you're right." Bess grabbed my arm and was on her way back in when she turned around and said, "You know what! Mama's cut glass pitcher wasn't on the stand in the dining room either. Oh, my Lord, Bee, what else is missing?"

"Bess, calm down," I warned her, as we both tried to go back into the house through the kitchen door at one time and got stuck. We both backed out and I let Bess go on ahead. Sure enough, the cut glass bowl, pitcher, sugar and creamer, and the crystal lamps were all gone. It seemed as if we had a very discriminating burglar.

Sheriff Ledbetter took a list of missing items and asked us to add anything else to the list as we worked. After giving us a discouraging look, he sauntered across the street to talk to Mr. Hodges. If Mr. Hodges was the only witness, I'm afraid we weren't going to ever know the truth about anything. Sheriff Ledbetter was in over his head, trying to pry anything useful out of that old man's mouth.

We despairingly started sorting through things. Sheriff Ledbetter stuck his head back through the door a while later, and called, "You in there, Ms. Bess?"

Bess despondently answered, "We're in the front room. Come on in."

"Ladies, the only thing I could get out of that old codger was that he thought he saw a person, dressed all in black with a hood over his head, running from the house. He didn't know anything else to add to the description, and I don't think we're going to learn anything else from that crazy old man."

"I've been trying to tell you all along, Sheriff. Elmo and Roscoe had nothing to do with these crimes!" I said in a determined voice. "I happen to know you have them locked up over at the jail right now, and that's where they were last night and this morning. Bess was here yesterday. Maybe now you'll believe me. I can't imagine anybody being so dumb as to leave fingerprints all over the place, but did you check to see if any were left?" I asked, thoroughly exasperated.

"We suspect our thief has worn gloves all along. Checking for fingerprints won't help us now. By the way, for your information, I let Roscoe and Elmo out last night."

"Sheriff Ledbetter, I hope you aren't thinking they had anything to do with this, for heaven's sake! No one is so stupid as to get out of jail one minute and go commit a crime the next! Heavens to Betsy! What do you have to go on so far, is what I want to know?" I questioned with a little too much fire in my voice. "I haven't heard any solid evidence against anybody. Just when are you going to have something to tell us? The citizens of this county are tired of feeling as if we can't even leave our homes for fear of somebody breaking in and stealing everything we have—not to mention all the damage left behind. We're ready for you to figure this thing out, and I mean soon. And leave Elmo and Roscoe out of it. Any moron would know they don't have one thing to do with all this!" I spouted off, waving my arms back toward Bess's house.

"Ms. Bee, I wish I had an answer for you, but I don't. We're doing the best we can with the means we have to solve this thing. You know, the county doesn't give me any extra money to hire more people or to buy the best equipment available. If it makes you feel any better, I'll leave a deputy here to watch this place for a couple of nights."

"Well, it doesn't make us feel one bit better! What do you think? Someone's going to break in the same place two times in a row? That makes no sense at all. Any idiot could figure that out!" I hastily shot back at him in my harshest voice.

"It doesn't help the situation for you to get hostile with me. If you think you can do any better with the evidence, let me know," he retorted, as he turned to leave. He had a lot of nerve, talking to me in that tone of voice like I was a schoolgirl. He needed to brush up on his etiquette as well as police detective work.

Bess and I spent the better part of the day putting the house back together. Bess was discouraged as we found more and more items broken and damaged. I thought at one point she was going to throw everything in the air and just walk out. Freddy did call later in the day and said as soon as he could get off work he would be on over. I decided I would leave as soon as he arrived, so they would have some time with just the two of them. Bess needed him now.

Freddy drove me home later that afternoon after he agreed to stay with Bess for the night. I went into the house with the heaviest of hearts. I had not felt that low since the day I'd had to go back home after we buried Will. I was in hopes Isabelle would be home this evening to keep me company and she was, as well as Preacher Henry. That was one time I was glad for his presence. My money was still short, but this was not the time to bring up my budget.

After telling them about the day, I asked Preacher Henry if he would consider staying the night with us since Freddy was planning on spending the night with Bess at her house in town.

He agreed.

"I'll be glad to, if you'll just allow me to run home for a few things first. I'll come right on back," he replied.

Knowing I'd have a man to protect us—that night at least—satisfied me. Just in case, I put the gun beside the bed. I could reach for it faster there than if it was in the corner. On second thought, maybe I needed to lay it on the bed beside me and keep my finger on the trigger.

CHAPTER TWENTY-TWO

Morning came all too soon. I felt as though I could have stayed in bed with my eyes closed all day, hoping the events of yesterday would float away with the time. There were things to do and the only way to get them done was to get at it, so my feet hit the floor. I worked up my courage to ask Preacher Henry for my much-needed money, and as soon as we finished breakfast I was prepared to confront the two of them about their obligation. He had skirted the issue and I was downright tired of it. I imagined if the lights went off because the electricity bill went unpaid, Isabelle would notice and bring that immediately to my attention.

I realized Henry had already left when I looked out of the window to see the new day. His car was gone from its usual spot, so I guessed I had missed another opportunity to talk with him about his financial obligation. He had said he had a busy day and wouldn't be around that morning, but I hadn't realized he'd leave at the crack of dawn. I don't see how he could have so many pressing matters to see about. After all, he really only worked a couple of hours a week.

I could already tell the day was going to be another scorcher, so I decided to drink cold milk this morning instead of my usual coffee. Coffee would make me break out in a sweat and make me sticky before I even dressed. I walked out to the porch with my glass, to sit and relax a few minutes, before starting my busy day. Vonion was out in the lot with the hogs, talking to them as if they could understand every word that came out of his mouth. There was quite a commotion going on as Vonion tried to spread the hog feed out in the trough so every one of them could eat at the same time. It always worried me he might get trampled to death by those greedy creatures as they pushed and shoved at anything that got in their way as they gobbled their feed.

As I sat there, I began to think about what we knew about all these burglaries. First, Old Man Peterson…he had complained about banks and the way they stole your money for as long as I could remember. Just about anybody could figure he had a good amount of cash hidden somewhere around the place. Floyd…it must have been common knowledge he kept money there at his house at night until he could bank. Shirley and Vera had their silver and things right out in plain sight for anybody to see. Someone had to have known that Earl had valuable coins, even though Mildred talked as if it was a secret. Of course, he did have guns stolen too. And then there was Bess. I just don't know who would have known she had her silver and other valuables hidden in the attic, of all places. Now that was really a mystery. Floyd was attacked and killed. Did he surprise this villain by being at home? Was he supposed to have been someplace else at the time of the break-in? I needed some answers to these questions.

As soon as I could get myself presentable, I was going over to Mildred's and see if I could speak to Earl. I also wanted to check on Bess and see if I could to be of any more assistance to her. Bless her heart. She was probably still too emotional to even think straight. More than likely she was still reorganizing drawers and cabinets. Just to think about her canned goods' labels facing backwards was more than she could tolerate. Why, I had noticed yesterday that all her stockings were folded and placed between pieces of perfume-scented tissue paper. Thank heavens the burglar didn't go into those drawers. That probably would have sent her right over the edge. Who, besides Bess, actually folds silk stockings, for goodness sake?

After dressing in the coolest dress I owned, and not even thinking about pulling on stockings, I went out to the car. A hint of Will's Sir Walter Raleigh pipe tobacco inside the car always took me by surprise and created a longing for past times. I sat in the car a moment and cherished the brief whiff and the memories. The hot air quickly brought me back to reality, so I cranked up and drove up the lane. My hair was just going to have to blow a little since I couldn't stand not having the window down at least halfway in this heat. I'm quite sure I looked a frightful sight by the time I made it over to Bess's house.

I wouldn't have believed what I saw if I hadn't seen it with my own eyes. Freddy's truck was gone, but right there in front of Bess's neat little brick house sat J.R. Kitchens' pickup truck at nine o'clock in the morning. What on earth would he be doing over there so early without an invitation? Mercy me, Bess still didn't have that temperamental old man out of her system! Well, she could just have him for all I cared. I went right on by without even slowing down or straining my neck to look through the window to catch a glimpse of what was going on. I presumed J.R. must have gone over this morning with all kinds of sympathy and apologies. She had probably swooned all over him and forgot that stuff about him wanting her to wash his dirty drawers. He was probably sitting at her breakfast table right now, eating soft scrambled eggs from my chickens and sausage from my last butchering. She had more than likely already allowed him to take his shoes off, and I was just hoping that was all he had taken off. I had been so concerned about Bess having to sort through those drawers and cabinets by herself this morning, and there she was drooling over the likes of J.R. Kitchens. Well, I had other things on my mind right now other than speculating on Bess's romantic escapades.

Mildred came right to the porch door after I knocked and invited me into the little front room of her house. I followed Mildred through the porch into the house. It was stifling. She must not have realized just how hot the day was becoming because she still didn't have a window up or a fan blowing. The air was so heavy I didn't think I'd be able to breathe, but I sat down and pretended to be comfortable. I looked for something to fan with, and seeing nothing but the church bulletin, picked it up, hoping to stir up a little air. Mildred must have realized I was roasting because she hurriedly walked back to the kitchen and came back in with a glass of cool water for me.

"Bee, I'm just horrified!" she said, as she offered me the water and walked over to open the front door again to let a little air come into the warm room. "A few minutes ago I placed a call to Madge, and Nellie told me about the break-in at Bess's house. Bess must be at her wit's end. I just can't believe it," Mildred sympathized, as she waved a kitchen towel, trying to move a little hot air around. "This situation is getting worse and worse. I know I need to go over and help Bess out, but I've got more to take care of here than I know what to do with. Please tell Bess I'm thinking of her."

"I will, and don't worry about Bess. She has plenty of help this morning," I said, as I pressed the cool glass to my forehead.

"Bee, I'm sorry it's so hot in here. We could sit on the porch, but I believe it's hotter out there than it is in here. It's going to be another scorcher. Can I get you anything else?"

"Mildred, I'm fine, but I was wondering if I could possibly speak to Earl." Just as I got the words out of my mouth, Earl walked into the room, dressed only in his unbuttoned faded overalls with nothing at all under those things. That man didn't have the decency to bother about shoes, socks, shirt or anything else; never mind combing his stringy, thinning hair. He was one of those people who looked so unkempt and untidy you just didn't want to look too close for fear of what you might see crawling around on him. How Mildred could endure the man staying in her house and sleeping in one of her beds was beyond me.

"Earl, I'm so sorry about your situation," I sympathized politely. "How are you holding up?" I reached over to take his hand to comfort him as he sat down on his broad backside. Without loosening his grip on my hand, he answered, "I guess I'm tolerable considering what I've been through this week. You know what I've been up against, don't you? It's been a real struggle just to get through the last couple of days, but I guess I'll make it with the help of my baby sister." Then, with my hand still clasped tightly with his firm grip, and without batting an eye or taking in more breath, he said, "You're sure a fine-looking woman. I know you to be unattached now, so what would you say to going out with me to eat sometime? It would be my pleasure to escort you anytime you're willing."

"I, er, don't really socialize too much anymore. You know, it's just not something I'm interested in at this time of my life. But thank you for asking." I pulled my hand back. This was going to be harder than I thought to get any information out of this horny old man. And if he thought for one minute that I would be interested in going through the back door to throw dirty dishwater out with him, he had another think coming. Trying to get down to business, I asked, "Earl, regarding your misfortune, do you have any idea who would have broken into your home and ransacked it?"

"I wish I did know, because I would break every bone in his body if I could catch up with him. It gives a body a bad feeling to know somebody has been through all their belongings like that. I don't know if I'll ever get my house back in livable condition again. Why, I had that place fixed up just like I wanted it before this happened. I'm just at loose ends now, it seems like."

Trying not to roll my eyes too far back into my head, I sympathetically said, "It's such a pity and I'm so sorry for all your troubles. But do you have any idea who could have done such a terrible thing?" My patience was right on the tip end of being lost.

"Naw, I don't rightly have no idea. If I did I would whip his ass though, before I strangled him and stomped him into the ground. If'n I knew, I'd knock his brains out just like he did to my old dog. A man that would kill another man's dog is lower than a tick clutched to a snake belly."

"I'm truly sorry about your dog, Earl. What was the poor critter's name?"

"Dammit, he was a good dog," Earl answered, shaking his head in disbelief.

Asking again, still trying to be patient, "Now, I know he was a good dog, but what was his name?"

"I told you already, Dammit. Dammit was his given name. I give it to him."

"Oh my, what an unusual name," I replied, turning a little red and beginning to get a little flustered. How anybody could name a dog Dammit was beyond my comprehension. I really didn't know if I could get any information from this seedy old man, and certainly, nothing that came out of his mouth would surprise me at this point. Persistently, I asked again, "Earl, why do you think your house was vandalized? I guess you must have had some nice things in there."

"Naw, I didn't have much in there anybody would have wanted except my guns and maybe a few coins I kept hidden. I ain't talked about them coins to anybody since I come about them. I been ashamed a myself fer gambling and carousing in my youthful days. I weren't too proud that I won them in an illegal poker game years ago. Them vandals found them, though, and now they're gone. I guess we won't ever know what happened to them, with that dim-wit sheriff we got in this county on the job. He's a real dumb ass. You sure you don't want to go out some

ANN COBB

evening soon? It would be my treat. You know, I got
better clothes than these," he said, as he gestured down
toward the worn patch in his overalls covering his left
knee. "I just have ordered a new set of bib overalls and a
new Dickies shirt from the *Sears and Roebuck* catalog that
came in Mildred's mail. I'm always teasing Baby Sister
about that there catalog being her other Bible."

"I really don't think so. Thank you again for asking
though." I'd have to hand it to him. He was persistent.
"So, you're saying nobody knew you had those valuable
coins hidden in your home?"

"No, I didn't say that. I had thought as of late
about giving them to some charity that could use the
money to do some good somewhere. I didn't know if'n
the church would want them since they might think they
was ill-gotten gain."

"Did you ever offer them to anybody or to any
organization?"

"Naw, I never did. I did look into it one time, but
then I 'bout decided to just leave them where they was 'til I
died."

"When did you talk to somebody about the coins?"

"I talked to the preacher at the Baptist Church in
town last year. You know that preacher. What was his
name? Preacher Jenkins. You know the one that died here
a while back. I didn't actually offer them to him then, but I
did talk to him about them and inquired if the church
would accept them as an offering. He said the church
could gladly accept them, so I give him a paper saying
when I died, the church could have them to pay for my
funeral and burial, and keep everything that was left over
to use any way they saw fit."

"Well, the man is dead now, so I don't guess he would be a suspect." I asked again. "Is there anybody else you can remember talking to about them being in your home?"

"Nobody but Mildred here. If'n we hear anything from the law, I'd be more than glad to come out to your house and talk to you about it, though. We could go to the diner for a bite to eat, and maybe a little dancing. I ain't shuck a leg in a while. That don't mean I can't though. There's still a little life left in this here old body." He pounded his chest, pretending for the moment to be like Tarzan.

Well, I wasn't Jane, but I thought I got what he meant. It was time for me to get out of there while the getting was good. I stood up, smoothed my dress and said, "Well, thank you for the information, Earl. If I hear anything about all this, I'll be in touch and you do the same." Hopefully he would just call on the telephone.

Mildred had stepped out but came back in as we walked towards the door. "Tell Bess to let us know if we can do something to help out over there," Mildred politely said. "I know she's fit to be tied, just trying to get her place back into order. I know she'll never get over losing her beautiful things. They were so important to her."

"I'll tell her, but I think you've got enough on your hands right here. Thanks for everything, Mildred. I'll see you later." I gave her a quick hug and as I patted her on the back, I wondered how she'd ever be able to deal with all this and stay sane at the same time.

Driving off, this time without hitting the curb, I said to myself, "And all this time, I thought the only man interested in my body was Mr. Lawson, the funeral director." Old Man Peterson and Earl here had proven me wrong. Oh brother, what a consolation! Well, Sister Bess wasn't the only one who could have a love life if they wanted one. Maybe that hair dye was just the trick. Romance wasn't for me, though, and it certainly wouldn't be with Earl Williford. He and Old Man Peterson were the last men on earth I would ever consider. Now Clark Gable—that was another story.

Getting my mind back to reality, I thought I'd see if I could catch Vonion and Ora Lee long enough to help me get those mattresses out in the sun for airing and clean the dust out from under the beds. I didn't want Margaret to come back home and complain about the dust again after I'd already been chastised. The first thing she'd do when she gets back home would be to check under those beds, just like a trained dictator. Well, no time like the present. I'd see if I could find Vonion and Ora Lee and get at it—that is, if Isabelle wasn't still lying right on top.

Vonion had to be back at his house by now, I thought, as I drove straight through my yard and on down the lane. He was sitting out under the old chinaberry tree in his yard, whittling with his pocket knife, looking as if he didn't have a care in the world. As I drove up, I noticed a bucket of pea hulls sitting beside him. That meant I'd have peas to cook today, and low and behold, he had even shelled them. I walked over, sat down next to him, and let out a sigh meant for him to hear.

Vonion started talking immediately as if he had something on his mind that needed to come out. "This morning early, I be in the kitchen up to yor house puttin' the milk in the icebox when I believe I heared that preacher man a'tellin' Miss Isabelle to hurry up and git her clothes together like they was in a hurry to go someplace. Ms. Bee, I be quiet and listened at the door of the kitchen long enough to find out he didn't have no patience in waitin' fer her."

"Vonion, what on earth are you talking about? Isabelle was getting her clothes together to leave and went off with the preacher somewhere in the car?"

"Yes ma'am, she did. And they didn't waste no time gettin' out da door."

"Well, that is strange. I guess they had a good reason for leaving in a hurry like that. I'm sure we'll find out all about the emergency when they return."

"Yessum. I tried to hear more, but dat be all I got. I 'spect you'll find out what the 'mergency be sooner or later."

"Vonion, you know it's not right to eavesdrop, but this time I think it's acceptable." I wanted to make sure Vonion didn't think I condoned what he had done, but I did want him to know I was grateful. "Vonion, do you think you and Ora Lee could come back to the house in a while and help me get a couple of the mattresses out in the sun to air? You know Margaret got on to me about letting all that dust accumulate under those beds, and this seems to be good day to start airing the mattresses and cleaning under the beds."

"Ms. Bee, you go on back up to da house, and me and Ora Lee, we be on in a minute or two. I'll bring them peas when we come. Ora Lee in the house washin' them now."

"Thank you, Vonion, but don't dillydally too long. I want those mattresses to catch as much sun today as they can. I want them smelling sweet by nightfall." It would clear my mind just to know that I'm not to be reprimanded again by my very own daughter.

CHAPTER TWENTY-THREE

With no real ambition to accomplish this task, I walked back into the house. I knew I had to get it done sooner or later. I had put it off way too long.

As I walked down the hall toward Isabelle's room, I noticed a slip of paper on the table, propped on the Roseville vase Mama and I kept there. It was a note, signed by Isabelle. I noticed the signature first, since I had a habit of reading the signed name before I ever read a letter. Isabelle wrote:

> *To Ms. Bee,*
>
> *One of mother's cousins has called Henry on the telephone and informed him our mother's health has deteriorated. He and I are needed to come to her as soon as possible, before it is too late. We feel as if we might always have regrets if we don't go to her now. Henry has talked to Tillman Hancock, Chairman of the Board of Deacons, and asked if he could find someone to fill the*

pulpit this Sunday. We'll be back in touch as soon as we have anything to report.

Isabelle

So that's why Henry was in such a hurry to pick up Isabelle this morning. She was probably lollygagging around, and he got aggravated waiting for her to get packed and ready. I sent up a quick prayer for their mother and for their safe journey to her.

It seemed as if I had more time than I expected to get this dreaded chore done after all. After removing all the bedding and piling it in the floor, I glanced around thinking, this is the first time in a while I've seen this room without clothes draped over every surface and shoes scattered all over the floor. I had forgotten what a pretty room it was. Mama's dark mahogany bedroom suite Granny handed down to her was about the nicest thing I owned. The walls of the bedroom had been painted a pale pink the year before Will died, and Bess had made some nice pink and white seersucker cotton panels for the windows. There was a picture of *Pinkie* and another one of *Blue Boy* over the bed. A few pieces of bric-a-brac were scattered about on the dresser. Nothing I had was very costly, but everything was sentimental to me in one way or another. I sat down in the upholstered rocker by the window, and as I waited for Vonion and Ora Lee, my eyes began to close. That's when I heard the scraping noise as Vonion and Ora Lee opened the screen door to the porch. They were muttering to themselves, something about being tired already and ain't even started yet.

The three of us pulled at the mattress until we had it at the porch door. We then slid it down the steps and over to the bushes where we leaned it in the sun. During the process, Vonion let out a few choice cuss words that

Ora Lee and I had heard—and ignored—a few too many times before. After that tug-of-war and with the looming task of manhandling that mattress back up those steps, the three of us collapsed right there on the yard bench. Ora Lee soon stood and wearily said, "Well, Ms. Bee, if we ever gonna clean under that bedstead, we better git at it. It ain't gonna git done by itself."

"You're right about that," I answered unenthusiastically and followed her back up the steps into the house.

I found a bucket and filled it with warm water, then picked up a couple of rags and a bar of soap. As I was setting the bucket down on the old pine planks of the bedroom floor, I noticed a slip of paper stuck to the side of the bedrail where the mattress had been. I reached down and picked it up. It was a telegram addressed to Irene Nelson, dated July 1st, 1946. Who in the world was Irene Nelson and what was that telegram doing in my house? I looked over at Vonion and as I was about to hand it to him, it dawned on me that neither Vonion nor Ora Lee could read. I'd have to tell them what it said.

"This seems to be a telegram sent to somebody named Irene Nelson, the first day of July this year," I said out loud, turning it over in my hand and inspecting the back.

"Well, we ain't gonna know notin' 'bout it till you open the thing," Ora Lee said, as if to give me the permission I needed to pull the telegram out of the envelope and read it.

"I don't know if I should read it or not," I said to Ora Lee, knowing full well I wasn't about to lay it aside and not read it. "Do you think I should?"

"Shore, you should. It be in yor house, ain't it? You know you gonna read it."

With permission granted, I pulled the slip of paper out of the envelope and read out loud.

"Strike while iron is hot. Meet at Resoto. August first. Signed, Billy Bob."

"That doesn't make any sense at all," I said, staring down at the paper. "What do you make of it?" I asked Vonion, as I sat down in the rocker and motioned to Ora Lee to sit down in the straight chair by the fireplace.

"I ain't got no idee what to make of that myself, but I reckon hit might be something Miss Isabelle had in here and forgot about. That would be my judgment," Vonion said, with a quizzical look on his old weathered face.

"Well, it isn't addressed to her, so what would it have to do with her?" I asked, as I folded the telegram and put in back in the envelope. I thought about laying it on the dresser, but instead, I tucked it into my apron pocket. I wanted to think more about it, and I thought I could think straighter with it in my pocket, closer to me.

"That date on that telegram ain't long gone. Who else been in this here room you knows of?" Vonion questioned.

"Nobody except Isabelle that I can think of," I answered. Remembering our task, I said, "Listen, we're wasting daylight thinking about it. Let's get this show on the road." I handed Ora Lee a rag and a bar of soap. After we finished cleaning in Isabelle's room, we went on to the other bedroom where Bess had been sleeping. We repeated the same process, this time a little slower. By the time the tasks were completed, our old bones were worn out, and we could hardly stand up straight.

I wanted to leave the mattresses out in the sun all afternoon to get the full benefit of the warm rays. We relaxed on the porch a while, drinking cool glasses of lemonade. Then Ora Lee and Vonion wearily plodded back down the lane to rest awhile before we brought the mattresses back in. They were both on their last leg from all that pulling and tugging. I knew they needed a rest. Before leaving, Ora Lee said, "Next time Margaret Girl want some cleanin' done, she best better be here to do it herself."

I totally agreed with her. Ora Lee was wise.

I sat back down in the porch rocker to rest a little more, but rest didn't come. I couldn't get the telegram off my mind.

I pulled it out of my apron pocket to reread it. I sat there staring at it and trying to imagine what the meaning could be, when it hit me like a ton of bricks! Like a lightbulb went on in my head, all at once everything was perfectly clear. I couldn't wait to get to the telephone!

"Nellie, get Bess, now," I said, trying not to let on how disturbed I was.

"I'll try, but she's probably out with you-know-who again. I'm sorry to hear about her troubles. She needs somebody strong to lean on in times like these, and I'm sure J.R. Kitchens has big strong shoulders. I'll ring her now and we'll see if she's at home. I give you fair warning; she's probably not alone though."

Exasperated, I politely said, "Thank you, Nellie," and waited. Bess picked up after four rings and I calmly said, "Bess, I need you to come to the house now."

"I don't know if I can come right now. Maybe a little later would be better for me. I'm in the middle of rearranging my china cabinet. It's not important, is it?"

"Bess, it is very important! Now come! And come alone! If you aren't here in ten minutes, I'm coming to get you!" I hung up and started shaking as I began to walk in circles, figuring what my next move was going to be. How on earth had I been so dumb? All this time…

CHAPTER TWENTY-FOUR

How could I be sure? Everything going through my head was absolutely unnatural. My head was spinning, and I wasn't sure I was even thinking rationally. Right now, all I could comprehend was that the pieces all seemed to fit together. It was like one of those big puzzles Margaret and Will sat for hours joining together, until it was one solid picture of mountains or forests. Before Bess arrived, I needed to get myself calm and collected, if that was at all possible.

Bee Martin, it's time for rational thinking, no make-believe, no nonsense. I stood there on my porch, not even daring to sit down for fear that if I moved, something would happen to my mind, and I wouldn't be able to think. I began to pray to God to give me the courage to tell Bess what was going through my head and let her decide if she thought I was absolutely losing it or I was on to something.

Everything around me was changing. In a matter of just fifteen minutes, I began to realize just how precious my life here was with my friends and Bess and Margaret. Vonion and Ora Lee were like rocks that never moved or changed. They were always there for me no matter what was going on in my life, and I wanted to always be there for them. Even though Will had passed away, his memories were as much a part of my being as the air that I breathed in and out every day. My home was my sanctuary, and all the sounds of the farm penetrated into my very being.

I prayed. "Dear Lord, please don't let anything happen that changes all this for me. I have so much to be thankful for. Please give me the strength and fortitude I need to endure whatever is coming my way. Be with me and guide me, I pray. Amen."

Bess's car was flying down the lane as I looked up, and I began to pray again her brakes would hold. At the rate she was going, her car could easily run into the front of the house and up the steps right into the porch where I was standing. Her brakes squealed and thank heavens the car stopped. She jumped out like a cat with its tail on fire. She was on the porch in record time for anybody, much less an old woman.

"Bee, are you all right? I don't know what's going on with you, but this better be worth my time."

"I'm fine. I have something we need to talk about." I was trying so hard to remain calm. I didn't want Bess to think I was completely insane after I finished telling her what I was thinking.

"Well, what is it, for goodness sake? I was in the middle of rearranging my china cabinet with the few pieces of china and crystal I still possess, and I had to drop everything to get over here. Now are you going to tell me what this is all about, or am I going to have to stand here forever? I'm waiting!"

"Bess, get a hold of yourself." I was beginning to shake now, and my voice was so high, I sounded like a screech owl. "I'm okay. Just let me get myself back together." I sat down and put my hands to my face, and then with all the inner fortitude I possessed, I looked up at Bess and said, "I'm pretty sure I know who killed Floyd and committed all these burglaries."

"Bee, what in the world are you talking about?"

"Just as I said, I think I know who burglarized your house and murdered Floyd."

Bess began to wobble around as if her legs were beginning to give way. "I'm feeling a little light-headed. Let me sit down before I fall down." She lowered herself to a chair and plopped down beside me. Looking confused, she said, "My gosh, Bee! How do you think you know such a thing? And if you say it's Roscoe, I'll never accept that."

"Bess, are you all right? I'll get you some water."

She grabbed my arm. "Oh no, you aren't going anywhere. Just tell me right now what you're talking about. You've just taken me by surprise."

"Bess, when did all these crimes start?"

"Oh, I don't know. Let me see. About the time Preacher Henry started at the church, I guess."

"Well, if you think about it, every person that has been burglarized is someone in our church. Preacher Henry has visited almost every member by himself, or with Isabelle, or should I say, Irene. I think that's her real name."

"Bee, if you are in any way thinking that our new preacher and his sister have anything to do with all this, you need to have your head examined. That is the most outlandish thing I've ever heard. Is that why you got me out here, to tell me that?"

"Listen to me, Bess. There's more to this than you think. I found this telegram in Isabelle's bedroom this afternoon when Vonion and Ora Lee were helping me take the mattress out into the sun. It somehow got stuck to the bedrail, and I saw it when we moved the mattress off the bed frame." I handed her the telegram. As she opened it and read it, I could see a puzzled look come over her face.

"What's this all about, Bee?"

"Bess, don't you see? It says, 'Strike while iron is hot. Meet at Resoto. August 1. It's signed, 'Billy Bob.' It was sent to Irene Nelson. Irene Nelson...Isabelle Newsome? Isabelle is Irene. Somebody named Billy Bob is telling her to act fast while she has the opportunity. They are to meet at someplace called The Resoto on August 1st. Today is July 31st. That's where they're going right now, to meet this Billy Bob. They left this morning to presumably see their mother who is supposed to be at death's door. Don't you think that is too much of a coincidence?"

"They left this morning?"

"Yes, this is the note Isabelle left me. She put it on the hall table for me to find."

After Bess read the note, she looked at me with that same quizzical look across her face that Vonion had given me. "This does not prove a thing. Bee, you're letting your imagination run wild. Be sensible, now."

"Listen, Bess, every time something happened around here, Isabelle or Henry was always out visiting in the same time frame as when the crime was committed. Everywhere that has been burglarized is somewhere they have visited and cased the place. They pretty well knew where everything was located in these people's houses because they've been there. Old Man Peterson made a point of talking about banking practices to whoever would listen. His place is between here and the church, and you know Preacher Henry has probably stopped by there going or coming from here several times. Why Old Man Peterson probably told Henry where he hid his money. Preacher Henry had a habit of going by Floyd's place every day for a soda, and he knew pretty well when Floyd had somewhere to be at night. He broke in, and for some unknown reason, Floyd came in on him, and Henry had to kill him to keep him from talking. Floyd probably caught Henry red-handed in his house. Shirley was at work while her house was being burglarized, so that was pretty simple. Preacher Henry and Isabelle knew she'd be at the library during work hours. She hardly ever missed a day. Isabelle and Henry had been over there before the theft, and you know how Shirley likes to show off all that stuff her mother and father left her. She had so much silver she couldn't have used it all in a hundred years. She had it all displayed in her dining room and front room, just for show, along with all those oil paintings and statuary stuff. Vera did the same thing. She kept all her nice things sitting out, and anybody that went in would just swoon over it."

"But Bee, Vera and Tillman's house was hit on the day of the funeral. Preacher Henry was pretty tied up that day."

"Preacher Henry was tied up, but not Isabelle! Don't you remember, Bess? Isabelle said she wasn't feeling well and needed to stay at home and rest. She didn't even attend the funeral. She evidently walked over to Vera and Tillman's during the time we were all over at the church. She did the dirty deed right by herself. You know, now that I think about it, Isabelle told me she didn't leave the house that day at all, yet Vonion informed me later that afternoon that he had seen Isabelle out taking a walk. Yeah, she was taking a walk all right. She walked over to Vera's, burglarized the place, probably hid the loot in the woods, and then walked back home, just as if she was out walking around for a little daily exercise."

"Bee, I don't know, I still think your imagination is running overtime."

"Bess, you don't know everything yet. Just listen. Earl had some very valuable coins he had won in a poker game hidden out in that rundown shack of his. He had talked to Preacher Jenkins before his death about giving them as an offering to the church. He wanted the church to pay for his burial and then keep whatever money was left over. Earl told me he had given Preacher Jenkins a piece of paper stating the church could take possession of the coins at his death. Now, I'm not sure about the exact location of the coins, but I do know he told Preacher Jenkins they were well hidden in his house. I think Henry must have come across the letter at the pastorium and decided to steal those coins while Earl was gone. He had to tear the house apart to find them, and he decided to take the guns while he was at it. Don't you see, Bess? They broke into your house and stole your stuff too. Remember the night you and I were sitting around talking about putting your valuables in the attic. Isabelle or Irene, or whoever she is, was listening to us as we talked. She was in the next room. She knew exactly where everything was."

"Bee, I don't know. Let me think about all this." Bess got up and walked over to the porch door and stood there a few minutes and stared out into the yard. She soon started shaking uncontrollably, so I walked over to her to steady her when she turned around and looked at me squarely in the face. "Bee, I don't always like to agree with you, but this time I think maybe you're on to something. I can't believe we've been so stupid. We've sat here and harbored these people while they've been terrorizing our community. Why I could just chew a nail in two! I'll bet a hundred dollars to a doughnut they stole your camera to keep you from having those pictures developed. Those low-down thieves probably stole your ring and locket out of your purse too."

"They stole my camera without the film. Actually, Margaret's camera had the film in it, and it was in her car. Margaret took her camera home with her and my camera was left here, without Preacher Henry's picture in it. They stole the wrong camera."

"We've been had, Bee! Now what in blue blazes are we going to do?"

"I don't know, but we're going to do something." I grabbed Bess and gave her a big bear hug as I contemplated what our next move was going to be. "You know, they never once offered to pay me one red cent for Isabelle's, or should I say, Irene's lodging. They must have taken me for a complete idiot. I guess, in a lot of ways, I acted like one. I've just got to get my locket and ring back."

"Bee, what about all my silver and cut glass? Those silver goblets and Mama's sterling silver flatware were my most precious possessions. Why, this is just unbelievable!

Do you think Preacher Henry really is a preacher and do you think Isabelle is his sister?"

"I have my doubts about all of that, now that I think about it. I never did see any favoritism between the two of them. You know, I don't think they have one characteristic in common, other than they're both tall. I just wonder how they really found their way here. That might be something we need to check into. In the meantime, Bess, I don't think I can stay here now. They could come back unexpectedly. Do you think that I might stay over at your house until we think this thing over and decide what needs to be done?"

"That's a good idea. Why don't you pack, and I'll go tell Vonion and Ora Lee something about you wanting to spend a few days with me while your boarder is gone. If they don't believe that, then I guess I'll just make up something else. I'll be back in few minutes. Hurry every chance you get. We could be in danger just hanging around here. Just thinking about you sleeping in the same house all this time with those murdering thieves scares me to death!"

"I'm trying not to think about it," I answered, trying to keep my emotions under control. "Tell Vonion to keep all the eggs and milk for now or give them to Eve Waters. I don't know how she's still surviving with that sorry husband of hers gone. I just wonder what's really going on with them. I thought I saw him the other day in town. I have my doubts that she is being completely truthful about their situation. She seems to be hanging on though. Oh, and make sure you impress on Vonion to keep a good watch on the place. Tell him to stay close to home."

"I will. And get the gun. We might need it."

That was a scary thought. As I was hurrying around trying to get my things together, the telephone rang. Two rings, one long, one short. That's me.

"Hello, Bee Martin speaking."

"Hello, Bee. It's Vera. Listen, I wanted to let you know somebody has come in at Millie and Tillie's house and gone through their jewelry box and taken their brooches. Those poor old ladies are beside themselves, according to Nellie. I made a call over to Madge a little while ago, and Nellie had just heard the news from Josh Brantley. You know him, J.B. and Nita Brantley's youngest boy. He just came back into town from the service, and he's gone to work part-time over at the oil mill with Mr. Rooks, that horny old man Eunice goes out with. Josh told Nellie all about it when he was making a call to his sister, Pearl. Did you know she has the gout and has had to stay off her feet? Poor thing, you know her sorry husband doesn't help her do a thing. I'll bet her house is a total disaster by now with all those children running around. They probably haven't had a decent meal…"

"Vera, get back to the twins. Now, what were you saying?"

"Oh, yes. Josh told Nellie, and Nellie told me, that when those two precious old ladies went to get their brooches out to wear to choir practice, they were gone. Well, they've looked high and low, and just could not find any trace of them. They've called Sheriff Ledbetter in on the investigation. I seriously doubt he will be of any use, but maybe it'll make them feel better if they think the law is on the job."

"Vera, those beautiful brooches were given to them on their twenty-first birthday by their father, when he realized they'd probably never get wedding rings. He reasoned that they were so attached to each other, no one would ever be able to come between them. I guess with identical twins, there's a special bond that others just don't feel. Why, they have worn those brooches to every social event and every church service for sixty-some-odd years."

"They sure have. One was a ruby and one was an emerald. They're the real thing too. That's the only way I could ever tell them apart. Millie wore the emerald and Tillie wore the ruby. Why, they have sat in that choir loft all these years with those things pinned right to their choir robes. Well, they're gone now. Those ladies don't have a clue about what could have happened to them. It doesn't appear anybody broke in or damaged anything. That's a blessing anyway."

"If nobody broke in, what happened to the brooches? How did they disappear? Didn't you say they always kept them in the same place when they weren't wearing them?"

"According to the ladies, the brooches were always kept in the jewelry box. They can't imagine what happened to them. They don't have many people visiting at their house, and they're home most of the time."

"Vera, do you remember the last time we were out at their place?"

"Oh, I don't know, maybe when we delivered those cookies we made for some of the elderly in the church. When was that, maybe two months ago?"

"That's right. They had the house and yard looking fairly nice and clean, and they always keep their appearances up pretty well. I don't think they're getting senile, do you?"

"No, I think they still have a grip on reality and would remember if they had put those brooches someplace else. I find it very unlikely they would do that, though. According to what Nellie overheard, they told Sheriff Ledbetter they always kept them in the same place. They're very proud of how orderly everything is out there, and they should be. When I'm their age, I just hope I'm alive," Vera added.

"You're right about that. Now listen Vera, I've got to go. I think I left my stove on, and I've got to go see about it before my house catches on fire. Thanks for calling and I'll see you later." Hanging up, I thought I was going to quit answering the telephone. All I ever get is bad news.

What a coincidence. The twins just happen to be members of the Baptist congregation, and I'm quite sure our new preacher and his sister have called on them one time too many.

CHAPTER TWENTY-FIVE

I told Vonion to get Roscoe to help get the mattresses in after a while. He didn't ask any questions but said to tell you they'd take care of everything." Bess, looking a bit flustered, relayed the message after running up the steps into the house. "I'm sure Vonion and Ora Lee will be okay. They know something's up but didn't ask any questions."

"Good," I said, as I checked to see if I had everything in my overnight case that I might need for the next day or two. "I'm ready."

"Okay, I'll go crank the car. Now hurry up and let's go. Did you think to get your pressure medicine and your toothbrush?" Bess questioned, as she started toward the door.

"I did. Oh, get the gun, Bess. I can't carry everything."

"Got it," Bess answered, as she carefully reached behind the door for it. "I sure hope we don't have to use this thing."

I looked back over the room before I closed my suitcase. "I'll get the mail and take it with me. I don't like leaving it in the box overnight." Then I had an idea. "Hey, Bess, listen. Why don't we go over to the pastorium and check it out? Maybe we can find out what's really been going on with Preacher Henry or whatever his name is. They're supposed to be out of town now, and who knows if they're ever coming back anyway."

"You mean break in, without being invited? You must be out of your mind, Sister. If you think for one solid minute I'm going to break and enter into another person's house, and it being a pastorium on top of everything, you're barking up the wrong tree. Why, it's almost sacrilegious to invade the House of God."

"The House of God?"

"House of God. You know, the pastorium. We could be put in jail for the next twenty years for doing such a crazy thing."

"Well, in case you haven't thought about it, it's either that or talk to that dim-witted sheriff. You know, the same one who waited a whole hour after getting the tip that your house was burglarized before even going over. If you think he would do anything with the information we have, you've got another think coming. What evidence do we really have? I mean substantial evidence that would hold up in a court of law. What we've got to do is find something concrete that points the finger right at Preacher Henry and Isabelle, or whatever her name is. We've got to get in there and see what we can find out. Now, let's go."

Bess grabbed my arm to stop me. "If we get caught, my children will disown me, and Margaret will never speak to you again, so I hope you know what you're suggesting. How do you think we can get in there anyway? I'm sure it's locked."

"We'll open one of the back windows, and I'll help you slide through. Then you can come around and open the side door for me to come in. It's going to be real simple," I answered, holding my breath that Bess would go along with my plan.

"How about if you slide in and come around and open the side door for me."

"Bess, you know as well as I do, you're the smallest and can get in through the window easier. You couldn't hold me up long enough for me to climb through."

"I can't believe you would even suggest a thing, Bee Martin. I'm not going through any window now or ever."

"Listen, Bess, you can do it. Think about poor Floyd, lying in the ground right now because that so-called preacher is greedy. And think about Mama's sterling flatware he stole right out from under your own roof. You know, I'm mad as fire about that. You always said you were going to leave it to Margaret when the time came, and now she'll never even see it again. And what about my ring and locket?"

"Oh, all right, let's go, but this is one time I wish I was bigger. We need some of those pedal pushers Mildred wears."

"You know, I was thinking about seeing if they come in larger sizes. I really think they would be comfortable. You know as well as I do, styles are changing fast and we need to change with the times," I sheepishly replied, and waited for Bess to scold me.

"I already have."

"You already what?" I asked Bess.

"Bought some. I just haven't had the nerve to wear them out in public yet. I hope I didn't waste my money. They probably make you wear ugly jailhouse dresses in prison. That'll probably be our next home after we break and enter."

"Well, at least we'll be together."

"What a consolation," Bess replied as she rolled her eyes.

After I grabbed the mail out of the box, we jumped in the car and Bess drove while I sat over in the passenger side of the car with Will's shotgun at my side. With the exception of running a stop sign and coming within two inches of missing the same big farm truck we narrowly missed just days ago—this time hauling goats—we made it into town without any difficulty. Nervously fingering the mail in my lap as Bess sped through town, I felt something a little bulky. I looked down and saw it was our photos. "Look, Bess, our pictures Margaret had developed came in the mail today. That was fast." I opened the package from the developing company, and right on the top of the pile of pictures was the one of all of us standing around in the front yard with Preacher Henry and Isabelle. I looked through the stack of pictures and realized what someone once said is true. *A picture doesn't lie.* Every one of my bulges showed.

"Bee," Bess said, with her hands clinched to the steering wheel, "we need those pictures. Preacher Henry never wanted a picture of himself and Isabelle taken. That's why he acted so out of sorts when he realized we had his likeness in a photograph. I'll bet that's why they deliberately stole your camera too. They didn't even know two cameras existed. Aren't those cameras identical?"

"They are...Oh my goodness, Bess, you are right! These pictures might be pretty important."

Bess was pulling into the pastorium driveway when I looked over at her and said, in an aggravated tone, "Bess, do you really think you should park in front of the house we're about to break into for everybody in town to see, for heaven's sake? Pull down to the next street and park in front of the insurance office. Nobody will think anything about your car sitting there. Don't you have insurance with them anyway? Do I have to tell you everything? Think!"

"Okay, but you don't have to be so demanding about everything. I've never broke into a house or anything in all my life. I guess my mind just doesn't work like a criminal."

We drove over to the next street, parked the car, and walked back over to the pastorium just as if we were taking an afternoon stroll through town. We casually wandered around to the back of the house, pretending to look at wild flowers, and then crouched down behind some overgrown nandina bushes.

Bess whispered, "I'm going to take a quick look over there behind the shed to see if I can find something to stand on under the window. You aren't going to be able to hold me up to it. It's way too high."

I silently nodded.

She dashed behind the shed and finally came running back with a five gallon lard can in her arms, looking as if she had found the prize in a box of Cracker Jacks. She placed it under the window and with a little push from me, climbed on top, holding on to the side of the house for support. As I held on to her backside, she attempted to push the window open... no luck.

"Bess, hold on to the windowsill a minute while I get that stick over there." I dashed over to pick up a small pecan tree limb that had fallen on the ground. "Take this and break out the window," I instructed, as I handed Bess the limb.

"Okay. Hold on to me, so I won't fall," Bess excitedly commanded, as she grabbed the stick.

Crash! She broke the window, and glass went flying into the house. "Please don't cut yourself," I warned, as I pushed harder against her backside, trying to keep her from falling.

"Just hold on to me while I pick the glass out of the window sash," Bess nervously answered, as she carefully pulled the broken glass out of the frame. "Now, that's got it." Looking from side to side to make sure we weren't being spied on by some nosy neighbor, Bess said, "I'm about ready to go in. Push me up... now."

I pushed, and before you could say *ginny squat*, Bess slid right through the opening. After I heard a thud, she peeked back out at me through the broken window, and with a lopsided smile, said, "That was easy."

"Easy for you, I did all the pushing. Now go open that side door," I ordered, trying to control the excitement in my voice.

"Come on around the house to the door in a minute, and I'll let you in," Bess answered. I could tell her enthusiasm was building too. "And don't be so bossy."

I gave her two minutes, then I casually walked around the house and knocked at the door, just like this was a friendly afternoon visit. Bess opened the door and I walked right in, as she was straightening her dress and patting her hair. Even in the middle of breaking and entering, Bess still wanted to look her best. We locked the door and looked at each other as if we had just won a hundred dollar bill. We were in!

We made a quick survey of the house. Exasperated, Bess looked around and said, "Can you believe what a slob the preacher is? I've never seen such a mess. Why, he never picked up a thing." Towels were thrown all over the place, wads of paper and dried banana peelings were running out of the trash cans, dishes covered with dried food were in the kitchen sink, and dust was an inch thick on every surface. The floor looked as if it hadn't seen a broom or mop in a month of Sundays. Bedbugs had probably made camp in the dingy sheets that covered the rumpled bed. A soup can filled with stale cigarette butts was turned over on the floor. "What a disaster! We better start searching."

As I watched Bess ease down to her knees to check under the bed, I said, "I don't see how a place could have gotten this bad in a few short weeks. I happen to know this place was spick-and-span before this so-called preacher moved in here. I was on the pastoral committee, and I personally inspected it. You know, Bess, if the other pastoral committee members could see this place now, they'd probably have the preacher thrown out with the dishwater, and then have him disrobed or disbarred, or whatever you call it."

"I'm sure there's going to be worse charges against this crook than messiness before this is over, Bee. A dirty house is going to be the least of this so-called man of God's problems... would you look at this!" Bess pulled a stack of girlie magazines out from under the bed and threw them on the bed. "Have you ever in your life heard of a preacher reading this kind of trash? This is absolutely revolting!"

"As a matter of fact, I have and I don't think Preacher Henry was reading. He was probably just looking at the pictures. Don't you remember Preacher Horace Hobbs who had a heart attack and died right here in this house about fifteen years ago? You remember him, he always stuttered when he got nervous—which was most of the time. You always said he looked like a big fat hog walking on his hind legs wearing a double-breasted suit. Well, I never said anything about it to anybody before now, but Preacher Horace was so heavy Mr. Lawson needed extra help getting all that dead weight out of the house and into the hearse. Will volunteered to come over here with Mr. Lawson to pick up his body after he died. They found that same kind of reading material on the floor by the bed. Will told me they destroyed it and decided not to talk about it. There wasn't any need to damage poor Preacher Horace's memory. I really shouldn't have said anything about it now."

"Bee, you don't mean? I guess preaching and praying wasn't the only thing the man had on his mind. You know, now that I think about it, he did love to hug on every woman in the congregation every chance he got. I know one thing, he could put away some fried chicken. I remember every time he ate Sunday dinner with us, I always had to cook an extra chicken and have two pans of biscuits."

"Bess, put those magazines back under the bed and let's get back down to business. You take the office and I'll take the front room."

Bess slowly pulled herself up and walked to the next room. Almost immediately she called. "Bee, come here a minute. I want you to see something."

"What is it? You've barely had time to find a thing," I answered, and walked into the room.

"Look at this!" Bess was sitting at the writing desk, reading from some papers. "These are copies of sermons that scoundrel ordered from some place called *Lessons from the Heart*, and this is the one, word for word, he preached last week! Can you believe that? He didn't even think up his own sermons. He actually paid two dollars apiece for them. That is absolutely the laziest thing I've ever heard of! Why would a man of God do such a thing! This is the last straw, I tell you. And to think, I actually hung on to every word he said from the pulpit, expecting to get a word from God!"

You'd think copying a sermon was the worst thing the man ever did. I sternly reminded Bess, "The man is probably a murderer. Do you really think he just sat around all day trying to think up sermons, for heaven's sake? Get real! We've got more important things to think about than those fake sermons. Now keep looking."

We went through every drawer and trash can. We looked under every piece of furniture and rug. The only thing of interest we found were advertisements for hairpieces, dyes, and lift shoes. We began to think Preacher Henry must have distorted his looks in every way. His hair probably wasn't the color we thought it was, and he probably had a false mustache by now. All we were absolutely certain of was he could change his looks, and he probably looked entirely different by now.

As we were just about ready to give up, I glanced across the room toward the fireplace. "Bess, look over there. Is this what we've been looking for?" I walked over and picked up a gold-looking coin sitting on the fireplace mantle, half hidden by a dirty coffee cup.

I handed it to Bess, and she examined it on both sides. "Bee, I've never seen anything like this before, but I'll bet it's one of those gold coins Earl won in that poker game years ago. They must have overlooked it when they left. This could be just the evidence we need. Let's go before we get caught and end up on the chain gang wearing those ugly gray dresses with all the other lady criminals. I'll slip it into my pocket and we'll look at it later. Now, let's get out of here."

We taped the window up with some newspaper and Band-Aids we found in the house, checked the lights, and walked out through the side door of the house. We headed back down the street, casually strolling along, as if it were just another day.

"Let's get to the house and plan our next move," Bess said, as we opened the car doors. "It's getting late and I'm tired. We need a little time to think. Do you think we need to call Sheriff Ledbetter?"

"Not yet. He wouldn't know what to do with all this evidence if it hit him square in the backside. I'm too tired and hungry anyway, and I need to use the bathroom. I hope you've got something besides carrot sticks and boiled ham at your house. I could eat a horse."

CHAPTER TWENTY-SIX

"What do you think Resoto means, Bee?" Bess asked, as we were making our boiled ham sandwiches. "If that telegram means someone is at some place called The Resoto waiting for Isabelle, and maybe Henry too, then they're either on their way or have already gotten there."

"That's exactly what the telegram says, Bess." I dug down in the bottom of my pocketbook and found the telegram. I read it back to Bess. "Strike while iron is hot. Meet at Resoto, August 1st. Billy Bob."

"Tomorrow is August 1st. That doesn't give us much time to figure out where the Resoto is. I've never heard of any place like that," Bess said.

"I have and I know where it is. Bess, do you have anything like potato wedges or saltines with cheese or something we can eat along with this ham?"

"I've got plenty of carrot sticks. I'll get them out of the icebox for you."

"No, that's all right. I was really thinking of something with a few more calories," I replied, as I thought to myself, I'd starve to death if I stayed around here very long. "Do you have anything sweet at all?"

"Listen, Bee, quit thinking about your stomach for a few minutes and tell me what you're thinking, for heaven's sake." As if she had a second thought, she added, "Oh, I do have some leftover chocolate cake. Do you want some of that?"

"That sounds great. I'd love a big wedge and maybe some sweet milk to help it go down. I know you've got milk. I sent Vonion over with some a couple of days ago."

"I think I'll have a little sliver of cake too," Bess sheepishly replied. "I've got to keep my strength up; after all, I don't have a clue what you'll have me doing next. Now, tell me what you're thinking before I lose my mind."

"Okay, Bess, now listen. The Resoto—it's that big hotel in Savannah. The very one Will and I stayed in a few years back when we went to the Cotton Growers' Convention. Don't you remember? I had to borrow one of your big suitcases because I needed three and only had two. We had the best time. We pretended we were on a second honeymoon. It's a wonder Margaret doesn't have a little sister or brother after that trip."

"Bee, I don't want to know everything. Just give me the basics, for heaven's sake."

"Well, I'm trying to tell you what I know, if you would just listen and not interrupt. We stayed in a big room overlooking the street, where we could look out and see Savannah's whole skyline. Bess, the landscaping there is so beautiful. The historic homes in Savannah are just magnificent. There are theaters, all kinds of shops, and you wouldn't believe all the restaurants. Well, I think that's where they went, to the Resoto Hotel in Savannah, and that's where we're going tomorrow."

"Bee, I can't go somewhere like that. I don't have a thing to wear and my hair's a mess. My porch flowers are dry as bones, and I really need to put fresh mothballs in my closets. Anyway, we can't just take off like a shot. I think we need to tell Sheriff Ledbetter what we suspect and let him do his job. We don't have a bit of business traipsing all over creation trying to catch up with those deranged people. They're dangerous, and we could be the next people on their short list of people to murder."

"Well, Bess, I'm going with or without you. Remember, those deranged people, as you call them, might still have your silver and cut glass, and maybe we'll have a chance of getting it back if we get a move on it. Now Bess, I think we need to leave Sheriff Ledbetter a note, telling him where we're headed and what we suspect, and then leave first thing in the morning. We need to be on the road by six in the morning. I remember how to get to Savannah, but we'll have to get directions to the hotel when we get into town. Hopefully, when we find the hotel, we'll find Henry and Isabelle, but that's going to be the hard part."

"And what do you think we'll do when we find them, is what I want to know, Miss Smarty Pants? I haven't noticed you practicing up on your wrestling lately."

"We'll call in the law."

"Bee, if I wasn't standing here having this conversation with you right now, I'd never in a million years believe what you're talking about. But I guess I'm game to go, under one condition."

"What's that?"

"You let me drive."

"Oh, I was counting on that all along, Bess. You know you can get us there a lot faster than I ever could." I was hoping Bess wasn't going to lose her nerve before we left.

"Well, hurry up and finish eating. Let's write that note to Sheriff Ledbetter and try to get a little sleep. Do you think we might do a little shopping in one of those shops you were talking about after this is all over?" Bess asked.

I couldn't help but roll my eyes. "Find some paper and a pen while I think about what we need to write," I instructed, as I started walking around in circles so I could think better.

"Let me see if I can lay my hands on that nice stationery Madge gave me for Christmas last year. It's so dainty with a little ivy border around the note cards and a little sprig on the envelope...oh here it is. I'll write while you dictate. I'm ready, now go."

"Okay, here goes. Write this..."

To whom it may concern:

Bee Martin and Bess Johnson have gone to the Resoto Hotel in Savannah on a lead to find the whereabouts of Preacher Henry Maxwell and Irene Nelson, also known as Isabelle Newsome. We firmly believe they are responsible for the murder of Floyd Screws and also the numerous burglaries that have taken place in recent days.

Bee Martin and Bess Johnson.

"We can stop by the jailhouse in the morning when we head out and put it on the sheriff's desk. He'll find it if he ever gets in to work in the morning," Bess said, after she wrote Sheriff Ledbetter's name across the front of the envelope. "Well, I guess that settles that. Now let's go to bed and get some rest. You can sleep in Freddy's old room."

"Okay, but Bess, we probably should take some big hats. We might need to hide our faces when we get to the hotel. Where are those big floppy things with the flower gardens and big clumps of fruit on top you wear to church sometimes? Don't you have two of them? Let's take them just in case."

"Are you insinuating you don't like my hats? They happen to be very stylish."

"No, of course not. There're just big and nobody can see over or around them when you sit in the congregation, that's all. But don't worry about that now, for heaven's sake."

"Well, I don't know why you'd bring something up about them now, of all times. But I'll get them and put them by the door with the note. Bee, I was thinking, why don't we drop that coin into the envelope we're leaving at the jailhouse? That way Sheriff Ledbetter will actually have that piece of evidence just in case, God forbid, something happens to us. We probably need to tell him where it came from too."

"That's a good idea, Bess. You're beginning to sound like a good private investigator. Put a *P.S.* at the end of the note and explain where the coin came from."

We cleaned the kitchen and fairly soon we were ready for bed. After Bess set the clock for five a.m., I said a quick prayer and closed my eyes. I finally drifted off with the melodious chords of Bess's snoring going through my head.

I felt as if I had just laid my head on the pillow when I felt Bess shaking me. "Wake up, Bee. It's time to get ready to go."

"Are you sure it's morning already?" I asked Bess, as I tried to open my eyes. "This fast living is just about to get the best of me."

"It's morning, and we need to get a move on it. I've already finished in the bathroom, so go on in. I've got the coffee brewing. I'll grab a thermos for the coffee and wrap some bran muffins in wax paper to take with us. We'll eat on the road."

"That sounds good," I said, thinking Bess was really turning into a regular trooper. "Just give me a few minutes, and I'll be ready."

After quickly making my bed and dressing, I was ready for our big adventure. I knew we needed to get out of the house hastily before Bess decided this would be a good time to mop and wax the kitchen floor since we wouldn't be here to track it up. Cleanliness was next to godliness in her eyes, and I mean it came in as a close second. She was arranging fresh towels on the rod in the bathroom when I said, "Let's go."

After stopping by the jailhouse and leaving the envelope with the note and coin, Bess and I left town before the sun came up. Driving toward Savannah carrying Will's shotgun and a Griswold cast-iron frying pan from Bess's kitchen for extra protection, we didn't have a clue as to what we were really getting ourselves into.

The blind leading the blind was the first thing that came to my mind.

CHAPTER TWENTY-SEVEN

That sign you just flew by said 'Savannah City Limits,'" I said to Bess, as she sat in the driver's seat—hands clutched to the steering wheel and staring straight ahead— as if she were in a trance. "Did you hear me? Are you awake?" I asked, and reached over and shook her to make sure she hadn't fallen asleep at the wheel.

"I'm awake, and don't shake me. I'm concentrating."

"What in the world are you concentrating on? For pity's sake, you look like you're in another world."

"How could I be so lucky? Any world would be better than this one right now. I feel like we're getting ourselves into something we can't climb out of. How could we have been so stupid as to think we could apprehend some dangerous criminals? We don't have the foggiest notion how to even get to the hotel."

"Now listen, Bess. When we left home, you said you were up to this. We can't have second thoughts now.

Pull over into the next gas station you see and let's ask for some directions. I need to use the bathroom, and we could get something to drink too," I added.

"I could use a break. My bladder is just about to bust."

"Bess, why don't you just sit here a minute and let me get out and do the talking," I said, as we pulled into a greasy little filling station that had a sign out front that said 'Free Restrooms.' "I'll check out everything and come back and let you know if the restroom looks clean."

"Listen, Sister. Right now, I don't care if the restroom is clean or not. I've got to go. I know how to use the bathroom without touching a thing."

We both departed, and Bess headed towards the back of the place where the lopsided restroom sign pointed. I walked into the front of the station to find a grungy-looking old mechanic standing in the middle of the room with some kind of small motor in his hand and a greasy towel draped over his humped shoulder. His coveralls hadn't been washed in the last decade, and he needed a haircut weeks ago.

"I was just on my way out to help you, young lady, but you beat me to the draw. What can I help you with? I got regular and I got high test."

It always made me feel young for someone, I don't care who it is, even some old codger like this, to refer to me as young lady. "Well, actually neither. I need directions to the Resoto Hotel. Do you happen to know where it is?"

"Young lady, everybody in Savannah knows where the Resoto is," he answered, wiping his sweaty forehead with the greasy towel. Just go three more miles into town and take a left turn at the intersection that has a billboard with a suntan lotion advertisement on it. It's the big one with a bathing beauty holding a bottle of suntan lotion in her hand. She ain't got much of nothing on. It's a real eye-catcher. Everybody around knows that sign. Anyway, go about two blocks and turn right at the lumberyard. The Resoto will be about two, maybe three miles on your right. You can't miss it."

"Thanks for the information. I'm sure I can find it." Bess had already returned to the car and was waiting for me with her hands on the steering wheel and the car cranked as I walked out and headed toward the restrooms.

"Want a drink and something to eat? I think I'm gonna get some crackers," I called to Bess after I rounded the corner of the station and headed back toward the front.

"No, but you go ahead. If I drink anything, we'd have to pull over, and I don't want to hold us up."

"Suit yourself. I'll just be a minute."

I walked back into the station and purchased two orange sodas and two packages of cheese crackers from the scruffy old man with a fresh twinkle in his eyes.

"How long you planning on staying in town, ma'am?"

"Not too long. I'm here on business," I answered as I opened the drinks. "I'll put the bottles in that crate outside the door on my way home, if it's all right."

"Sure, that's fine. I didn't charge you for them. I could show you the sights if you're willing. I know this town like the back of my hand." He gave a little cough as he chewed on the stub of the cigar he had clinched between his stained teeth. I could see a slight grin spreading across his face behind his straggly, unkempt whiskers.

"I, err..."

He quickly interrupted me. "There're some swinging places around here and I know them all. I do a mean jitterbug too." He did a little shuffle with his feet, and asked, "What do you say?"

Completely astonished, I answered, "It sounds like fun, but I won't be staying long enough to enjoy the night life. Maybe some other time would be better." By that time, I was backing out of the heavy front door with our drinks and crackers. "I'll be sure to return the bottles. Thanks for the information and...err, the offer." I stepped over a greasy spot in the doorway and made a hasty exit. Still reeling from all the attention, I thought to myself, I should have changed my hair color sooner. Maybe the next time I had my hair done, I'd see about having a facial too. My skin had felt a little dry lately, and Thelma had advised me that one would help put new life back into my tired old skin.

I hurried back out to the car. "Here, take this," I said, as I handed Bess a soda and a pack of crackers through the open window.

"Okay, but don't blame me if we have to stop again before we get to the hotel," Bess said, as she reached for the drink and crackers. "If I hung around you much more, I'd weigh two hundred pounds. What in the world were you and that nasty old man talking about so long? I could have written a book out here waiting for you."

"He asked me to go dancing with him. He said he could do a mean jitterbug."

"I hope you told him not to get his hopes up. You did tell him you didn't dance, didn't you?"

"I did not. In fact I told him the next time I stopped in, we'd talk about it. I just don't plan on stopping when he's here, if I can help it."

An hour and a half later, we pulled up to the Resoto, after making at least fifteen right turns and more than twenty left turns. My ears were reeling from all the grinding and grating those gears had made as Bess changed them repeatedly. Bess had fought that city traffic like a trooper. She honked her horn at oncoming cars, made signs of all kinds with her left hand, and came close to several fender benders. At one point, Bess asked me if I would get out and direct traffic so she could get through a dangerous intersection. I looked at her and asked, "Bess, have you completely lost your marbles? You can't drive through here, and you want me to walk out into the middle of the street and hold my arms up to direct cars. Now I know you've lost your cotton-picking mind. I'm not getting out of this car in this traffic, now or ever, so don't even think about it."

She hung in there, even though half the people we passed were idiots—at least that's what she called them. Bess really put that car to the test on those city streets. I was just hoping she hadn't torn something up under the hood with all that stopping and starting. We still needed to get home in that car. We had ridden just about all over town when we finally just happened up on the hotel. "Either that old mechanic didn't know where he was, or he didn't know where the Resoto was," Bess remarked as we drove up to the front of the hotel. "He must be completely senile. We wouldn't have made it here in a month of Sundays following his directions."

"Bess, we need to pull around to the next block so nobody will notice your car. I thought I had already taught you that. You know Henry and Isabelle might just walk out any time and see it. They'd know right off we were here."

"I was just about to suggest that. I'll wheel around, and we'll find a nice little secluded spot to park." Bess paid no attention to the sign by the road that said one way and pulled right into oncoming traffic. With directional arrows pointing one way and Bess driving the other, I could actually see the horrified expressions on drivers' faces as Bess drove right toward them. Several motorists even yelled out the window and waved their arms as Bess charged on, dividing the traffic as she drove, just like Moses divided the waters of the Red Sea.

We eventually found a place to leave the car after circling the block again, without a head-on collision, thank heavens. With the greatest relief, Bess parked the car, and I thanked the good Lord for his protection and vowed to myself that if we made it home, I'd keep Bess on country roads from now on.

"Finally, I can get out from under this wheel and stretch," Bess said, completely unaware of how close we had come to prematurely meeting our maker. With our pocketbooks and floppy hats in tow, we opened the car doors and stepped out. We slid the frying pan in Bess's large purse but left the shotgun in the car trunk, thinking that if we toted heavy artillery as we walked into the hotel, we might look a little suspicious. "I hope we can get across this street without being run down by one of these stupid, reckless drivers here. I just wonder where all these irresponsible people come from. They need to keep themselves home until they learn a little bit more about city driving."

With that remark, I had to almost slap myself to keep from saying something I'd be sorry for later on. "Well, you did great," I lied to Bess, as we crossed the street. I didn't want her to get any more flustered than she already was. "Now let's just calm down and get ourselves back together before we get to the hotel lobby. Let's do some deep breathing."

"Bee, you were so right. This place is just luscious. I've never seen such beautiful tropical flowers. Do you think they would mind if I pinched a few cuttings to take home?"

"Don't you dare touch a leaf!"

"You can be so bossy. I wish we could vacation here a while and just soak all this atmosphere up. Wouldn't it be nice if J.R. and I could..."

"Bess, for pity's sake, keep your mind on business!"

With our heads concealed by artificial green grapes, purple plums, and pink azalea blooms, we marched onto the hotel's covered porch with anxiety in our hearts and determination in our steps. "Bess, why don't you wait over on the other side of that potted palm over there while I go into the lobby and ask the cashier if Henry and Isabelle are here? I have their picture in my purse, and I'll show it to him if I have to," I said as I gestured toward a wrought iron table partially hidden by some large foliage. "Maybe he'll know who I'm talking about. I'm going to pretend to be Isabelle's mother."

"All right, but be careful and watch that staircase. They could come walking down any minute. I hope we haven't jumped to conclusions, thinking they might be here. It's such a long shot."

"Bess, don't give up now. I just know we're on to something. We didn't come this far for nothing." So after straightening my dress around my hips and adjusting to my best posture, I walked into the lobby. Spotting an elderly bald-headed man leaning against the registration counter, I strolled across the room, flashed a big smile, batted my eyelashes, and asked, "Young man, have you, by any chance, seen my daughter this morning?"

CHAPTER TWENTY-EIGHT

G ood morning, madam. Excuse me, I'm a little hard of hearing. Now what were you saying?"

"Pardon me, sir. I was merely asking if you had seen my daughter this morning. She's a very pretty young woman, twenty-two years old, tall with very good posture, and is traveling with a young man. Here is a fairly good likeness of her." I handed him the photograph Margaret had taken out in my yard.

"Oh, you're inquiring about Irene Coleman, Mrs. Lester Coleman, in room forty-two. Lovely young couple, yes indeed, they are quite a dashing pair. I believe they are here on their honeymoon, seeing the sights. We have honeymooners here all the time, you know. I, oh, well, if you're the mother, what are you doing here? I mean, if they're on their honeymoon, shouldn't you be somewhere else?"

"You're quite right, sir. I discovered after they left for their honeymoon, Irene left her medication, and knowing her like I do, I knew she wouldn't be bothered to come back home to get it. So being the thoughtful mother that I am, I decided to bring it to her. You see, she takes a medication that keeps her from having seizures. It is imperative that she takes it daily, and she should have taken a dose this morning. I'm being brutally honest with you when I say she really does not understand the severity of her condition."

"Oh, my goodness, I completely understand what you've been going through. I have a son with a severe liver condition; therefore, I realize the importance of daily medication. Without the help of a wife, all the responsibility falls on me."

"I'm so sorry to hear that. Maybe we could get together and discuss our burdens sometime. We seem to have so much in common." I could hear a loud cough coming from the potted palm that alerted me I better get back to what I came in here for. "Mr., oh, I'm sorry, I didn't catch your name."

"Honeysuckle, Jasper Honeysuckle. Please call me Jasper."

"In that case, Jasper, is there any way you might allow me to put my daughter's medication in her room?"

"I'm so sorry, madam, but we're not allowed to let anyone in the rooms that are occupied. You're quite welcome to leave the medication here with me, and I'll be sure to give it to her when they come back in. I believe they've gone out dining, and then I believe I overheard them saying they would be shopping for a new car. Isn't that something, a young couple with the means to have a nice honeymoon and purchase a new car on top of everything? They must be financially established. Lester seems to be quite the businessman. I believe he mentioned he has an export business."

"Yes, he is quite a businessman all right. Maybe I can catch up with them at the restaurant and, if I can't, I'll come back and wait for them. Irene needs her medication as quickly as possible."

"That seems like the best plan, madam. I'm so sorry I can't help you further."

"Oh, you've been quite helpful, Jasper. Maybe we'll run into each other again sometime."

"That would be my pleasure, madam," Jasper answered, with a little glimmer of hope in his eyes.

With a plan already formulating in my mind, I walked toward the outside door of the lobby, found a seat on the side veranda and waited for Bess, who was making her way over to join me. Bess sat down beside me between the ferns and the swaying palms and complained, "Well, that took long enough. We don't have all day, you know."

"Jasper was such a gentleman, Bess, and he has the nicest manners."

"Bee, he's paid to have those manners. Now what did you find out?"

"Bess, they're in room forty-two. Would you believe it? That's the very room Will and I stayed in all those years ago. That just defiles my memories of that room. I had such good memories. Did I ever tell you...?"

"Yes, you told me. Now spare me the details. Can we get into that room or what?"

"No, he said he wasn't allowed to let anybody in that room while it's occupied. But Bess, if we could get by Jasper, we could go on up to the hall and maybe get in some other way, even break in if we have to."

"I can't believe I'm agreeing with you again, but I do. Now how are we going to get past old Jasper to get to the staircase?"

"We'll just have to watch through the window here, and when he leaves his post, we'll hurry across the lobby. Hey, I know. Let's send a note by the bellboy asking him to check on something in the coffee shop, and when he leaves, we'll sneak right by his desk," I answered, feeling rather proud of myself for coming up with another solution without even giving a whole lot of thought to it. This detective business must be getting easier all the time.

"Bee, that is a good idea. Do you think it will work?"

"It's gonna work. We've got to get up to that room in a hurry. Now where is a notepad and pen? I know you've got one in that gigantic pocketbook you lug around."

"I do. I try to stay prepared for any emergency, unlike some people I know who don't keep a handkerchief or anything in their purse half the time and have to borrow everything from their sister."

For the next few minutes, Bess rummaged around in her purse and ended up pouring half the contents out on the table, along with the frying pan. She finally came up with a pen and some paper from the very bottom. "Look what else I found—my grocery list from the other day. I looked everywhere for that thing after I got in the store." Glancing at the list, Bess said, "I forgot to buy foot powder. I knew there was something I overlooked. I think I'll keep this list and add aspirin. If we ever get home, I'm going to have a terrible headache. I can already feel it coming on."

"Bess, please just write what I say and keep your mind on what we're doing, for Pete's sake. Okay, say this:

Sir, I am in great distress! Please come to the coffee shop immediately. My legs seem to have lost all feeling in them and I need some immediate assistance.

Then sign it, oh, I don't know, make up some name."

"How about Mrs. Smith?"

"That sounds good. It doesn't matter. He'll come no matter who it is. Okay, now give it to the bellboy when he goes by."

Bess folded the note and as we were impatiently waiting, I glanced over at Bess and noticed the color draining from her face. "Bess, whatever is the matter with you? You look like you've seen a ghost."

"Oh, Bee, I can't believe what my eyes are seeing. I haven't seen a ghost, but I think that's J.R., standing there at the cashier's desk with that home wrecker, Eunice Donaldson."

Slowly turning around in my chair, I saw what she was talking about. Over by the lobby desk stood J.R. Kitchens, all five feet, ten inches of him, dressed in a light blue suit, Panama hat, wingtip shoes, and a wide tie with a palm tree design. He was what you call dressed to kill. Beside him was Eunice Donaldson, in a tight purple dress at least two sizes too small and a feathered plume hat perched on her bleached head. She was hanging onto J.R.'s arm with a look of total excitement plastered across her heavily made-up face. J.R. reminded me of a sheep going to slaughter as Eunice eyed his wallet when he pulled out several bills.

"That's him all right, with that floozy Eunice that lives over on Jackson Street. You know, that 'double d' who works with Thelma at the beauty parlor sometimes when she gets behind. How could he do this to me? There he is, in broad daylight, going into an expensive hotel with a woman half his age, when he wouldn't take me anywhere. Why he never spent a dime on me. If he bought me a drink from a filling station, you'd have thought he was doing me a favor. Why, he is the horniest thing that ever put pants on, or should I say, who took off pants. I'll bet he wasn't even faithful to Minnie Lou."

"Who, on God's green earth, is Minnie Lou?"

"Don't you remember? His dead wife. Bee, you don't listen to half the things I say. Why, he's not anything but a low-down, sneaky snake in the grass, and that's the nicest things I can say about him. If he thinks he can get away with this, he's got another think coming. I think I'll go in there right now and knock that smile right off his..."

"Oh, no you're not," I said, as I grabbed Bess's arm and almost pulled it out of the socket. "You can attend to that situation later. We're staying right here until we see Jasper leave. Now just calm down and here, fan yourself with the note." I knew Bess was fit to be tied so I gave her time to compose herself before I said anything else. "Do you have yourself together now? For goodness sake, this is not the time to fall apart."

She nodded and deviously said, "I just wonder what room they have? We might want to break into more than one room before we leave. They probably wouldn't give us any more time in the state penitentiary for committing two crimes. I might just commit murder too, and I think you get a life sentence for that. Bee, I'm so upset, and I need to go to the bathroom. I'm getting nauseated, and I need to eat a little something too."

This situation was getting worse all the time. "Bess, I know your heart is broken, but that two-timing coward isn't worth getting yourself all worked up over. I knew all along he wasn't for you, but you wouldn't listen. Can't you wait to go to the bathroom? Try not to think about your stomach for a little while."

"I'll wait, but Bee, please don't start getting so preachy right now."

Sure enough, a bellboy walked by just as we were about to give up hope. Bess handed him the note and asked if he would give it to the man at the desk. He nodded and walked into the lobby. We watched through the window as he handed the note to Jasper just like we asked him to. Jasper responded by rushing over to the coffee shop and disappearing through the door.

Bess and I didn't know we could move so fast, but we hightailed it through the lobby and up those steps faster than a couple of jackrabbits with a seasoned hound dog after them. I just hoped Jasper wouldn't come looking for us too soon. He would certainly question the bellboy to get to the bottom of the mystery when he discovered there was no one in the coffee shop with a leg malady. He'd start to put the pieces together sooner or later. I just hoped it was later.

"Bess, let's hide in this broom closet for a few minutes just to be sure Jasper isn't going to catch on and check on things up here pretty quickly. That bellboy is sure to tell him who gave him that note. Old Jasper might be a little cleverer than you think. We could get arrested just for sneaking up here."

"That's good thinking."

We closed the door and stood in the closet until we thought the coast was clear. Bess peeked out and said, "I don't hear anything or see anything. Let's go." We walked out of the closet, looked both ways to be on the safe side, and closed the door behind us.

"There's room forty-two down the hall, Bee. Hey, wait a minute. A maid's coming out. Let's see if we can get in."

Just as if we were paying guests, we strolled down the hall and took a left turn right into room forty-two as the maid struggled to get her cleaning cart out. We nodded to her and thanked her for the service. Bess even went so far as to give her a tip. I thought that was going a little too far, but what the heck, we were in. Closing the door, Bess looked at me the same way she did after we broke into the pastorium—just as if we had won another hundred dollars.

"Now let's search everything as fast as we can. We might not have much time. We've got to find some real evidence. Without something concrete, we're up the creek without a paddle," I excitedly told Bess, as I began going through a suitcase lying on the bed. "And, Bess, be careful and don't make a mess. We don't want them to know we've been here."

"You're right. I'll be careful. Now look fast," Bess answered, as she rummaged through Isabelle's overnight bag that lay on an overstuffed chair in the corner.

"Oh, Bess, look at this," I excitedly said, as I held up a black shirt.

"What's so important about a shirt? Lots of men have black shirts, for goodness sake. We're looking for some evidence here, not a piece of wardrobe, Bee."

"But I think this is evidence, Bess," I said, as I started examining the shirt for missing buttons. "Look, Bess, one of the sleeve buttons is missing. I picked up a button similar to the other buttons on this shirt in Old Man Peterson's yard the other day. I believe I put it in my change purse."

"Well, hurry up and look, for heaven's sake. Bee, you know we're in real danger up here. Do you have it or not?"

"It's a match, Bess!" I hastily held up the shirt and the button to show Bess. "This button was probably lost as Preacher Henry ran from Old Man Peterson's house after he robbed the poor old man."

"Keep looking. We probably need more evidence than that. More than likely, Preacher Henry visited Old Man Peterson several times. He could have lost that button anytime."

"You're right, Bess, but I'll bet he never wore a black shirt on any of those preacher visits. You know full well, men don't wear black long sleeve shirts in the heat we've been having. I never saw the man in anything but a grimy white shirt and tie."

"I always wanted to snatch that dingy thing off that man's back and give it a good washing. He didn't know beans about how to launder or iron a shirt."

We were about to give up finding anything else when I heard Bess exclaim, "Bee, I've found what we need." She waved a small piece of paper in the air like it was a small flag. "It's a receipt for sterling silver flatware and a sterling tea service from some place called Champion Pawn Services, made out to somebody named Fredric Salter. I swear, those people have more aliases than pigs in a litter. Can you believe they got four hundred dollars for just those two items? That was my flatware too, what do you want to bet?"

I grabbed the receipt, and sure enough, it was just what Bess said it was. More importantly, it was the evidence we needed to put those ruthless impersonators under the jailhouse. "Bess, we've got what we need, now let's get out of here," I said breathlessly, as I was beginning to lose my nerve. "I don't think I'll ever trust another preacher again as long as I live."

Just as I gave the receipt back to Bess, and she was tucking it in her pocketbook, we heard somebody walking down the hall. I frantically motioned for Bess to get into the bedroom closet, and I stumbled in right behind her, just as someone put a key into the lock in the door.

CHAPTER TWENTY-NINE

O h baby! We're free at last. No more sneaking around with that old busybody watching us all the time. I don't know if I could have stood being cooped up in that stuffy old house with those creaking floors and scraping doors much longer. I've still got those gospel songs from that hick radio station running through my head. Have you ever heard of the West Family with Mom and Pop, Orville and Irma Jean? I don't know which sounds the worse, them or all those animals bellowing all the time. And all that country cooking just sitting in my stomach and souring. The milk manufactured by Hortence the cow—with those giant bags—just minutes before we drank it. It was disgusting! Promise me you'll never leave me in the sticks again."

That was Isabelle's scratchy, high-pitched voice. I would have known it anywhere. As Isabelle complained and whined, I longed for the familiarity of my home and yearned to be there again. I squeezed Bess's arm to let her know I was right there with her and wasn't missing a thing. She moved over a little and snatched her arm back. It was dark, but I gave her a look I'm sure she could see through pitch black.

All kinds of thoughts were running through my head as we stood side by side, trapped in that three-foot-square closet. If I had minded my own business, I could be home on my own porch right now, daydreaming about the prospect of Margaret's next visit. What had we been thinking about, running off to Savannah like this. We must have been out of our minds.

This time the voice was masculine. "Baby doll, I'm relieved it's all over with too. If I'd had to preach another sermon to those sanctified people back in that podunk town, I think I would have thrown up. Just standing behind that podium looking out at Mrs. Bess Johnson with that big hat on top of her head made me think I was preaching to a salad plate. And that Miss Shirley, after she made that play for me, I could hardly go near her again. What I should have done is blackmail her. That would have taught her a lesson, and we probably could have made a little extra spending money too." That's when Bess almost pulled my arm out of the socket and I stepped on her foot.

Preacher Henry began to breathe harder. "That guy at the pawn shop didn't even have enough sense to question where we got those sterling goblets."

I could feel Bess tense up again.

"I hope we don't have any trouble when we go back to the art dealer to pick up our money," the preacher said, breathing even harder. "I always hate it when they tell us we have to wait until the oil paintings are authenticated. That's just a waste of our time. The guy said we could come back about two o'clock today, so that gives us plenty of time to have a roll on this nice feather mattress. You know, I went without this pleasure for a while. Come on. Time's a'wasting."

I thought I'd bust a blood vessel right then and there. If Bess and I had to stay in such close quarters much longer and listen to what I believed was about to take place, well, it was just about more than I could handle. Bess was pinching the tar out of me by now, and it was all I could do to keep from jabbing my arm right into her stomach.

"Okay, but let's talk a few minutes before we get too carried away," I heard Isabelle, or should I say, Inez say. "We've got to get out of here as soon as we can finish all this business with Billy Bob. He's probably sold the load of stuff we gave him yesterday, so he should be ready to divide the profits by now. Didn't you say he left a note with that dumb Jasper down in the lobby that he should be here about four o'clock with the cash? I hope we can still trust him. I know he's always been reliable, but you never know. We need to be ready to hit the road as soon after four as we can. I want to drive when we leave. You know, you haven't let me drive the new car yet."

"We don't have a lot of time. Let's get out of these clothes and get down to business."

"My, oh my, that feels so-o good. Do that again." There was that squeaky voice again. "You are no gentleman, Hershel Snodgrass."

"And you, Inez Frogmore, are no lady."

Could that be their real names?

Bess was breathing so hard by this time I thought she was going to fog up the whole closet. We stood in there for what seemed like an eternity listening to moans, groans, and whispers like I'd never heard before. I thought at one time Bess was going to pass out. I was completely holding her up by then. We were trapped in that closet for the duration, and my life will never be the same. Bess didn't move the rest of the time, but leaned on me until I thought I would lose all the feeling in my arm and side. We finally heard them come up for air after they had had enough time to do their business three or four times, according to my standards. If I had known making whoopee could have been like that, I would have enjoyed it so much more when I had the chance.

"Darling, I've really missed you these few weeks. Next time we need to pretend to be a married couple, so we don't have to be without each other's company," Preacher Henry said. It sounded as if they were moving around in the room now with their feet on the floor. "I saw an advertisement in the classifieds by a wealthy widow woman over in South Carolina who is in need of a butler and a maid. We could go as a married couple with all the benefits of sleeping together and probably have full access to the house. What do you think? I'll bet the house is loaded with expensive stuff."

"Do you think I'd have to cook and clean? You know how I hate to do that sort of thing," I heard Isabelle say in that squeaky voice I knew I'd never forget. "You know, I don't really know how to cook anything but toast, and cleaning is so bad on my hands and nails. Feel how soft they are."

"Oh, sweetheart, your hands are wonderful. Just keep moving them like that. I think we have time for one more romp in the hay," I heard Hershel breathlessly say, as Bess started sinking to the floor. As I grabbed for her, I accidently knocked a box off the closet shelf with my elbow. *Crash!*

"What was that?" screamed Isabelle.

We froze, and then after what seemed to be an eternity, the door to the closet flew open to expose us. But Preacher Henry Maxwell was exposing much more!

"Get out of there, you nosy old bags! I thought I had seen the last of you two!"

Preacher Henry grabbed us and slung us over to the bed as Isabelle was jumping off. Bess landed right on top of me, and we had to scramble to keep from falling off the side of the bed. Preacher Henry, Hershel, Fredric or whoever, took his gun from the chair and held it on us as Isabelle struggled to wrap her robe around her bare body. "Here, take this gun and let me get into my clothes, Inez," Preacher Henry said, as he stood there as naked as the day he was born.

"You ladies have messed up now. Why couldn't you two just let things rest? We were gone and everything would have gotten back to normal," Isabelle adamantly said, as she held the gun directly at us as if it was something she was accustomed to doing.

As Preacher Henry grabbed his underwear and stepped into them, I nervously spouted off, "Nothing is normal anymore!"

"We know who murdered Floyd now," Bess retaliated, not even thinking about that gun pointing right at us. "How could you two be so evil? Why you, whoever you are," Bess said pointing toward Preacher Henry, "performed the funeral for the very man you killed, and then let poor defenseless people be blamed for it!"

"I didn't want to kill the old guy. He came home at the wrong time. I didn't have any choice. Now be still so I can tie your hands. Hand me my necktie, Inez," Preacher

Henry said, as he grabbed my hands and tried to put them together.

"We know everything you did. You'll never get away with it!" I defiantly said as I struggled against Preacher Henry's strong arms.

"You'll never live to tell it," Preacher Henry angrily retorted, as he grabbed the tie. "You two are going out of here in bags, and the rest of your short lives will be spent in the trunk of a car!"

Just as he started tying my hands, the door flew open. Sheriff Ledbetter barged in with a shotgun pointed right at Isabelle, yelling, "Drop that gun or I'll blow your head off! Get over by that wall, both of you, now!"

Isabelle dropped the gun on the floor as she tumbled over to the wall right on top of Henry. They fell all over each other but ended up side by side against the wall.

"Don't anybody move unless you want to get ripped open by a bullet!" shouted Vernon, the deputy, a second later as he ran in with another shotgun. He was followed by poor old Jasper, with a stunned expression plastered across his face.

"Ladies, move very slowly out into the hall now, and stay out there together," Sheriff Ledbetter demanded in an authoritative voice I didn't even know existed.

"With pleasure!" I heard myself answer. Sheriff Ledbetter might have been weak-minded, but at least he had good timing.

CHAPTER THIRTY

B ess and I stood out in the hall, shaking and huddled together, as Vernon and Sheriff Ledbetter led those two misfits of justice in handcuffs out of the hotel room and down the stairs. *Thank heavens!* Preacher Henry had finally been able to get both legs into a pair of trousers. Bess and I had seen more of him than we ever wanted to see again. We wobbled behind the band of law enforcement agents and their prisoners down to the lobby. Bess and I triumphantly watched as Sheriff Ledbetter personally put Hershel Snodgrass and Inez Frogmore in the police car that had been dispatched to pick them up. What a relief to see that car pull off with its lights flashing and siren blaring!

The sheriff walked over to us after the car pulled off and asked if we felt like talking to Vernon and him a few minutes.

"We'd be more than glad to," Bess shakily answered.

"Just wait in the lobby and I'll be back down shortly. I have to go back up and secure the hotel room and make some calls to the pawnshops."

"Wait a minute, Sheriff. We need to tell you something before you go up," I excitedly exclaimed, not wanting him to get away.

"Okay, what is it, ma'am?"

Not having had the time to calm down yet, I started out with my mouth in overdrive. "Billy Bob, we assume he's the dealmaker between Hershel and Inez and those people who are buying a lot of this stolen stuff. He's supposed to be back at the hotel at about four this afternoon with the money he collected when he sold or pawned some of the silver and other items. You know that was my mama's heirloom silver. Can you believe they took it and didn't even care if my daughter ever inherits it or not. Why, the very idea that Mama's silver is sitting in some pawnshop along with her locket and wedding ring this very minute is almost more than I can bear."

"Lady, just calm down," Sheriff Ledbetter gently said, as he put his hand on my shoulder and patted it in an attempt to compose me.

Bess took over from there. "Let me tell you, Sheriff. Bee and I have a receipt from the Champion Pawn Services that we took from the hotel room after we broke in earlier today. Now I don't want to be the one to tell you what to do, but you probably need to hurry up and call those people on the telephone before anything gets gone. We overheard something about an art gallery too. We aren't sure which gallery they were talking about, but I have an idea it could be that nice one Bess and I passed earlier in the day as we were riding around town trying to find this place. You know, it's on the street that's about two blocks over towards that big office building that has the roses blooming by the front door. You know the kind that has the big yellow double blooms."

"Just the facts, lady. Just give me the facts."

I jumped back in and said, "Well, that's probably all we can tell you right now, but…"

"That's good, ladies. Now the two of you go on all the way to the back of the coffee shop right now and don't come out under any circumstances. I'm about to seal off the hotel and call in some other officers to wait for Billy Bob. In the meantime, I'll get somebody to work the telephones to get in touch with that pawnshop and try to find out about that art gallery. Could you trust me with that receipt from the pawnshop?"

Bess handed over the receipt but had to add, "Now don't lose it. We might have to have it later on."

I wasn't sure Bess and I could even wobble over to the coffee shop on our own, but with a little help from that nice Jasper and the bellboy, we made it to a back table and sat down. Jasper offered us something to drink, and we gladly accepted it.

It had been a long and eventful day. We were both still trembling as we attempted to drink our iced tea. Bess wasn't any better off than me, but I knew she had a bee under her bonnet about something.

It was a while later before Sheriff Ledbetter finally came in and sat down. "We've just picked up Billy Bob as he entered the hotel. He was recognized immediately by one of the officers as a known fence for crooks. Ladies, we couldn't have captured these criminals without you. Our department is eternally grateful—not that we condone what you did. You put your own lives at risk, but I guess we can say it turned out all right. After reading your note this morning, I made some inquiries and discovered Hershel Snodgrass was staying at the same boardinghouse with Henry Maxwell a month or so ago, when the young preacher decided not to take the appointment in Jeffersontown. Henry Maxwell, an unmarried young man, turned down the appointment by writing a letter to the church that was never posted. We think now that Hershel intercepted it from the mail table at the boardinghouse. The rest is history. Hershel then came to the church impersonating the real preacher. He figured he could get into the church members' good graces and be invited into their homes where he could familiarize himself with the layout and gain access to them. He knew exactly where the nice, expensive items were. With the help of his girlfriend, Inez, they planned to burglarize as many homes as possible before they skipped town. That was his sole purpose in coming to our little community. We have now put two and two together and come up with four. That is with your help. You two seemed to have figured out most of it before we had a chance. It seems Hershel and Inez— we still aren't sure about their real names— are wanted in several states for theft by taking. They're now being held for theft and murder."

"Well, of all the low-down things I have ever heard, this just takes the cake," Bess interjected, in a disgusted tone. "I will never trust another preacher as long as I live. Did you know he even bought the sermons he preached? Now I ask you, have you ever heard of something like that? I just can't wait until I can talk to some of those so-called deacons who were supposed to have checked this man out."

"Well, I'm sure they'll be on pins and needles waiting to hear from you. By the way, there's a nice reward, so come by the sheriff station in a day or two and fill out all the paperwork. It'll be waiting for you. The whole community is indebted to the both of you."

"What about all the stolen items and Floyd's and Old Man Peterson's money? Will it be returned?"

"From what I was just told, Billy Bob is already squealing like a stuck pig, so it won't be but a matter of time before we know where most of the stolen items are. Unfortunately, they've probably spent a great deal of the money, but hopefully we can retrieve most of it. We have officers working on that right now."

Sheriff Ledbetter stood up and pushed his chair back under the table. As he adjusted his gun holster, he said, "Ladies, I have work to do now. Would you like Vernon to assist you home?"

"We got here by ourselves, and we can certainly get home by ourselves," Bess answered indignantly. Thinking she might have sounded a little abrupt, she added, "It's very kind of you to offer though. Thank you, but we'll manage."

After he left, I said, "Bess, I just wonder how much that nice reward is. I know one thing, I sure can use it. My little business venture didn't turn out to be quite so profitable, and being a landlady just isn't for me. I wonder if we could use the reward to start a small business doing something. What do you think about us starting up some kind of detective agency? I think we would make good private investigators, and it could bring in a little money."

"I think you're daydreaming, that's what I think. If you think for one minute I'm going to put my life out on a limb again for anything, you've got another think coming. But Bee, I do have a little more business I need to attend to while we're here, if you don't mind."

"Bess, I know we talked about shopping, but I'm just wiped out. Can't we come back another time?"

"I wasn't really talking about shopping, Bee."

"Well, what business do you have now?" I asked exasperatedly. "Bess, we've done what we came to do."

"I haven't finished what I need to do yet," Bess answered, as she got up from her seat and then marched out to the lobby where Jasper was standing talking to the bellboy. "Excuse me, Jasper, but Bee was telling me you might be able to assist me with something. I believe there's a couple registered here under the name of J.R. Kitchens. I was wondering if you could give me directions their room. I need to deliver them a little something from home."

I'd tell you what happens next, but that's another story.

Made in the USA
Columbia, SC
28 April 2021

36620479R00181